GREY
HOWL

D0208576

Previously published Worldwide Mystery titles by
CLEA SIMON

MEW IS FOR MURDER
CATTERY ROW
CRIES AND WHISKERS
PROBABLE CLAWS
SHADES OF GREY
GREY MATTERS
GREY ZONE
DOGS DON'T LIE
GREY EXPECTATIONS
CATS CAN'T SHOOT
PARROTS PROVE DEADLY
TRUE GREY
GREY DAWN

GREY HOWL

Clea Simon

WORLDWIDE®

TORONTO • NEW YORK • LONDON
AMSTERDAM • PARIS • SYDNEY • HAMBURG
STOCKHOLM • ATHENS • TOKYO • MILAN
MADRID • WARSAW • BUDAPEST • AUCKLAND

For Jon

Recycling programs
for this product may
not exist in your area.

Grey Howl

A Worldwide Mystery/January 2016

First published by Severn House Publishers Ltd.

ISBN-13: 978-0-373-26974-7

Printed in U.S.A.

Acknowledgments

All storytellers need an audience, and I have benefited greatly by my early readers, who help both me and Dulcie stay on track. For such services, I'd like to thank Jon S. Garelick, my editor Rachel Simpson Hutchens, copy editor Nicky Connor and agent Colleen Mohyde of the Doe Coover Agency for their inestimable services. A full troupe of cheerleaders kept me going, and so a shout-out to them, as well: Vicki Constantine Croke, Caroline Leavitt, Lisa Jones, Frank Garelick, Naomi Yang and the wonderful Sophie Garelick. You keep me going, and this book is for all of you.

ONE

Darkness fell too quickly on this dim and dismal day. Grey shadows faded into black, as the thrusting shapes of trees, skeletal hands grasping at the sky, reached out to the unknowable in the growing Gloom. Turning at last from the window, where Night's curtain had fallen with a fervor, she found little solace in the lone Candle, that one meager taper whose sickly light seemed neither to illuminate nor to warm the spare and comfortless chamber which she, so lonely, occupied. E'en that light failed in its purpose, to her grief-shrouded eyes, casting the drafty doorway in looming shadow. More shadows flickered, as if engaged in climbing the bare walls into a dim beyond, there to hover and wait, poised in threat, ready to swoop in and suck out the life within. The room was grim and poor. A churchman's cell, if any church could condone the fate that sent her here. Yet, through the mist of tears and sadness, there seemed a Memory to awaken, to form a counter Image in the shadow. A Traveler, cloaked in grey, whose eyes were Bright as the new green leaves of springtime, offering solace. A hope, a promise, and yet his Words were full of dread.

'We are not what we seem.'

'I don't know, Dulcie. I don't think it's safe.' Mina sounded worried. 'It's nearly midnight, and it's so,

I don't know, *grim* out. Maybe we should just wait until tomorrow.'

'No, it'll be fine. Tomorrow will be crazy,' Dulcie replied, shaking her head. Her friend's warning sounded too much like the passage she had just read. She needed to dispel those echoes. Besides, Mina didn't yet understand how hectic the campus was about to get. 'And I really should get that paper from you. I'll be by in a half hour.'

Before Mina could protest further, Dulcie signed off. 'See you soon!'

It wasn't like Dulcie wanted to go out again. Her friend's dorm room was a good half hour from her own cozy apartment, and the December night was frosty. But the walk would do her good, chasing the last of those spooky echoes from her mind. Besides, she had been the one to encourage the younger student to go old school while looking over the paper. 'Forget track changes,' she had said. 'Sit down with an actual printout and a pen. Take your time with the part where I used your research, and feel free to mark it up.'

Dulcie was not officially Mina's tutor. Dulcie was a grad student in English and American Literatures and Language, while Mina was an undergrad concentrating on History and Literature. But they'd met during a trying time the month before and shared intellectual interests as well as friendship, and Dulcie had taken the younger woman under her wing. Recently, she'd been trying to teach her that part of learning—and loving—the eighteenth century texts they both studied was accepting that, sometimes, paper was still the best medium.

As soon as she hung up, however, she began regretting her decision. 'What was I thinking, Esmé?' As she reached for the thick hand-knit sweater that served as her coat, she looked around for her companion. 'Well, you won't mind if I run out, will you?'

'*Chrr—rr—rr.*' The plump black and white cat appeared out of nowhere, as was her wont, and proceeded to rub against Dulcie's legs as she trilled. *Chris?* The question sounded like an echo in the back of Dulcie's mind.

It was an answer of sorts. Just not the one Dulcie wanted.

'Let's not tell him,' she said, as if she had heard the name out loud. 'He worries too much, you know.' With that she bent to stroke her pet's smooth black fur and to scratch around the base of her ears. But even though the feline purred, her voice reverting to the low rumble, Dulcie sensed the little tuxedo cat was annoyed. La Principessa Esmeralda—Esmé, for short—was not a normal house cat. She didn't like to be dismissed.

'It's the conference, Esmé.' Dulcie squatted on the floor to be eye level with her pet. 'The next four days are going to be crazy, and I really want to make everything go smoothly.'

Esmé tilted her head slightly but did not deign to respond. Dulcie waited, to no avail. It wasn't that her pet didn't understand her, Dulcie knew. As she had learned over the last two years, the little tuxedo cat had inherited many of the strange powers of her predecessor, the late great Mr Grey. Like being able to communicate, at least fleetingly, with a kind of conversational, if intermittent, telepathy that always made Dulcie feel like she was hearing a real voice from just behind her.

The problem was more in the opposite direction: Esmé loved to make herself heard, particularly when she felt slighted or like dinner service had been slow.

What she didn't like was listening—or responding to anything like a request. Although the little tuxedo was barely two years old, she acted like Dulcie was the kitten of the family, and a not very bright kitten at that. Mr Grey, who still appeared to Dulcie on occasion, might advise her, but he never took the tone Esmé did. It wasn't that Esmé was overbearing exactly, it was more that she exuded an air of entitlement. Or privilege.

'*I am the Principessa.*' The voice that cut into Dulcie's thoughts illustrated her point, even as it brought her back. So did the claws that reached up to pierce her jeans.

'Esmé, that's rude.' Dulcie tried to sound firm as she carefully removed the claws. Tone, she assumed, might be as important as content, since she still didn't know how much the little cat understood. Clearly, she could 'hear' comments that her human hadn't voiced out loud.

'*Well, I am!*'

Dulcie sighed and stood up. She wasn't going to win this argument.

'Yes, you are,' she responded in resignation. The black tail flicked once in acknowledgement. 'And, yes, I should call Chris. I'll tell him later, I promise. It's just that I really want to have Mina's paper to give to Professor Showalter first thing tomorrow. Once the conference gets started, we're not going to have a moment to spare.'

Esmé turned away, suddenly captivated by the sight of her own tail. Dulcie had to smile. Maybe it was simply a function of age. Mr Grey had been a mature cat by the time he passed on—and Dulcie had only heard him speak after his death. Esmé, despite her protests, was still a kitten at heart. And living with two humans and a venerable ghost, maybe it was understandable that she tried to look more important than she… Dulcie wouldn't say 'than she was'. That was unfair. The little cat was as dear to her and to Chris as, well, as they were to each other. But with her limited knowledge of the world—Esmé was, after all, a house cat—it was debatable whether she was as wise as any of her companions.

At any rate, Dulcie thought as she buttoned up her coat, neither of them would be able to tell Chris anything before morning. Dulcie's boyfriend, a graduate student in computer sciences, had recently changed his schedule to something more like normal hours. The overnight shifts in the computer lab paid the best, but the toll they took on his studies—not to mention their relationship—had begun to be untenable. Now Chris was doing more tutoring—and getting his research done. And she got to come home to the lanky computer geek most nights. He'd been called out tonight, however, for some kind of emergency fill-in. The lab, in the basement of the Science Center, had had some kind of animal infestation or something—Dulcie didn't even want to hear the details. For once, however, Dulcie was grateful for his absence.

'I'll be fine,' she said now to reassure herself as much as her feline mistress, as she detached the white mittens that once again clasped around her ankle, lifting the cat up as she did so. 'You just play with your catnip mouse for a while and take a nap. I'll be back before you know it.'

With a shove against her chest, the cat freed herself, jumped to the floor, and stalked away, and Dulcie smiled. She was short too. She knew how hard it could be to salvage one's dignity. However, she used the break to head to the door. The sooner she got over to Mina's, the sooner she'd be back.

'Mr Grey, do you think maybe you could talk with

her?' Dulcie was on the street by the time she voiced the request. It had taken her a few minutes to find a way to phrase it that wouldn't be insulting to the younger animal, and now she walked swiftly along the empty sidewalk, the only sounds the distant roar of traffic. 'Reassure her that I'm not completely brainless?'

To all intents and purposes, she was alone. Wednesday, a week before Christmas, and the city was as quiet as it would get. Still, the glow of lights behind window shades was cheering, and Dulcie held out hope. Mr Grey had also been an indoor cat, but often as not these days he came to her out in the world. He seemed especially fond of appearing in the library, or in the tiny office she shared with another grad student, but he'd been known to make himself heard out here, particularly as the wind off the river picked up.

Now it whistled softly, threading its way through the old brick industrial buildings and the worn-out triple deckers. Dulcie didn't pause—the night was too cold— but she listened, hard. Often, she heard Mr Grey's voice. Sometimes she saw him, the flare of his wide white whiskers or the soft plume of his grey tail, silhouetted by the dust motes in a shaft of light or in the shadows like the one cast by the bare maple she now passed under. Sometimes, she still thought she imagined his visits. He did tend to come when she was sleepy or distracted, after all.

'Mr Grey?' She peeked up at the sky—at the moon overhead caught in those spiky branches. 'You are there, aren't you?' But she kept her voice low, and after a moment's search, her eyes went to the street again, to the dun sidewalk and the blue shadows that crossed it. As much as she had dismissed Mina's concerns—and Esmé's—Dulcie wasn't foolish. The street might seem quiet, but this was still a city, and as a young woman walking alone close to midnight, it made sense to be aware of her surroundings.

'*Lost in the inky dark...*' The phrase, from her earlier reading, came to mind. She sped up a bit, but still her mind wandered. '*As in her black-hued thoughts, she felt her fancy wander, searching down the dim paths by which she had arrived. Or been led, she pondered, the dark of night thick'ning before her burning eyes.*'

No; she shook her head to clear it and felt her curls break free of her knit cap. Now she was just scaring herself. The city might be quiet, and a little eerie, but it wasn't as bad as all that. Besides, as much as Dulcie enjoyed the Gothic conventions—ghosts and intrigue, all wrapped up with a dollop of romance and, at least in the case of her favorite author, a heroine with enough spunk to see it through—she knew the difference between fiction and real life.

Into the Square and back—that was all the midnight journeying Dulcie was doing tonight. She'd get Mina's annotated paper and bring it home; the undergraduate had contributed some genealogical research, and Dulcie had wanted to make sure she had used it correctly. Then she could read the whole thing through again, quickly, before presenting it to the visiting professor in the morning. Odds were, the professor—who was coming for the conference—wouldn't have time to critique it thoroughly between the constant panels and presentations that would re-energize the otherwise deserted campus. But she'd said she'd look it over before Saturday—meeting's second full day—when Dulcie was going to be giving a short talk about its contents. It was only one of the morning presentations, to be held in a small room off the main lecture hall. But it was Dulcie's first time presenting an academic paper at such a gathering, and she was a tad nervous. Even the sketchiest thumbs-up would be appreciated.

ELLA—as the Association of English Language Literatures Academics was known—was a big deal. And although the conference convened biannually, this was the first time it had met at the university since Dulcie had been here, and since the last two had been in Dubai and Oxford, both a bit beyond Dulcie's travel budget, this would be the first time she had ever attended.

Dulcie had heard the same gossip as all her friends— the hook-ups arranged over dialectics, the marriages made—or shattered—between panels. Even Chris had made some comment about the rumors, although Dulcie suspected him of feigning his concern about the reception she—and her paper—might receive. He wasn't really the jealous type, and besides, she suspected not many people would come to hear her anyway.

It didn't matter. All Dulcie cared about was the research. While some of her colleagues, Chris included, might be surprised at the number of real breakthroughs that were announced between the romantic comings and goings, Dulcie knew better. Newly uncovered texts, radical attributions, and revolutionary reinterpretations were constant and as vital as the discovery of the Higgs boson—and ELLA was where they were announced.

Not that she expected a thunderclap of acclaim for her own work. She—and her paper—were too small to make much noise, at least right away. Still, in three days, Dulcie would present, even if nobody but Mina was there to hear. Then, she hoped, the paper would develop its own momentum. Over the next month, she'd revise it and file it with the ELLA-associated journal. If she were lucky, she'd hear back by spring from the review board—whose members would, of course, expect her to spend her summer making minute and often contradictory revisions based on their particular areas of interest or grudges against each other. Then, sometime next winter, it would—goddess willing—be published. The size of the rumble then would be commensurate with how bright she could shine here. She had to make this presentation count.

Even without her own work, the next few days would be busy. Tomorrow—Thursday—the guests would be arriving—dozens of grad students and other low-level scholars and three top-flight academics, all of whom were candidates for an open position here at the university.

On Friday, the conference would kick off for real, with Martin Thorpe, the acting head of the department, giving the keynote speech. For the rest of the weekend, Dulcie knew, in addition to polishing her own paper, she was supposed to attend back-to-back talks from nine until three, not to mention the numerous gatherings that would follow. The guest lists for these could be political, but Dulcie figured as a member of the hosting university she'd receive invites to the major ones. She hoped so, anyway. That's where she and all the other aspiring academics would have their chance to mix and mingle with the tenured set, almost, sort of, on equal terms.

Some of her fellow academics, she acknowledged, would be here just for the socializing: the conference's reputation had to have some basis in fact. But with any luck, a few of them might also come to hear her present her paper—'The Moon in the Branches: Tracing the Family Tree of a Gothic She-Author'—setting in motion the kind of relationship she desired—the kind that, in a year or two, might lead to a job.

It was exhilarating but also, Dulcie had to admit, exhausting. In some ways, she thought to herself as she made her way into the Square, she just wanted life to continue as it had for the last five years. Looking at the hallowed brick buildings around her, she thought about how easy it would be to do research here another five years, spending her days in the library—and her nights with her newly present boyfriend. They'd come through some, well, interesting times, and survived them intact. Now their domestic routine seemed the epitome of comfort. Plus, she still wasn't sure about that title. If only she could have some sense of the future.

'I guess I chose the wrong field for that, huh?' The moon over her head didn't answer. Maybe that was because it was well overhead, far from the spare branches of the sickly street tree. It didn't really matter. While Dulcie could have continued researching her topic forever, and, in fact, hoped to make it her life's work, she was nearing the end of her thesis.

For the last five years, she'd lived and breathed *The Ravages of Umbria*, a little-known Gothic novel that she'd fallen for, hard. Only two fragments of the novel survived, but Dulcie had managed not only to extract its themes but also to piece together some information about the work's anonymous author. Recently, she'd even identified a later—possibly greater—work by the same author. And now, with Mina's help, she was closing in on giving that author a name. The paper she was presenting at the conference would be her third on the mysterious author and her haunting works. By this time next year, Dulcie would probably be defending her dissertation, if she could somehow come up with a way to sum up everything she had discovered—and was learning still. 'The Mysteries of *The Ravages*'; she rehearsed her latest title for that in her head, not daring to speak out loud this close to the library. 'The Political Ramifications of the Unfinished *Umbria* Author'.

Well, she was going to have to work on that, too. Somehow, she decided as she swiped her university ID, she needed to get in that her subject might still be anonymous. But also, she amended as she jogged up the stairs, that Dulcie had uncovered a lot about her. And while she felt compelled to acknowledge that the author's great work was incomplete—there, that was a better word than 'unfinished'—the author herself seemed to have lived quite a full life. Including, Dulcie suspected, giving birth to one of Dulcie's great-great-grandmothers. One of whose other descendants might be the undergrad upon whose door she now knocked.

'There you are.' Mina Love opened the door, relief washing over her pale, round face. 'I was beginning to worry.'

'Esmé,' said Dulcie, by way of an explanation. Ever since they had met, Dulcie had found the younger woman surprisingly easy to talk to and therefore often didn't have to say much at all. One reason for this was that they shared certain interests. Although the undergrad was in a different department, focusing more on the sociological side of things, they were both studying the same anonymous author. That was partly because they had both begun to believe that they might be descended from that author, making them cousins of some sort.

Maybe it was all just wishful thinking, Dulcie thought. Following the young woman into her dorm room, she noticed how Mina's hair—a true auburn—waved, rather than curled, how her few extra inches of height put her curves into perspective. Despite the childhood accident that left her often reliant on a cane, Mina was like the idealized version of what Dulcie ought to be, she thought with a touch of rue. And the younger woman didn't even seem to notice.

'Do you want some cocoa?' Mina called from the other room. Dulcie was tempted to say yes. Growing up the only child of a single mother, Dulcie had not had much in the way of family. Too many years moving around had forced her to rely on herself or her books, and by the time Dulcie's mother had settled them into the commune—what her mother called the 'arts colony'—she'd grown used to her solitude. Since coming to college, she'd found a soulmate in Suze, her longtime room-mate. But even a surrogate sister was not a blood relative.

'Oh, I shouldn't.' And work was still work. After all, not only was Dulcie presenting at the conference, she—or, okay, her department—was the unofficial host. That was an honor, but it was also time-consuming. It didn't help that her thesis adviser had recently been named interim chair of the department. He was up for the permanent position, and Dulcie suspected that if he could just hold on long enough the wheels of the university would eventually turn in his favor. But she knew the balding, nervous scholar didn't see it that way, and instead viewed the temporary post as merely a stay of execution. And while the conference gave Thorpe an opportunity to strut his stuff, it gave the same to his competitors—and also various chances to schmooze with the university's sundry deans and senior faculty. By this point, Dulcie almost didn't care who got it. Well, that wasn't really true: she favored another candidate— Professor Renée Showalter—but despite his flaws, she also felt bad for Thorpe. He hadn't been that terrible an adviser. If she could help relieve some of the pressure, she would.

'Thorpe wants me at the departmental headquarters bright and early to go over the scheduling, and you know he'll have a million errands for me,' Dulcie called into the other room. 'I'll call once Showalter has gone over this.'

'I hope she likes it.' The younger woman came back in, slowly, the paper in her hand. This hour of the night, she leaned heavily on the cane. 'I can't believe I'm getting a credit on this.'

'Hey, you did the preliminary trace on the genealogy.' Dulcie smiled at her. 'Everyone at the conference should know that.'

'Still, thanks.' Mina didn't have to say what they both knew: that student researchers were often uncredited. 'Are you going to hear Roebuck, too?'

Dulcie nodded as she pulled on her coat. 'I think I have to.' She looked at the other woman for understanding. 'As little as I care about all that postmodernist stuff, she's a big deal. Supposedly she's going to deliver the biggest breakthrough our field has seen since…since, I don't know.'

'Since you tracked down the anonymous author of *The Ravages of Umbria*!'

Dulcie couldn't help returning the younger woman's smile. Or her compliment. 'With the help of a certain History and Literature major.'

With that, she gave the other woman a gentle hug, tucked the marked-up paper under her arm, and headed out into the night.

'The Moon in the Branches…' Dulcie let her mind wander. The presentation was already in the conference program, not under her title but under the workmanlike but decidedly unpoetic rubric of 'Additional Theories on an Anonymous Gothic Author'. That had been Thorpe's doing. 'Let's not overreach,' he'd said. Now, in the light of the moon, Dulcie wished she'd pushed harder for something that captured more of what she would actually say. Caught in the branches, like that mysterious moon...

Wrapped up in her own poetic vision, she started to cross the empty street. It was all so exciting; the bright moonlight seemed designed to reflect her mood. Only two years ago, she'd been foundering, her thesis stalled. In the last year, however, she'd not only identified additional writings by the anonymous author, she had practically confirmed a long-held suspicion. The author had emigrated, probably fleeing some kind of abuse, and brought her fiery writing style to the new Republic. That was the kind of breakthrough that made an academic's name, she thought as she crossed the quiet street. This was—

'Watch it!' The bicyclist hit her arm, throwing Dulcie sideways and the pages she held on to the street. 'Share the road!' he yelled behind him.

'Jerk.' The voice behind her was almost as startling. Still, she was grateful for the firm grip on her other arm that steadied her; then the man, following her gaze, bent to retrieve the papers. 'Share the road yourself!' he called after the cyclist.

'I wasn't looking,' confessed Dulcie, as the stranger stood and handed her the papers. 'And, well, I was thinking of other things.'

'I figured that, from the way you were gesturing.' The man smiled. It was a nice smile and made him look younger than the salt-and-pepper hair implied. 'Are you an actress?'

'Oh, no.' Dulcie looked down, to hide the growing flush, as they walked. Maybe the blue-white light of the street lamps wouldn't show her crimson cheeks. 'I'm a student. A graduate student. I was just thinking of a talk I have to give.'

'On the genealogy of a Gothic novelist?' He'd guided her to the opposite corner, but now stopped.

'Wait, you know it?' A cold chill replaced the warm flush. Had Mina shared her work with someone else?

But her companion was shaking his head. 'Those pages.' He pointed. 'I saw the title.'

'Are you here for the conference?' Dulcie might not know everyone at the university, but surely she knew anyone interested in Gothic literature.

He nodded. 'Paul.' He held out a gloved hand. 'Paul Barnes. From Humbard.'

'Of course.' Dulcie nodded. Then belatedly reached out to shake. 'Sorry, I'm Dulcie, Dulcie Schwartz. I'm organizing ELLA.' It was an exaggeration, but perhaps an understandable one. Paul Barnes, after all, was one of the luminaries of her little field. Which meant that he probably knew Thorpe, as well as the dean. 'I mean, I'm helping with the organizing,' she amended her claim. 'I'm a doctoral candidate.'

'I know who you are now.' He was nodding as if he did indeed recognize her. 'I read your last paper. You're presenting?'

Somehow, without bursting, she gave him the details about her paper—and about her latest discovery. 'It's just one of the small talks,' she confessed. 'And Martin Thorpe thinks I've gotten a bit off track. He thinks I should have defended my dissertation a year ago.'

'There's no such thing as a "small talk", and don't let anyone rush you.' The visiting scholar's face turned serious. 'There's so much work to do, and you want to do it correctly.'

'Thank you,' she whispered, and stood there smiling as he walked off down the street into the night.

'Paul Barnes,' she said, as much to the moon as to herself. 'Paul Barnes knows who I am! Maybe he'll even come to hear me speak.'

It wasn't, she told herself, that he was a star. A dashing star who had rescued her. It was that he had recognized her. She couldn't wait to tell Chris. Except then she'd have to confess to being out walking, close to midnight. Well, it wasn't like they were married, she told herself as she picked up her pace. And even if they were, she'd still be able to make her own decisions. It wasn't like in the days of her author, when a woman gave up everything. She was a person in her own right.

And he was Chris, she reminded herself. He didn't even want to be out nights any more. Said he was sick of moonlight, that he felt like the nocturnal schedule was depleting him somehow. Poor dear. She looked up at the moon, now so bright it might as well be a street light. He'd gotten so turned around by the schedule changes that he could barely sleep through the night, especially when the moon was so bright. In a way, she admitted to herself, she was glad he was working tonight. Full moon like this, he'd have been tossing and turning. Better he should earn some money. And she should get home and get some more work done. *Carpe diem* wasn't the only rule academics followed. *Carpe noctem*, too. Especially with conference prep to do in the morning.

She turned off Mass Ave and down the long street that led to their apartment. The wind had picked up, coming straight off the river, and she hugged her sweater—and the pages—closer. Before going to sleep, she'd type in Mina's changes and print out a clean copy. The professor had requested a hard copy. They were book people, paper people, in a way that Chris and his colleagues would never understand.

Paul Barnes would. The traitorous thought snuck in, like a draft between her buttons. Paul Barnes may have been out on a similar errand—she hadn't asked him. At any rate, his timing had been fortuitous, not that the cyclist had done her any real harm. One block left, and Dulcie cradled her elbow. It was sore where the cyclist had hit it. She hadn't even seen him coming.

Maybe it was dangerous to walk around the city at night. Maybe Chris had a point. Well, once he was completely off the overnights, she'd give up that particular bad habit. It was too cold to be out here anyway.

I wonder how busy he is? she asked herself as she unlocked their building's front door. I could call, just to say hi. She let herself in, careful to make sure the door latched behind her. The old tile floors were loud, but she enjoyed the clatter as she made her way up to the fourth floor. A skylight, old and pigeon-grimed, let that cool blue moonlight in.

'Esmé, I'm home!' Her stage whisper was simply for effect. The little cat knew when she was arriving without an announcement. When she opened the door, however, there was no pet to greet her, and Dulcie looked around with dismay.

'Esmé? Esmeralda?' She called, and wandered into the kitchen. There, silhouetted against the moonlight, she saw the seated feline form. From her perch on the window sill, the cat's green eyes seemed focused not on the street below but on the moon. Listening.

It was a trick of the light, surely. Or the wind, which

now whistled off the river, looking for a way in. From out in the city, Dulcie heard it. Lonely, and as cold as that moon: a howl.

TWO

Violent as a blade ripping through sable velvet, the night was pierc'd, not by stars but by the shaft of lightning that tore the darkness, heralding the storm to come. In its wake, grey against the new-inked midnight, thund'rous clouds rolled in, lowering on to the roof-tops and the river beyond. Yet, safe, for now, within the stone confines of her tower keep, She stood fast against the terror of the storm. No Spectre, nor any Spirit ephemeral as those clouds, approached. The one she awaited would forge a path through the deepening gloom. O'er the river, she could spy the faintest glimmer. Dawn, perhaps, or its earliest Herald, reflecting off the storm-toss'd waters. But, no, the hour was not near. 'Twas a different glow, a hellish light, spreading as she watched, her eyes grown wide with Horror. Whipped by hellhounds Atmospheric and dark, the phantasm grew, threatening the Town below, that eerie Wind foretelling its arrival, a Howl upon the dark.

Dulcie woke with a headache and the feeling of fur in her mouth. If the hour she'd finally gone to sleep explained the former, the bright green eyes that peered down at her from the back of the sofa gave plausible grounds for the latter.

'I know, Esmé, I should have gone to bed.' She picked a cat hair from her lip as she sat up. 'I just wanted to go through this one more time.' The laptop, warm on her legs, brightened as she pulled it toward her. On the screen, her presentation, incorporating Mina's latest edits, came to life. She must have fallen asleep while proofing it, Dulcie realized. At least she'd been saving as she went along.

'Oof!' With a thud that belied the young cat's size, Esmé jumped from the sofa back, landing on Dulcie's legs. The spot must still be warm from where the computer had lain, but the tuxedo's arrival—and the furious purring that commenced as she kneaded—sent her back to other, colder thoughts.

'Was that you, purring, last night?' She thought of the dream, of the rumbling thunder. It made sense, in a way, considering that she'd been rereading that passage about a dark night only hours before. And in the dream, the thunder hadn't sounded ominous, not that she recalled. More like a message, a harbinger of a storm to come. 'Or was it just my laptop?' She looked at the cat, hoping for an answer. The thunder in the dream hadn't been scary. Still, something in it had left her unsettled.

'Meh.' The soft exhalation could have been a reply or simply a comment on the afghan Dulcie had pulled over herself at some point in the night.

'Was it Mr Grey, Esmé?' Dulcie asked, her voice going soft. The relationship between the two felines in her life was complicated. At times, she had thought of Mr Grey as a parent figure for the living cat, even though that wasn't physically possible. Sometimes she thought the two discussed things behind her back, conspiring how best to manage the humans in their household. Recently, however, it seemed that Esmé was rebelling against the spirit. Having worked to free herself from her own mother's influence, Dulcie understood the need for the younger cat to assert herself. She worried, though, that simply by being here, by being the actual living pet in Dulcie's life, Esmé would end up banishing her spectral companion, not seeing how Dulcie—and even Chris—could love them both.

'*Huh.*' This time, the voice sounded in her head, even as Esmé circled and lay down. '*Like you'd listen to anyone right now. You don't even listen to yourself.*'

'What do you—' Dulcie stopped herself. She knew what her pet meant. For starters, she had set herself up to fall asleep on the sofa, working well past the point of exhaustion. In truth, she'd gotten used to Chris being there. When he wasn't, not even the presence of a cat or two could make the bed feel quite right.

Was it that sense of unease that had caused the dream? From where she sat, Dulcie could see the sky through the window. It loomed grey, thick with clouds that seemed to presage snow. She'd experienced thunder snow, as odd as it was rare. And as for a lightning strike starting a fire? No, she would have heard sirens.

It was a metaphor. It had to be. But with that dream in mind, she wasn't going to get back to sleep. Maybe it was just as well. The conference guests would start arriving in—she checked her alarm clock—two hours, and it wouldn't hurt to have an early start. In truth, she didn't have to look any further to identify the huge undertaking, looming over her dream's horizon. And as for the approaching traveler? Well, that could have been Chris, if in her sleep she'd been waiting for him to come home. Or it could have been Professor Showalter or any of the other dignitaries she would soon be greeting.

'Excuse me, Esmé.' Dulcie extracted her feet, earning a dirty look from the cat. That sense of foreboding, or warning, was her own internal clock, making sure she didn't oversleep on the brink of what could be the most important weekend of her life.

And the howl? Dulcie thought about that as she showered. She'd heard something, maybe, when she'd come in last night. Or had she? Toweling off, she tried to remember. She'd been thinking of so many other things: the conference, her paper. Paul Barnes.

Maybe, she admitted silently, the sense of danger came from the handsome scholar. She wasn't interested. She hadn't even flirted. He'd been the one to approach her, appearing out of the night like that to save her from a potentially fatal, or, well, painful accident.

But she'd enjoyed the attention, she had to be honest about that. Paul Barnes was a rising star in early American fiction, and he had recognized her. He'd read her work—and it sounded like he would attend her presentation. And, yes, she had found him attractive, grey-flecked hair and all.

Maybe there was a reason for the conference's reputation, she thought. And if so, it was just as well that Chris would be around tonight. At the very least, maybe he could fix their printer. For now, she shoved her laptop in her bag. She could print out a clean copy of the paper at the departmental offices. She could get coffee there, too, she knew. Chris would want to sleep once he got home, so there was no sense in making a pot here.

'Ciao, Esmé!' The twitch of an ear acknowledged her farewell. 'Bye, Mr Grey!' Clattering down the stairs, Dulcie realized her headache had evaporated, banished like the steam in the shower. Maybe that rumbling had been a purr after all. But, if so, why had it felt like a warning? And had she heard a howl for real, or only in her dream?

She'd have to take it up with Chris tonight, she decided. For now, she had to get to work.

THREE

'MISS SCHWARTZ, YOU'RE EARLY.' Martin Thorpe made the statement sound like an accusation.

'I thought I could help you get a head start on the day.' Dulcie decided she might as well turn it into a credit. Behind her adviser, she could see Nancy, the departmental secretary, making coffee. 'As soon as I've gotten caffeinated.'

'How early did he get here?' she asked the plump secretary once she'd joined her in the little room that served as both Nancy's office and an informal grad students' lounge. 'How early did you?' It wasn't even nine, pre-dawn by the grad student clock, but Nancy only smiled.

'Only a little earlier than usual, dear. I suspected he might be a bit tense today.'

Dulcie raised her eyebrows at the understatement, but kept her mouth shut. Nancy was a staunch ally, and her maternal tendencies had made life easier for the graduate students as well as their irritable leader. Besides, she made great coffee.

Filling her mug, Dulcie changed the subject. 'Who's coming in today?' While Martin Thorpe was the titular head of the conference, Nancy handled most of the actual organizing.

'Hold on.' The secretary retreated to her desk, although Dulcie suspected she had the schedule memorized. 'Stella Roebuck, from Tech. She should be here by noon. Marco Tesla from Cal—'

'Marco Tesla?' This was news. Marco Tesla was *the* rising star in postmodern criticism, which was *the* hot discipline. Then again, that was Stella Roebuck's area of expertise, too. 'Isn't that, ah, a redundancy?'

Nancy nodded. 'Yes, we didn't expect him. I gather he's had some trouble recently with his work. But he got in touch and, well, he is a prestigious name and so Mr Thorpe insisted that we make room for him.' Nancy went back to her notes, and Dulcie saw her jot something down. She didn't have to ask: scheduling Marco Tesla and Stella Roebuck so that they appeared complementary and not competitive might be tricky.

'And they are all candidates for the job,' she said, half to herself. 'Poor Thorpe.'

'Not necessarily,' said Nancy, finishing her notes. 'We also have Paul Barnes coming in.'

Dulcie couldn't tell if that was a non sequitur or the result of the secretary giving her papers a last once over. What she did notice was that even Nancy used hushed tones on his name.

'He's here already,' said Dulcie, trying not to sound too excited. 'I met him last night. In the Square.'

'Really?' Nancy looked up at her, then back down at her notes. 'He didn't check in with us yesterday. Though I gather he has friends in the area...'

'It was late. Maybe he just went to the hotel.' Dulcie felt a bit odd, like she'd ratted the academic star out. 'He was probably tired.'

'Maybe.' Nancy was still staring at the schedule. 'Oh, dear. This must be a mistake.' After looking back and forth between two sets of papers, she reached for the phone.

'What?' Nancy's raised hand shushed her, and Dulcie listened, drinking her coffee as the secretary asked to be put through to the conference hotel.

'Miss Schwartz? If you really are here to help out, I could use you.' She turned. Martin Thorpe was standing on the stairs. With his head turned sideways to see into the little office, he looked like nothing so much as a worried vulture.

'Sorry, Mr Thorpe.' She turned to top off her mug. 'I'm coming.'

'No, I understand about the block of rooms, Ms Swift.' Nancy was seated now, and seemingly engaged in negotiation. 'But there are extenuating circumstances. Don't you think you can find something?'

Dulcie paused, waiting for a break. If she could help Nancy sort out a housing problem, she would. The older woman looked up, though, and waved her away. For once, her smile looked a bit forced, but Dulcie smiled back, in support, as she headed toward the stairs.

'You have to find another room for the professor, Ms Swift.' Nancy turned her attention back to the call. 'You see, the two of them can't be running into each other. The success of this conference depends upon it.'

FOUR

'For starters, you'll need to check on the media techs.' Thorpe hadn't looked up from the papers on his desk since Dulcie had stepped into his office. Seeing the pile, she wasn't surprised. It was a little awkward, however, addressing the bald spot on his head.

'Mr Thorpe?' She waited. He didn't look up. 'I kind of thought that as a presenter, I could fulfill other duties for the conference.' Nothing. He seemed to be reading one of the papers. 'Like, perhaps, I could go over to the conference hotel and greet the guests who are arriving today.' It wasn't just that she hoped to spend some time with Paul Barnes, Dulcie told herself. The other academics might need help, too. 'Make sure their accommodations are what they were expecting, and all.'

'Oh.' He looked up and blinked, his eyes wide behind his thick glasses. 'No, I've got that covered. I was hoping, you know, because of your special connections...'

Chris. Dulcie couldn't regret that her adviser knew her boyfriend. They had met when they had helped Thorpe adopt a strange, stray kitten Dulcie had found. However, it did mean that her adviser now viewed her as having the inside track to anything technical. Even if he just wanted her to make sure the conference would have sound and computer connections; Chris's work was far more advanced.

'Of course.' Dulcie wasn't really in a position to refuse. She could, however, drive a bargain. 'But since

I'll be working on the conference, I assume I can skip our meeting this afternoon?'

'But...your presentation? Don't you want to...' He stopped himself and blinked, his eyes going wide as comprehension dawned. His top grad student was getting help from one of his top rivals. 'Fine.' He bent back over his papers.

Dulcie knew she'd been dismissed, but she couldn't go yet. Her preference for Renée Showalter wasn't personal, or not entirely, and she had to let Thorpe know. 'How's Tigger doing?' The marmalade kitten seemed like a safe subject.

'Fine,' Thorpe repeated. Then, as if he'd really heard the question, he looked up. 'Though I have to say, he's a strange little fellow. I thought dogs were the ones that howled at the moon. For the last few nights, as the moon has been waxing, he's been sitting in the window and staring at it. I swear, after I go to sleep, I hear him making the strangest sounds.' He paused and waited, but Dulcie didn't venture a response. 'I guess I'm just not that familiar with cats,' he said, finally, bending back over his papers.

Returning downstairs to the student lounge, Dulcie sent her paper to the printer. There was a queue, however. Someone's spring syllabus was being spit out, page by page, and Dulcie found herself looking through the papers that had already piled up. A reading list: Hawthorne, Mather, Irving. And under that, more titles. 'The Look of Love: Deconstructing Gender Attraction in the Romance Novel'. Surely that wasn't part of the core curriculum? No, it had been spewed out earlier. She balanced her empty mug on the pile to read more.

'Is that the end of the pot, Dulcie?'

Dulcie looked up guiltily, grabbing at her mug. She'd

thought Nancy was too preoccupied to notice her. 'Do you want me to set up another?'

'No, no.' The older woman stood. 'I can use the break.'

Dulcie watched as she pulled a canister from the cupboard and counted out scoops. 'And two for the pot,' Nancy said, to herself.

'So that's the secret.' The department's coffee was legendary.

'It's not exactly rocket science, dear.' Despite her words, she looked pleased as she added the water and set the machine to brew. 'When I first came here, Professor Bullock told me that strong coffee was the key to holding the department together. Of course, things were a little less hectic in those days.'

Dulcie nodded. Back then, it had been difficult to get the go-ahead to study a Gothic novel, never mind a romance. She'd considered herself lucky when Bullock had taken her on. Her original adviser, as well as the last actual chairman the department had had, he'd been a full university professor, too, with an endowed chair in eighteenth century literature, and a score of graduate students doing his work. But all the perks and all the supporters—and Dulcie counted herself among them—had only helped hide his precipitous decline into dementia, which had left the department in a bit of a mess.

'Do you think that's why the university hasn't named a new chair yet?'

Nancy shook her head, though she seemed to follow Dulcie's train of thought. 'I don't know, dear. I do know that Mr Thorpe seems to be better these days.' She leaned in. 'Having a pet is good for him.'

Dulcie smiled. Nancy had been instrumental in pairing the man and the kitten.

'I only hope…' Nancy cut herself off. 'Well, we shall see. There, I believe it's brewed.'

'What?' Dulcie ignored the coffee. 'Have you heard something?'

Nancy made a fuss about finding her own mug and wiping it out before turning back to Dulcie. 'I don't believe anything is certain, dear. I do know that several of the candidates are being given special treatment.'

'I heard you on the phone.' Dulcie reached for Nancy's mug and filled it, while trying to think of a way to ask which candidates were being so demanding. 'And I know how these conferences can be.' It was the best she could come up with. 'I'm sorry, I didn't mean to eavesdrop.'

If Nancy didn't take the bait, at least she was too polite to call Dulcie out on a lie. 'I'm afraid that was my fault, Dulcie. I must have overlooked some of the paperwork.'

'Oh?' Dulcie poured her own coffee and waited, but Nancy only shook her head.

'I've gossiped enough.' She walked back toward her desk, and the pile of forms that awaited her attention. 'And I believe your paper finished printing several minutes ago.'

FIVE

WITH NO OTHER excuse to linger, Dulcie gathered her pages and headed out for the Science Center. Although the big, modern complex wasn't her department's usual turf, the Center had the university's two largest lecture halls, as well as smaller classrooms that would work for presentations like hers. That made it perfect for the conference. From tomorrow's opening keynote through Sunday, talks could run simultaneously. With one central location, scholars could gather, meeting and chatting in the center's spacious lobby no matter what the New England winter threw at them. It might even mean more people would be likely to step in to hear her and the other junior speakers.

At least, that had been the plan. It was reading period at the university, the time between classes and exams, and that had originally been seen as a plus. Dulcie, for example, only had a few study groups to monitor—she tried to avoid the word 'babysit'—rather than her regular, overfull teaching schedule. However, with most of the students already away on their holiday break, someone in facilities maintenance had decided these two weeks were optimal for renovating the modernist building's less-than-modern plumbing. By the time the conflict had been pointed out, the work was already under way.

Now construction crews were working at a frenzied pace, trying to get the lobby cleared out and the taps turned back on before attendees started to arrive. In a supreme act of faith, Thorpe had decided to trust that they would. Faith or, Dulcie realized, desperation. Not only would it look bad for the conference to have to deviate much from its published schedule, it would create a logistical nightmare. The Center, with its jumbo lecture halls, had had everything. Moving it anywhere else meant lost time, lost opportunities, and, undoubtedly, lost academics, wandering through the wilds of wintry Cambridge.

It didn't bear thinking about, Dulcie decided, unconsciously siding with her adviser. Better to hope for the best, and as Dulcie skirted a canvas drop cloth, she made herself do just that. Besides, the building hadn't been entirely shut down by the work. Down in the basement, the university media services and the computer lab were still at full power, unaffected by the construction and plumbing crews. Not even facilities maintenance would dare mess with those, she thought as she descended the stairs. After locating the building's one working bathroom, she went in search of Chris's office, which opened off the lab.

'Knock, knock.' Her boyfriend's door was open, but she suspected he was asleep in his chair. The way he jumped up confirmed it.

'Dulcie!' He turned toward her, pale but smiling. 'My God, what time is it?'

'After ten.' She shook her head. 'You must have been really out. I wasn't even sure if you'd still be here. Why don't you go home, get into bed?'

The smile faded. 'I don't know. I've got to be back here at one for my section.'

'Poor dear.' She closed the door behind her and came

over to put an oversized blueberry muffin on his desk.
'I didn't think the café was functioning, so I picked this
up on my way over. But I'm sorry I woke you. Was it
a crazy night?'

'I—I don't know.' He ran his hand through his hair,
pushing his long bangs off his face. 'It's the craziest
thing. I feel like it was hectic, but I don't really remember.'

'Maybe you slept more than you realize.' She hoped
that was true. 'Unless,' she took in his waxy complex-
ion, the purple rings around his eyes—and the fact that
he hadn't yet inhaled the muffin—'you're coming down
with something.'

'No, it's been wonderful to be down here without
hearing someone clanging on a pipe. I feel great.' He
stood and yawned, before looking down at the plate.
'I'm not even hungry.'

'Chris Sorenson, you are sick.' She tried to sound
like she was joking, but this was worrisome. She broke
off a piece of the muffin top for herself, and—out of
habit, she suspected—he reached for the rest. 'What
happened to your hand?'

'My hand?' He held up the one with the muffin and
turned it over, so they could both see the scratches that
broke the skin. 'Wow, I don't know.'

'Were you playing rough with Esmé again?' She took
his hand in hers. The scratches looked too deep—and
too widely spaced—for the little cat's claws. 'Or did
someone bring a dog in?'

'A dog…' He seemed lost in thought. 'Maybe that was
it. I thought I heard something last night. Howling…'

'Down here?' Dulcie couldn't even hear the construction down here, only the quiet whirr of machinery.

'I think so.' He put the muffin back on the plate. 'Maybe it was a dream. Maybe that's why I feel so rested.'

Dulcie bit into the pastry to keep from replying. Her boyfriend might have said he felt fine, but he didn't look like himself. And his dream seemed a little too close to hers.

Not until he had eaten the rest of the muffin did she feel comfortable leaving him. Even then, she convinced him to close the door behind her and to nap for an hour, at least.

'We'll go to bed early tonight,' she promised.

'With the conference starting? Not likely.' The grin that opened up his face reassured her, somewhat. And with a kiss, she went off to do Thorpe's bidding.

'HALL A AND HALL B the next three nights.' The media tech seemed amused by Dulcie. 'Then B for the final presentation. Got it.' The tech—Kelly, she'd said her name was—swung her terminal around so Dulcie could see the schedule, each box filled out with the acronym ELLA and the last name of the presenter. 'Assuming the building is open, we'll get it done. We do know our job, you know.'

'I know.' Dulcie felt she owed the boyish tech an explanation. 'It's Thorpe, my department head. He's a little nervous about the conference.'

'I figured.' Kelly gave her a conspiratorial grin. 'He called three times yesterday. "Barnes must have Hall A and Showalter Hall B, and do be sure that you don't mess up the slides."'

'He said that?' Dulcie cringed. Kitten or no, Thorpe was not doing well. Then again, Showalter was an ac-

tive candidate for his job. And Paul Barnes was, well...
Paul Barnes.

'That wasn't the worst of it.' Kelly scooted her chair
closer. 'He was asking about the renovations, about the
exits, about access and when the new bathrooms will
be ready. Really going on and on. I mean, we're completely ADA compliant, he should know that.'

'I didn't realize...' Dulcie caught herself. Dishing
about Thorpe within the department was one thing.
Gossiping with a stranger quite another. 'I'm sorry.'

'That was the weird part.' The tech looked thought-
ful. 'The plumbing is going to be out for another day
on the main floor, but we have everything working in
the basement. Only, he didn't want to hear about ramps
or how to work the lift to the stage. He only seemed to
care that people could come and go without running
into each other. I mean, you're all in the same field,
aren't you?'

Dulcie flopped back against the wall. 'It's this conference.' She thought about trying to explain and gave
up. 'And about the job.' That was a little easier. 'So
Thorpe's the interim chair,' she was winding up, five
minutes later. 'But even after the search, the deans declined to name him—or anyone—to the position. And
he has to host this conference, basically, and it's in his
best interest to attract the top scholars.'

'Several of whom might want to steal his job.' The
tech filled in the blanks. 'I get it.' She looked up at Dulcie. 'Who do you want to get the gig?'

Dulcie hesitated. Kelly was being friendly, and the
urge to confess was strong. Then again, the university
was a really small place.

'I can, you know, make sure someone has a better mike.' That grin turned devilish as Kelly raised

an eyebrow. 'Maybe arrange for some static or lighting problems.'

'Oh, you couldn't!' She should never have said anything.

'I'm joking.' Kelly leaned back, laughing. 'Sorry. I should know by now not to tease anyone about tenure here.'

'It's okay.' Dulcie shook her head. 'It's just been so tense.'

Kelly nodded. 'I believe it. I've been working here for four years, and I've seen it all. But I'd be careful, if I were you.'

Dulcie looked up, expectant.

'Your Martin Thorpe might be on the right track with the separate exits and all.' She motioned Dulcie closer and dropped her voice. 'I wouldn't be surprised if someone was looking for a way to sabotage a rival, or even the whole conference.'

Dulcie was about to interrupt—to explain that the conference was better known for love triangles than for anything more dire—when Kelly continued.

'When I came in this morning, I found one of the back doors propped open, when it should have been locked tight,' she said, her voice still low. 'It might just have been a prank, but it looked like someone had been working on the latch—hacking at it with a screwdriver or something. Positively clawing at it. My crew is responsible for making sure everything here is secure when we close out for the night, so I didn't want to report it. I just cleaned it up. But, Dulcie? There was something else strange about the doorway. There was something sticky on the lock—and a little on the floor. I'm not sure, but I think it was blood.'

SIX

'BLOOD?'

That was only one of the many questions Dulcie had, and possibly the least articulate. It didn't matter. No matter how she asked, Kelly was unable—or unwilling—to elucidate before Dulcie had to leave.

'I don't know,' the slim tech had concluded. 'Maybe it was an animal, trapped in here and desperate to get out. But, like, how?' She'd shaken her head and turned back to her terminals, her heavy, dark hair hiding her face. 'Maybe someone was pranking us—or maybe pranking your conference.'

Dulcie didn't entirely agree. For all the high-jinks ELLA was known for, pranking wasn't one of them. But without anything further to add, she'd let Kelly's comment stand. At any rate, the media tech clearly had the mechanics for the auditoriums under control, and Dulcie had a study group scheduled.

It really was babysitting, she thought twenty minutes later as she looked at the students assembled around her. Reading period made the undergrads a little frantic, and the ones who were still here, well, they tended to need even more coddling than usual. She ought to be more sympathetic, she knew that. They were nervous, and it was her job as a teaching assistant to be here to help them. All she could think about, though, was the idea of an animal…and that howl.

'Ms Schwartz?' A nasal voice broke into her reverie. Tom. She'd been fielding his queries all semester. 'What do you say?'

'I'm sorry.' She had to be honest. 'Would you repeat the question?'

'I said, "Why does anyone care, anyway?"' The whine didn't improve the grammar.

'You *asked*,' Dulcie corrected him. Teaching could be a trying proposition on the best of days. Teaching sci-fi—she mentally corrected herself, 'early speculative fiction'—was nearly impossible. Especially to a group of students who had no sense of fun. 'And the reason we spent so much time this semester on this aspect of *The War of the Worlds*, Tom, is because it's a window on readership and perspective.'

'But it was all a sham,' Marcie chimed in. Somehow, she got two syllables out of the last word. 'Didn't they get mad?'

'Some people did. Why? Would you?' Dulcie knew she was prevaricating. With all the preparation for the conference, she'd fallen a bit behind on her prep for this section. Still, she figured she could at least use it as an exercise in critical thinking.

'I don't know.' Marcie shrugged. 'Maybe.'

Dulcie bit her lip and made herself pause before responding. For all she knew, this girl was a whizz at chemistry. 'Anyone else?' Eight sets of eyes stared at her blankly, twelve if you counted the glasses. Dulcie fought the urge to stare blankly back. She couldn't blame them. At this point in the semester, they were thinking more about how to pass the final exam then they were about any deeper meanings in what most of them had probably assumed would be a gut course.

'Let's look at this another way.' She stood up—that helped—and started walking around the table. 'Let's look at what we bring to any artistic experience. When we go to a movie, for example, aren't we sometimes expecting to be entertained?'

The eyes followed her, but the mouths stayed still. 'Or TV. I mean, don't we all turn on the television sometimes knowing that what we're going to watch will be dumb, but because we know that, somehow we can still let it captivate us?'

A shrug. She jumped on it. 'Julie?'

'I don't watch TV,' said the sophomore. 'Only downloads.'

Dulcie resisted the urge to shriek: *It doesn't matter!* She managed to keep her voice even. 'The question is, don't we often set ourselves up to believe in the experience? To enjoy it? Because we want to be entertained?'

'Well, if it's good.' Julie gnawed on the end of her pencil as if she could taste the answer. 'Like, I don't know, that *Glee* rip-off?'

'But that sucks this season,' one of her classmates, Dulcie didn't know his name, chimed in. 'Ever since they got rid of the blonde girl...'

'Okay, everyone!' Dulcie was not at her wit's end yet. She was, however, close. 'Stop it. Here's the deal. What I want you to think about... No.' She had to be literal with this group. 'What I want you to be prepared to discuss is the role of the reader, of the audience, in any creative endeavor.' She paused for a moment while they wrote that down. Or at least texted themselves some version of her assignment. She decided to bulletproof it.

'I am not, repeat not, saying that this will be on the final. But I think it will be useful if you can tell the study group about a book or a television show or a movie—some form of mass media—that you had an idea about. That could be as simple as thinking that you were going to like it. Or not like it. And then be able to tell us how or why that idea—that preconception—influenced your actual experience.' She paused. It was pointless. The moment she'd said this wouldn't necessarily be on the exam, most of them had stopped taking notes.

She had one more shot in the locker. 'Are any of you going to the ELLA talks this weekend?'

Silence.

'You do know that as members of the university, you can attend the conference's public lectures. Don't you? And that many of these same questions of authorship, of reader, even of point of view, will be covered by some of the leading minds in our field.' Dulcie left out that she would be speaking. Surely someone would ask.

As she'd hoped, a hand went up. 'If we go, will we get credit?'

She watched them pack up their tablets and phones with an almost unreasonable flood of relief. At the very least, when she next met with this particularly obtuse bunch, the conference would be over. Maybe she'd have some new ideas by then.

For now, she was off the hook. This group wasn't the sort to hound her with questions. If that was indeed what their vague articulations were. Maybe, she thought, she should be teaching semiotics.

Gothic literature still had her heart, though, and Dulcie scooped her own papers into her bag with a sense of urgency. Professor Showalter should have arrived in Cambridge by now. They'd been emailing and made plans to meet at the Science Center café. Dulcie hadn't realized, then, that the little eatery would be out of commission, but it was still a convenient rendezvous. Besides, the professor had wanted to see the hall where she'd be speaking. Then they could go out, get some lunch, and talk about their plans.

It was almost too good to be true. To have the backing of an esteemed academic, a professor who just might become the head of her own department...

With a twinge of guilt, Dulcie thought of Paul Barnes. Before last night, she had only known the greying academic by reputation. Now that she'd met him, she realized he fit the bill, too. And she had to admit it wouldn't be the worst thing in the world if he got the job either. It wasn't that he had been so solicitous of her well being, though that had certainly been nice. It was also that he was an old school academic, like Renée Showalter—and like herself. Paul Barnes focused on early American fiction, like Showalter did. The fact that he hadn't published much recently—nothing since his groundbreaking and provocatively titled book *So Many Cities, So Many Hills: the Great Awakening in the New Republic*—undoubtedly had more to do with the shifting trends of academia than with his talent. Fashion favored the super-modernists, like Marco Tesla. But the pendulum had to swing back, Dulcie told herself. At any rate, she probably had another year before she'd be out, looking for a job. And after this weekend, she'd have presented at a major conference. Presented in the presence of—and maybe even worked with—two of her idols. Either one of whom might end up here at the university.

Dulcie had a bounce in her step as she made her way back across the Yard, despite the icy wind that buffeted her as she walked. The early morning clouds had parted, exposing a pale winter sun. Even though it didn't give much warmth, the flat white light brightened Dulcie's mood. Time for her own work and most of her students gone: an academic's dream. She laughed as the thought formed; it was such a truism. She was still chortling when her phone rang, which was probably why she answered without looking to see who it was.

'Dulcie, thank the goddess.' Dulcie fell back to earth. Her mother had that effect on her. 'I'm so glad I reached you!'

'Hi, Lucy,' she answered in as calm a voice as she could muster. It had taken a while, but Dulcie had finally learned to ignore her mother's constant drama. 'What's up?'

'Do you still have that cat by you? You know, the special one?' Despite her annoyance at the interruption, Dulcie found herself smiling again. Lucy was so predictable, always starting her phone calls as if they were in the middle of a conversation, leaving Dulcie to piece together whatever she had missed.

'They're all special, Lucy.' She might be amused, but she still couldn't resist ribbing her mother as she walked. 'Isn't that what a devotee of Bast should know?'

'Don't fool with me, Dulcinea Schwartz.' Her mother's tone stopped Dulcie in her tracks and she found herself staring at the phone in the weak sunlight. Sadly, the flat device gave no clue as to what cue Dulcie had misheard—or what the earlier part of the conversation might have been—so she started listening, and walking, again. 'You know the one I mean. The little marmalade. The...the...the tiger cat.'

'The were-kitten?' Dulcie wasn't sure what she'd missed, but she regretted the words the moment they were out of her mouth. She had no proof that Tigger, Thorpe's little orange tabby, had any unusual powers, and was only going on a half-remembered and distinctly fuzzy impression of something she might—or might not—have witnessed about a month ago. She had told her mother about it in a moment of weakness, simply because Lucy was one of the few people on earth who wouldn't automatically assume she was crazy.

'That's the one, dear.' Dulcie had gotten it right. At least partly. 'But you know, "were-kitten" is a misnomer, "were" implying a human element. Unless you've noted other transformative powers?'

Her mother sounded so hopeful, Dulcie hated breaking the news, but she was coming up to the Science Center now, and this didn't seem like the kind of conversation she'd want to continue in anybody's presence. 'No, I'm sorry. And really, Lucy, I'm not even sure what I did see. It's just that…' She paused outside the glass doors. How to explain that she thought she'd seen the tiny orange creature grow into a tiger when she had been threatened? Dulcie had been dizzy from a blow to the head at the time, which made what she thought she had seen even more unlikely.

Maybe the best path was not to explain at all. 'Tigger is now living with Martin Thorpe, my thesis adviser.' Silence on the other end of the line. 'He really needed a cat, Lucy.' Her mother had to understand that.

The depth of the theatrical sigh implied that she did. 'I was afraid that was the case,' Lucy said, after the requisite dramatic pause.

'Why? What's going on?' Even with the weak sun, the day was frosty, and Dulcie wanted to hurry this conversation along.

'Because that means there's another.'

Dulcie rolled her eyes. 'Mom? I'm kind of busy here.'

'Shape shifters aren't all bad, Dulcie. But they don't always know their own powers.' She must have heard Dulcie's intake of breath, because she cut her next dramatic pause short. 'They can be dangerous, Dulcie. Never forget that.'

Dulcie looked once more at the phone, but it had gone dead in her hand. Knowing Lucy, that could have been intentional. Her mother had been known to hang up in a fit of pique, especially when she felt her daughter was not taking her seriously. Then again, it was just about equally likely that her mother had accidentally disconnected her—or that she or one of her co-residents had forgotten to pay the communal phone bill again. Either way, as Dulcie opened the door to warmth and noise of another sort, Dulcie suspected that she'd be hearing more about the kitten or—what was it?—shape shifters soon enough. It was time to get her own life into gear.

SEVEN

'DULCIE!' RENÉE SHOWALTER'S SIMPLE, enthusiastic greeting, audible even above the construction noise, was much more satisfying. And although her thick red hair was beginning to come loose from its old-fashioned bun, the visiting academic also looked a lot more like the woman Dulcie would hope to be one day than did her own mother. At least professionally, Dulcie amended with a flash of guilt. Lucy couldn't help who she was, just as Dulcie would never be as tall as the woman beaming down at her. 'How are you?'

'A little harried.' Dulcie was suddenly aware of her own flushed cheeks. She'd spent so long dallying with her mother that she'd dashed through the lobby to the hall. 'Thorpe has me checking on the audio-visuals for the conference.'

'Ah.' Professor Showalter nodded. She clearly understood, and Dulcie was pierced by another pang. The jackhammers didn't help.

'He just wants everything to be perfect,' she backtracked, once the noise had died down. 'And it does mean I get to meet everyone. Though, of course, I already know you, and I ran into Paul Barnes last night.' Too late, Dulcie tried to mask the lift in her own voice.

'Paul Barnes?' Showalter must have heard it, too, but she refrained from commenting further.

'I think he must know my work.' Dulcie couldn't resist a little brag. 'He seemed to recognize my name.'

Showalter nodded, as if she weren't surprised, and Dulcie felt another flush of pride. Maybe she did have a career in this field, after all. Then again, she realized, Showalter might be thinking that she, Dulcie, preferred the male academic. Which, of course, she definitely did not.

'So anyway, helping Thorpe is no big deal, really,' she said, to change the subject. 'I'm happy to help.'

'Of course you are, but…' The older woman bit her lip. Another bout of hammering interrupted whatever she might have been about to say. 'Well, it can be very easy to take advantage of grad students,' she continued once it stopped. 'Free labor and all.'

'Thanks.' Despite the noise—which had now turned to a strange whining—Dulcie really was thrilled to be here. Being recognized by Paul Barnes was an honor. But what she had with Renée Showalter was special. It wasn't simply that the red-haired academic was actually interested in her specific field—the 'she-authors' who penned the majority of the great Gothic novels. And it wasn't simply that she had uncovered a trove of letters that were already proving relevant to Dulcie's thesis. It was that she had handed those letters over without conditions. Clearly, she still remembered what it was like to labor in the lower levels of academia.

'Anyway, I'm here,' Dulcie said once that whining— maybe it was a drill?—stopped. She had two hours free to spend with the scholar. She wouldn't waste it in complaining. 'And here's the paper.' With a flourish, she brought forth the printed pages. 'The café is out of commission for the duration, but I know the best lunch place in the Square. I can go ahead, get us a table, if you want to find a quiet corner to take a quick look.'

Renée Showalter reached for the pages, but for a moment Dulcie was hesitant to hand them over. There was something about her. A look like she was trying to say something. Or would be, but for that drill.

'I revised these after our last conversation,' Dulcie jumped in at the next quiet moment, hoping to pre-empt whatever problem the professor was about to bring up. 'And I got Mina's input, too. She finished her edits last night. I mean, she didn't have much to say about the actual drafts, but her biographical research might mean a lot.'

'I'm sure it will, but Dulcie?' A pained look flashed on her face. 'I'm really sorry about this, but I'm not going to be able to do lunch. Something—well, some old personal business has reared its ugly head.' She forced a smile on her face, but it was a sad smile. 'I'm sure you understand. Maybe we can sneak in a quick chat tomorrow—before the conference starts?'

Dulcie felt her heart sink. The conference was only three days long, and the hours leading up to the opening address were going to be some of her busiest. Still, the professor was already being so generous. The return of the jackhammer gave her time to compose herself. 'That will be great,' she made herself say, once the noise subsided. 'Maybe I can actually sneak in some library time.'

'Thatta girl.' Showalter's smile looked more real. 'But don't forget to get something to eat, too.'

SOMEHOW THE IDEA of Lala's three-bean burger had lost its appeal, so Dulcie ducked back into the cold and walked one block further, to the wrap place for a tuna roll-up. If she could talk the counter person into chopping some pickles up for a bit of crunch, it would still be a good lunch.

The problem, ultimately, wasn't the pickles. Although the woman behind the counter had raised her eyebrows at the request, she had done a neat job with them, dicing some dill chips into matchsticks. However, once Dulcie had the sandwich she wasn't sure what to do with it. The tiny storefront focused on takeout, but the day was too cold for eating alfresco. The few tables squeezed in like an afterthought seemed to have been commandeered by a seminar. From what she could hear, Dulcie guessed they were refugees from the Science Center, or else they simply liked discussing basic ASCII. When she finally spotted an empty chair, she made a beeline for it, thinking she could drag it away from the group, and just as quickly realized that in her current mood, any pleasure in her meal would be negated by the assembled crowd.

It wasn't that they were geeks. She lived with one, quite happily. And the language was vaguely familiar, from too many overheard conversations between Chris and his friend Jerry. But as she had listened the tone had turned from the usual mellow nerdiness of ones and zeros to something more personal—and nastier.

'As soon as there's a girl in the story, it all goes bad.' That was the line that had stopped her, just as she was reaching for a chair. The applied math department was still largely male, and that could breed misogyny—especially among the younger members.

'I know he's got a girlfriend now, but really…' Jealousy, Dulcie knew, was largely to blame, and she snuck a peek over at the speaker, expecting to see a spotty face on a body either way too skinny or too round to attract its own mate. All she could see, however, was a thatch of dark hair, unfashionably long. 'He should know bet-

ter than to get involved with one of those high-mainte-
nance chicks, is all I'm saying.'

'Maybe there was an emergency?' The equally
shaggy friend—Dulcie guessed freshman—sounded
somewhat more reasonable. 'Maybe she was sick? Or
he was?'

A third geek turned back toward the other two,
nearly dislodging a pile of parkas with the move. He
grabbed at them. 'Did anyone get an explanation?'

Dulcie hung back as he re-stacked the coats, but the
little café was small. Through a chorus of 'nuh-uh' and
other assorted demurrals, she got a better look. Hood-
ies, jeans…no more spots than usual. As much as she'd
wanted to dismiss these anti-girlfriend activists as com-
plainers, she had to admit they looked like ninety per-
cent of the male university population, down to their
salt-stained sneakers.

Anyway, the direction of the complaint seemed to
have changed, or at least softened. 'I guess I shouldn't
blame the girl,' the first speaker was saying, the whin-
iness in his voice toned down, too. 'He's the one who
made the commitment. He's the one who let us down.'

'Right.' The sarcasm was unmistakable as yet a
fourth student chimed in. 'And he couldn't leave a note.
Or get someone to cover. I mean, hell, he was supposed
to be the cover. No way. These grad students,' the student continued. 'They forget what it's like to be an undergrad and flailing, especially during reading period.
I mean, it's not like they're helping us for free.'

It was too close to home. She hadn't missed a reading period help group—not yet—but as distracted as
she had been recently, Dulcie could too easily imagine
her own students complaining about her in this fashion.
Although she was seized by the urge to grab the fourth

student and yell at him—*Quit saying 'I mean!'*—Dulcie resisted. Better to eat elsewhere, and not let herself get drawn into someone else's fight. First, she needed to nab some napkins: tuna could be drippy. But as she navigated around the crowd toward the condiment stand, she couldn't resist eavesdropping further. Someone must have noticed her interest, however. Whether because she was an outsider, or because she was of the suspect gender, the voices had all dropped, and Dulcie found herself pretending to be oblivious, as she stuffed napkins in the sandwich bag.

Of course, she told herself. Some of them would recognize her. She'd come by when Chris was working often enough to meet some of his regular tutees. She'd even brought her own laptop by over the last few months, happy to work in Chris's company, as he helped guide hapless undergrads over the basic programming hurdles. That had to be the reason they were now staring at her, she decided. Or, perhaps, she should not have taken quite so many napkins.

Well, too late now to do anything about that, she decided, rolling the top of her bag closed. It was their fault that she couldn't sit here, anyway. They were the ones forcing her out into the cold. Besides, it was probably simple familiarity that caused them all to watch her as she made her way back around the chairs and out. After all, she was pretty sure she heard at least one of them say 'Chris'.

EIGHT

Two minutes later, she was regretting her timidity. Better she should have stayed, meeting any barbed comments with a few piercing words of her own. At least she'd have been warm. Instead, she had left the warm storefront to find the pale sun gone, replaced by thin clouds and a biting wind that seemed determined to toss every bit of grit into Dulcie's face.

Nothing for it, she decided, but to get back to the Science Center and to work. Thorpe, at least, would be grateful for her getting a jump on all the preparation. And maybe Paul Barnes would be early.

As she bent into the wind, Dulcie found herself wondering about the cold at the heart of the average undergraduate. All they cared about were their exams, their grades. Was it possible to make them understand what she and Chris loved about their fields? Was it possible even to make them care about their teachers as people?

'We weren't like that at their age. Were we?' She didn't expect an answer as she scurried through the Yard, her voice torn from her by the wind. It was comforting to address Mr Grey, however. It helped her feel that she had truly left that hostile crowd behind.

'*You needn't have retreated, you know.*' The voice seemed to come from right behind her, perfectly audible through the din. Feeling its warmth, Dulcie turned. '*Not all is as you perceive.*'

'Mr Grey!' She couldn't help it. She paused to look

around. But as she could have predicted, the Yard was almost empty. Early afternoon, and only a few stragglers—reading period refugees like herself—braved the blustery weather. Bending once again as a particularly fierce gust blew her curls about, she hurried along, feeling more alone than before.

'*There, there, little one.*' As she reached up to push her hair out of her eyes, she felt his fur, as soft as his voice, brush against her ungloved hand. '*You are among friends here, no matter that it appears otherwise.*'

This confused her. 'Mr Grey,' she murmured. 'Are you saying those students weren't blaming some poor girl for, well, everything?'

A rumble, part chuckle, part purr, seemed to echo the roar of the wind. '*We look for explanations when we do not understand, little one. When intellect and experience fail us.*'

Dulcie waited. When no other words followed, she asked the obvious. 'So, I just made up the misogyny? That first guy didn't blame someone's failing on his girlfriend?'

'*There's more here than your natural philosophy can reveal.*' The voice was fading. '*More for you to learn...*'

Dulcie was alone again. While she couldn't have explained how she knew that, she did, Mr Grey's final words echoing in her ears as she ran the last few hundred yards to shelter. So there was more for her to learn here? She mulled that over. Did he mean about male undergrads? She hoped not. There was something unnerving about the scene she had just left. It wasn't that they were that angry, and she certainly didn't think they'd be dangerous. Just...something unsettling and almost, maybe, familiar. Something she couldn't quite place.

Natural philosophy...that meant 'science', basically,

Dulcie recalled, as she once again pushed open the big glass doors. Although the author of *The Ravages* was more concerned with tumult of the heart than of any alchemical experiments, Dulcie knew enough to recognize the older term, in use long before the disciplines separated so completely in the later nineteenth century.

'Looking for explanations'—well, that was what she was doing, wasn't it? Was Mr Grey urging her to study science at this late a date? Looking around, she paused to consider the question. From that glass entranceway to the huge silver Möbius strip here in the lobby, everything about this place was alien to her. Even the flyers that lined those white walls, luring her colleagues to various talks, seemed to swim with numbers rather than words, unless you counted the occasional bit of Greek.

It was an odd place for the English department to hold a conference. And there was little chance, she realized with a sinking feeling, that the construction would be finished by tomorrow. Already, her relief at being out of the cold was giving way to a feeling of helplessness. How could they host international scholars with only one set of working bathrooms? As if on cue, Dulcie felt something splash on her foot, and looked up, worried. But no pipes were running overhead, dripping or not. Wrapped only in wax paper, her sandwich had begun to leak. Maybe this was her cue. Maybe she was supposed to go back into that café and face down those undergrads. But that could wait until after lunch, couldn't it?

Holding the sodden bag away from her body, Dulcie glanced around for options. 'Kelly!' The media tech had come out of Lecture Hall A, leaving the door swinging behind her. 'Kelly!' Dulcie called again. Some female company would be welcome right about now.

Her voice was drowned out, however, by the squeal

of something mechanical, and the media tech disappeared down the stairs. The computer center—the one place Dulcie most certainly did not want to follow. Well, she could wait.

Still being careful with her sandwich, Dulcie walked over to the lecture hall. Yes, the door was unlocked, and as Dulcie let her eyes acclimate, she saw that not everything was dark. To her right, she could see through the open door to the sound booth. Inside, the sound board glowed as multiple screens seemed to wait with bated breath. To her left, down the steep slope of seats, was the stage area. One spotlight picked out a podium, obviously set up for the conference speakers who would be arriving soon. The house lights were down, but Dulcie didn't need to see to eat. Careful not to trip—or to get more mayonnaise on herself—Dulcie found her way to the back row. It was pleasant in the dark. Maybe, she thought, here in the quiet Mr Grey would come visit again.

BY THE TIME Dulcie was halfway through her sandwich, she'd given up on Mr Grey. He'd been in a riddling mood, but he'd clearly wanted to cheer her up—and he had. She might have felt better anyway: the sandwich was good, and coffee alone was not enough to sustain one. With some food inside her, even the scene at the café began to seem less ominous. Sure, some undergrads were peeved at a section leader or something. That wasn't a big deal. Dulcie couldn't imagine missing a meeting, but she'd occasionally shorted her office hours—getting there late or sneaking out a bit early. She'd have to ask Chris about how applied science handled such things. Maybe his department was much stricter, being as how they were all into numbers and precision and all that. Of course, he was such a straight arrow that he probably wouldn't know if any of his colleagues were bending the rules.

Like she was, sitting here. Eating. Students were allowed in the hall. Food wasn't. Well, she'd clean up after herself, she resolved, and took another bite, dropping one of her napkins in the process. Down below, stage right, a door opened. Kelly, the media tech, entered and walked to the podium. Dulcie watched, her mouth full, as the other woman attached a microphone to the podium's stand. Dulcie chewed faster, watching as Kelly unspooled a long cord. She should announce herself. Wave hi, at the very least, before she startled the boyish tech.

Tucking the last third of the roll-up back in its bag, she looked around for a trash can. Another napkin would have been helpful too, she realized, as she wiped the back of her hand across her mouth. Well, people probably brought their meals in during classes all the time, rules or no. She stood, ready to hail Kelly, when she realized that the tech had ducked back into the wings.

Maybe she should just descend to the stage. Only, just then, Dulcie felt something. A soft brush—something moving—right by her leg. She looked down and didn't see anything. Only that lone napkin, white against the dark, and she remembered: claw marks. Like an animal had been trapped inside, desperate to get out.

The lack of a trash receptacle took on a darker meaning, as did the prohibition against food. Rats, thought Dulcie. Or, no, a rat couldn't reach the door lock, could it? Something bigger: feral cats. Feral dogs? The memory of that howl popped into her mind. That couldn't be what Mr Grey had wanted her to find out about, could it?

She really hoped not, and suddenly the idea of finishing her lunch—even of socializing with Kelly—was a lot less appealing. Not that she'd risk leaving anything here for any…thing to eat. Conscious of all the mayo on that napkin, she ducked down to retrieve it.

'Hello!' A woman's voice, stretching the single word out like a melody. By the time she stood up, the woman had already passed by. 'Anyone there?'

Dulcie was about to respond when Kelly appeared.

'Ms Roebuck?' The slim tech shaded her eyes from the stage light, peering up into the dark.

'I know I'm a bit late,' said the newcomer. 'Personal things…' She waved her tardiness away with one hand and stepped into the light. 'But I'm here now.'

Dulcie leaned back on her seat, watching. So this was Stella Roebuck. The scholar, a rising star in postmodern circles, looked the part in a tight, tailored suit that might have been designed for an anorexic man. Gender roles: Dulcie flashed back to what she'd seen in Nancy's office. Something about 'deconstructing attraction in gender roles'. 'The Look of Love', that was it—the title of her talk. Seeing Stella Roebuck, Dulcie had to admit it was perfect: the academic intentionally mirroring the subject and simultaneously throwing it into disarray, or something. It was stagy, but maybe she had to be—teaching English at Tech. Still, at this rate, Dulcie mused, she'd end up dressing like a Georgian noblewoman. At least the big wigs would give her some height.

Stella Roebuck, however, had chosen her look—if not her subject—wisely. As she ascended to the stage, the lights caught her dark, short hair, throwing blue reflections off of what were obviously carefully crafted angles, and the hands that now turned in to rest on slim hips ended in black nails.

'Well, this is something.' She turned to look out at the seating area, and Dulcie shrank back. It wasn't Roebuck's work per se. As much as Dulcie disagreed with the current fad for deconstructing everything down to its vowels and consonants, she'd pretty much conceded that fight. Academia had its trends, just like everything else, and she held on to the thought that at some point, if she persevered in her career, people would get back to reading for its own sake again. And although Stella Roebuck—'the beautiful Stella', she'd heard her called—was probably within a year or two of Dulcie's age and already such a big deal, it wasn't professional jealousy. Roebuck focused on criticism. That was a world unto itself.

No, it was more basic. Dulcie looked down at her sweater, at the bag she held. Stella Roebuck was glamorous, from that blue-black hair to the high-heeled boots that seemed particularly inappropriate for a New England winter. Kelly was slim, too, but this woman made the dark-haired media tech look positively masculine by comparison. Stella Roebuck was a star, made for the big hall, just as Dulcie might forever be relegated to the small seminar room down the hall.

'Now I'm being silly,' Dulcie muttered to herself, and looked around. This would be a good time for Mr Grey to show up with some encouraging words about how they were all different, and how the most beautiful trait in any person was compassion.

'Stella, darling!' a voice called out, but it belonged to a human male. A door on the other side of the auditorium swung open and a tall man strode in. 'You ran off so quickly...' He trotted down toward the stage, as if to illustrate.

'Some of us have appointments.' From her place on the stage, it was natural for her to look down on the newcomer. Dulcie sensed that she liked it that way.

'Ms Roebuck?' Somehow Kelly had gotten over-looked with all the entrances. She was standing there, holding a clip-on mic. 'Did you want to try this out?'

'Why would I want that?' Another flap of the hands, dismissing the dark-haired tech.

'I was told you had some concerns about our set-up here.' Kelly was holding her own, and Dulcie wished she could support her. 'That you might not want to use the podium.'

'Not the best way for me to make a presentation. Is it, darling?' She strode across the stage, assured and leggy in those boots. 'But I didn't come by to try out your little gadgets.'

'Ms Roebuck...' Poor Kelly, she was trying.

'No, what concerns me is the security in this hall.' The stylish academic stopped short, peering into the darkness. Dulcie shrank back, hoping for invisibility. 'The fact that I could walk in means little. But that *he* could...' Another outflung hand, this time dramati-cally pointing to the man who had reached the stage. He looked familiar, the stage light reflecting off the silver in his hair.

'I'm going to be making a very important announce-ment here tonight. Groundbreaking, if I may say so. And I don't want to risk anything happening—anything or anyone getting into my system.'

'You don't have to worry—' Kelly didn't get to fin-ish her sentence.

'Of course I have to worry.' Stella Roebuck cut her

off, as she strode to the edge of the stage. 'I have enemies here. Enemies and, worse, former lovers. But you would know about that. Wouldn't you, Paul?'

That last bit was directed at the man at her feet. The man who had greeted her so affectionately, and who had come to stand, like a supplicant, beneath her. The man, Dulcie realized with a sinking feeling, she now recognized as her savior, the great Paul Barnes.

NINE

THIS NOT ONLY didn't concern her, she might as well be invisible. Dulcie stood frozen for another few moments, as the great professor pleaded with the woman above him to be reasonable, and Dulcie remembered Nancy's words. Was it Paul Barnes and Stella Roebuck who couldn't be roomed near each other? It sounded like Stella had another lover, or more, in the wings, and for all Dulcie knew the entire conference was a hotbed, so to speak, of exes and currents, all seeking to hook up or dodge the others. She shook her head in disbelief. This wasn't what she'd expected when she decided on a life in academia. Thank the goddess that Chris was not only not in her department, but also a sane and faithful type.

Meanwhile, Kelly was standing by, looking increasingly impatient. If Dulcie could have rescued her, she would have—pulling the tech backstage by pretending to worry about wiring or room assignments. She certainly shouldn't be kept waiting, like a lesser serving person. But to announce herself now just seemed like it would make more trouble than it was worth, and so, garbage in hand, Dulcie made her way to the back of the auditorium and carefully, quietly, out to the lobby.

Only to run into Renée Showalter. 'Professor!' It was a happy surprise. 'I was hoping we could talk before tomorrow.'

'Dulcie?' The professor sounded startled. 'Did you...?' She looked over at the lecture hall door.

'I'm supposed to run interference, help the speakers get set up. But they don't need me in there,' Dulcie explained. 'You weren't looking for me, then?'

'No, no.' The older woman smiled sadly. 'I'm sorry.' She turned away to look at the door.

'You can go in,' Dulcie said, and reached to open it for her. 'Stella Roebuck is setting up, but I can't imagine she'll take long.'

'No, never mind.' Showalter forced something that looked like a smile on to her face as she looked down at Dulcie. That smile faded as she looked up, beyond her. 'I should go.'

'Of course.' Dulcie watched, confused, as the scholar took off. Only as Renée Showalter disappeared around the corner did Dulcie realize that she was hurrying after Paul Barnes, who must have emerged from the auditorium's other door and been standing there, looking for her. And that she—Dulcie—was missing an opportunity.

'But Professor Showalter, wait!' she called, and hurried after her. 'Did you get a chance to look at the paper?' In her long camel-hair coat, Showalter should have been easy to keep track of, even as she hurried to join the other scholar, but with the crowd in the atrium she lost them both. Dulcie paused, looking at the auditorium's other door. Maybe Paul Barnes had changed Showalter's mind and they had ducked back inside. She reached for the door, only to be stopped by a hand on her shoulder. She turned.

'Oh good, Professor—' Dulcie said.

And stopped in mid-sentence. The blue-black hair in its artful spikes. The fitted suit with those ridiculously pegged pants. The figure that had stopped her had turned away, but Dulcie wouldn't forget those particular fashion signifiers. Had Stella followed her out only to sneak up on her?

'Oh, miss, maybe you can help me?' The slim figure before her spun around, and Dulcie found herself face to face with a man. 'I'm looking for Lecture Hall A?'

'Right—right behind me.' Dulcie couldn't stop staring. The man before her had a square jaw and just the right amount of beard to make him look masculine. In fact, the tightly cut suit and the bedhead hair seemed to play up his male good looks as much as they had Stella's female ones. 'You must be—' She caught herself. Better to ask a question than to make an assumption. 'Are you looking for Stella Roebuck, perhaps? Because she's in there now, up at the podium with Kelly.'

'God, no.' He tossed his head back so the little points of hair bobbed. 'But thanks for the warning, darling. I guess I'll have to do my soundcheck later.' He leaned forward, as if to kiss her. Dulcie held her breath, mesmerized. But all he did was touch her cheek, gently, with one outstretched finger. 'Pickle,' he said, and he was gone.

TEN

'I CAN TELL YOU, Mr Griddlehaus, because I know you can keep a confidence.' Dulcie was safe, safe in the bowels of the Mildon Rare Book Collection. 'Some of our visiting scholars are beyond the pale.'

'Really, Ms Schwartz?' The wide eyes blinking behind the enormous glasses didn't look any more curious than usual. They didn't look disapproving, either. Dulcie had never gossiped with her favorite librarian, but she was too full of news right now to worry about his censure.

'I don't know if he was her twin or her lover. Or how Paul—' She stopped herself. Actually naming one of the parties would be going too far. Especially since he was the one she admired. 'Or how they all ended up at the same conference.'

'Rather like one of those English house parties, isn't it?' He was amused, definitely amused. 'Perhaps we'll have a—' He stopped himself. 'Oh, I'm sorry.' The university had had a murder recently. It wasn't a subject for fun. 'Would you like to examine Box Five?'

As if embarrassed by his near slip, the little clerk retreated. Dulcie let him. She'd been working in his territory long enough to earn some rights, including the freedom to follow him into the archives. Right now, however, they both could use some space.

'Just the first document, if you please,' she called

after him. 'I'm afraid I have to get back to the—ah—party soon.'

She really didn't have more than a half hour. She shouldn't even be here. Only no matter what Thorpe had said, it was quite clear that nobody needed her at the Science Center. Not yet, anyway.

'Must you?' Griddlehaus poked his head out. 'But it's been days.'

'I know.' She nodded, feeling grim. 'I've been working on my paper. And I did get it to Professor Showalter, but then she bailed on me.' She shrugged. 'I guess I should be grateful. If she hadn't, I wouldn't even have this time.'

'She's not part of that…confusion.' Griddlehaus's voice was barely audible over the hum of the climate control system. Still, Dulcie thought the pause was intentional, and discreet. 'Is she?'

'I hope not.' Dulcie sat while the mousy clerk returned and carefully placed a folder before her. 'I assume she knows Paul Barnes. But Stella Roebuck? Oh.' She blushed, realizing what she'd revealed.

Griddlehaus had turned away and was at least pretending not to notice. 'Well, even respected researchers have been known to have their heads turned.' Dulcie looked over at him. 'Intellect not being a safeguard against everything.'

'Mr Griddlehaus…' Dulcie paused, unsure how to proceed. Was the clerk confessing an unwise passion? A foolish affair of the heart? Or was he simply joining in her gossip—and, if so, what did he know about her would-be mentor? 'Is there something you want to tell me?'

'No, no.' He ducked back into the archives. 'Nothing.'

'Mr Griddlehaus?' Dulcie called after him. 'If there's something I should know…'

'Honestly, Ms Schwartz, I suggest you stay out of it.' His voice sounded stronger now that she couldn't see him. Echoing slightly and deeper, and for a moment Dulcie wondered who was speaking. 'Some people bring trouble on themselves.'

Partly because of her limited time and partly, if she was being honest, because of the strangely feline feel of that last comment, Dulcie didn't push for any more. Instead, she focused in on the letter fragment before her. Tattered and stained, it had been hidden in a file of un-identified documents until the recent gift to the Mildon Collection of a newly uncovered set of letters had al-lowed Dulcie to put it into context. That gift, engineered by Professor Showalter from a library in Philadelphia, was only one of the reasons Dulcie adored the profes-sor. The main one was that the older academic trusted Dulcie's instincts and urged her to do the same, even encouraging her desire to expand her thesis beyond its original scope.

While Dulcie had originally set out to analyze a lit-tle-known Gothic novel, *The Ravages of Umbria*, her re-search had led her to attempt so much more. The book, of which only two fragments survived, was all that Dul-cie had hoped: a discussion on the roles of women in eighteenth century society, cloaked in an exciting ad-venture. But the anonymous author had not stopped there. Dulcie had already found several political essays that more clearly outlined the author's proto-feminist views, and she had been able to link them to the novel through the use of repeated phrases. That alone had brought her a tiny bit of acclaim—as much acclaim as could be expected for articles in academic journals about a lesser-known two-hundred-year-old author. It had also, at least in the eyes of her adviser, threatened to derail her. Five years in, Dulcie should be finishing up her dissertation, Thorpe had said, not pursuing new avenues of research.

Dulcie was writing; she'd be crazy not to at this point. But every time she thought she was done researching, something like this would turn up. Something that would entice her to read just a little more, and to tweak her focus ever so slightly.

Glowing with the molten light of embers, deep within the stove, the heavens above gave up their last light, leaving her upon the flagstone, lost in the inky dark as in her own black-hued thoughts.

What Showalter's gift had made clear was that this fragment, this bit of paper, was part of the author's lost second novel. Never mind that Thorpe remained dubious about the book's very existence, not to mention its being penned by the writer of *The Ravages of Umbria*; to Dulcie, this was gold.

The source of her sorrow, the weight that bore down her very soul, she held within her hand. One letter, a missive short, its words unclear, had sunk the barque that was her hope. 'Beware the one you trust,' it read. Although the passing light had left the page as blank as the clouded night, the words once read could not now be forgotten. 'Beware the one who gives you succor, the one upon whom you would lay every Future hope.'

It was a plot twist that Dulcie hadn't expected. True, she hadn't read that much of this book. There had been some kind of crime, some violence that had caused the heroine to flee, alone, through a storm. She had been helped by a stranger, a Frenchman, who may or may not have had some supernatural qualities, this being a Gothic novel, after all. And at some point later, a young lord—handsome, but possibly evil—had been killed. Dulcie did not know for sure whether that lord was the abuser, but she believed he might be. Nor did she know if her protagonist had killed him, possibly in self-defense. That, she was a little leery of finding out. Could a woman justify murder in self-defense back in those days? For that matter, how easy would she find it now?

And now this, another plot twist. Clearly, the heroine had thrown herself on the mercy of a friend or relative. Someone who, perhaps, could not be trusted. It was a good development, one that promised to add more intrigue to the book. Only right now, it made her a bit uneasy.

Pre-conference nerves, Dulcie decided. Just because Stella Roebuck seemed to be juggling hearts didn't mean that anyone Dulcie knew would ever be so cavalier, or so careless. Still…now that the pixie-like scholar had invaded her train of thought, Dulcie realized her ability to concentrate on her own work was gone. 'I think I'd better get back,' she called out. Griddlehaus's oversized lenses accentuated his look of surprise.

'So soon?'

She nodded. 'I can't really concentrate anyway. Not while the known world is descending on us.' Taking the prerogative of a long-time scholar, she began ever

so gently to return the document to its protective case.
'You're probably going to be besieged, down here.'

The Mildon had one of the country's largest col-
lections of rare manuscripts, and Dulcie could easily
imagine the clamor as the visiting scholars descended
to read its folios, codices, and more.

'I don't know.' Griddlehaus looked more than a little
perturbed as she closed up the folder, and she was sorry
she'd brought it up.

'Will you need help?' Dulcie wasn't sure what she
could offer, besides the acid-free case she now handed
over. She wasn't going to leave the little clerk in the
lurch, however. 'You can always limit how many people can come in at once.'

'Oh, no, it's the opposite.' Griddlehaus took the box
from her with both hands, holding it level as he carried it over to a cart. 'In fact, we've had a drop off in
the number of requests from visiting scholars over the
next few days.'

'What?' She watched his back; he slowly shook his
head. 'Maybe the conference attendees don't know the
protocol,' she said. Members of the university were per-
mitted access to the collection, provided they signed in
and showed an appropriate ID. Visiting scholars, however, were supposed to apply in advance for permission
to use the archives. The collection was too big, and its
staff too small, to function otherwise.

'Perhaps you're right.' Griddlehaus turned toward
her, but the furrow in his brow belied his confident
assertion. 'Perhaps that's it. Though, considering our
collection of eighteenth century documents, you would
think...well, never mind. Now, you had a bag, am I
correct?'

Dulcie followed him to the front desk, where her bag

and laptop had been locked into a cabinet. Her friend seemed to be fussing a little more than usual with the paperwork, his head down over the old-fashioned ledger that recorded comings and goings.

'I'm certainly going to try and sneak away again,' she said. Something was going on that she couldn't decipher. For some reason, Griddlehaus seemed to believe he—or the Mildon—was going to be abandoned.

'I'm sure you will, Ms Schwartz.' He looked up, blinking. Dulcie didn't think his myopia was to blame.

ELEVEN

'MR GREY, DO YOU know what's going on?' Dulcie addressed the air as she walked. For a moment, she thought she would get a response: a fat, grey squirrel had stopped in the middle of her path, frozen in place. 'Is something happening with the Mildon?'

It seemed unlikely that the collection would be in any danger. It had an international reputation, and in terms of upkeep was probably less expensive to maintain than any of those fancy new projects Chris was always talking about.

'Mr Grey?' She stopped, too, staring at the squirrel. But just at that moment, a shadow appeared. A hawk, perhaps, or maybe a cloud. And the little creature turned on its fat bottom and scampered up a tree.

'Well, so much for spectral intervention.' She pulled out her phone to see two messages: one from Lucy, and one from an unknown number with a 415 area code. A new worry grabbed her. She shouldn't have played hooky. Someone had been trying to reach her. She skipped over her mother and went directly to the unknown number.

'I assume I've reached Ms Dulcie Schwartz of ELLA?' a man's voice asked. It was familiar, but she couldn't place it, and her stomach sank further. Not Thorpe, but someone connected to the conference. 'Paul Barnes here. Maybe you remember me from last night?' She stopped in her tracks. Surely he hadn't seen her back at the Science Center. Was he going to accuse her of eavesdropping? The message continued. 'I was hoping we could talk about your work while I was out here—your work and mine. I have, as you know, been very impressed by your research, and I have some ideas that you might be interested in.'

Dulcie stood there, staring at her phone. Paul Barnes—the Professor Barnes of *So Many Cities, So Many Hills*—wanted to share some ideas with her?

'I have a particular paper in mind that could use your input. Of course, please keep this confidential,' the message concluded, leaving Dulcie with her mouth agape. Paul Barnes wanted to work with her. With *her*. On a paper!

Trembling with excitement, Dulcie hit callback—and immediately regretted her haste. There was too much she should do first. Too many questions she needed answers to from her adviser—and from Showalter. It was with relief, then, that she heard Barnes's recorded voice.

'Dulcie Schwartz returning your call.' She worked at keeping her voice level and calm. 'I would be happy to speak with you,' she said, and left it at that. Her breathing was still ragged as she started walking again; her mind was racing. It was her presentation—the paper that he'd gotten a look at last night—that had attracted Professor Barnes's interest. Her hours of work were paying off. Maybe by spring she'd have a co-credit on a paper by Professor Paul Barnes. Or maybe a book?

He would undoubtedly make use of the Mildon over the next few days. In fact, maybe he had already applied. Could Mr Griddlehaus have misplaced his application? Was it possible that he didn't know about the application procedure? Or maybe—Dulcie's heart soared—Barnes had been waiting to approach the spe-

cial collection; waiting because he wanted to make sure
Dulcie was available as a researcher. As a colleague.
Maybe he would get the job here—and she would be
able to work under him, here in Cambridge, while Chris
finished his degree. Or, if she had to, she'd go out to
San Francisco, just for a year or two. It was an unbe-
lievable opportunity.

She stopped short. She owed this all to Renée Showalter, of course. If Professor Showalter hadn't directed
those letters toward her, she never would have been
invited to present at the conference at all. Her current
paper wouldn't have been possible, and Paul Barnes
would never have seen the work that so obviously in-
trigued him. Was that why he had asked for her to keep
quiet about the offer? Was he trying to poach her?
Should she not have called back so quickly? Then again,
maybe he knew that Showalter had never offered her a
credit on any of her own publications. Besides, Barnes
had said he'd heard of her other article, too.

She looked down at her silent phone and breathed a
sigh of relief. The call had come in while she was at the
Mildon. She'd seen Showalter go after Barnes before
then. They must have spoken. In fact, Dulcie thought,
she just might owe this opportunity to Renée Showalter,
too. Maybe this was the 'personal business' her mentor
had been referring to—something she hadn't wanted
to tell Dulcie about until it was set up. Either way, all
she had done was return a phone call. She would talk
to Showalter before she decided on any further steps.

She couldn't wait to call Chris. Luckily, he answered
on the first ring. 'Hey, Chris, I've got great news.'

'I was about to call you,' said her boyfriend. 'It's the
strangest thing.'

'Did you hear from Mr Grey?' She'd almost gotten

over being jealous of his connection with *her* cat. Then again, maybe he'd told Chris about the Barnes opportunity. 'What did he say?'

'No, it wasn't Mr Grey, though I have to say, Esmé is being very odd today.'

'Oh?' Dulcie kept walking. She'd spring her news as soon as he was done. 'So is that what was strange?'

'No, not really.' Chris didn't sound like himself. Lack of sleep, Dulcie thought. 'I'm, like, not tired. Dulcie, I couldn't even go to sleep once I got home.'

So much for that theory. Still, this was easily explained. 'Well, you were asleep when I came to see you, Chris,' she said, eager to dispense with these pleasantries. 'I think you're just out of practice. You probably slept through your shift.'

Saying that reminded her of something—those undergrads at the café. 'Hey, Chris, what's your department's policy on missing a shift?'

He laughed. 'Don't worry, Dulcie, I'm not on overnights for the foreseeable future. Not any more.'

'No, not you.' She smiled. It would be good to have him around. 'I overheard some students complaining. Their section leader never showed up or something.' In retrospect, it seemed like such a minor thing.

'They should talk.' Chris was eating. Something crunchy, and Dulcie began to regret that lost half sandwich. 'I had a bunch of appointments set up last night. That's one of the reasons I took the shift; I knew some of my students needed time with me. But Dulcie, none of them showed up. Not a single one!'

'Maybe they just didn't have the heart to wake you?' Dulcie knew the feeling.

'Not these guys. They're hardcore, and we're too close to examine period.'

'Huh.' Dulcie had arrived at the Science Center. Besides, she saw she was getting another call. It was Paul Barnes again. 'Chris, I've got to go, but what's up with Esmé? Does she seem sick?' It was probably nothing, but the little cat was too dear for Dulcie to ignore. The other call went to voicemail.

'No, nothing like that.' Whatever Chris was eating was definitely crunchy. 'Not at all. But she hissed at me when I came in this morning. Then she swiped at me and ran and hid. I watched her run, Dulcie. She wasn't limping or anything. And she'd eaten and everything. It was just, well... I had the feeling that she was afraid of me.'

'That's crazy.' Dulcie pondered, ignoring the urge to rush off the phone. 'Esmé isn't afraid of anything.'

'Maybe you can talk to her when you get home.' Chris sounded hurt. 'She won't say anything to me.'

'You're home tonight, right?' So much had been going on, Dulcie couldn't remember.

'For the foreseeable future,' he said. 'Assuming, that is, Esmé lets me stay.'

'She doesn't have final say.' Dulcie was joking, but something was wrong here. 'Mr Grey does.'

TWELVE

SHE HADN'T TOLD HIM. It wasn't the confidentiality issue that had stopped her. Surely Paul Barnes would expect her to share such news with her boyfriend. Odds were, he simply meant to warn her about bragging to her colleagues, as if she wasn't already aware of how hurtful professional jealousy could be.

It wasn't even that Chris hadn't asked, even though she'd said she had great news. That stung a little, she had to admit. Basically it was that he'd sounded so perplexed, Dulcie didn't have the heart to bring up her own happy surprise again. Well, she told herself, as she clicked through to voicemail, good news is always more fun shared in person. Besides, this latest call might mean she'd have even more to tell.

It didn't. Paul Barnes hadn't left another voicemail, and Dulcie tried to counter her disappointment with reason. After all, she had just called him back; he had probably been hoping to reach her in person. But just as she was about to try the visiting professor one more time, her phone rang again—a number she knew too well: Martin Thorpe's office in the English and American Literatures and Language department.

'What do you mean, you're *not* at the Science Center?' Martin Thorpe sounded more frantic than angry. 'That was the only thing you needed to do this morning.'

Dulcie caught herself. Yes, he was being factually

inaccurate, if not unreasonable. And, yes, it did seem like, perhaps, other candidates for his very job were treating her with a lot more respect these days. But he was, for now, the head of her department, as well as her thesis adviser. And he was under a lot of stress. And so, taking a deep breath, she responded as calmly as she could, explaining how Kelly, the media tech, seemed to have things under control with Stella Roebuck.

'It's not Ms Roebuck I'm worried about.' Thorpe's voice was high and tight. 'It's Marco Tesla. He's experienced some setbacks lately, I gather, and no matter what I—what we—think of his work…' Her advisor caught himself about to make a supremely politically incorrect comment and changed course. 'At any rate, he's due at the Science Center, and he's expecting to be met by a departmental representative. He is, well… he is rather important. Remember, you're representing the department, Ms Schwartz. I need you to do your job, and your job, today, is to smooth some feathers.'

Reprimanded, if not enlightened, Dulcie apologized again only to have it register that she was talking to a dead line. In addition, because of Thorpe's hemming and hawing, she realized she had no real idea of what exactly she was supposed to do. Because Marco Tesla was a late addition to the schedule, Dulcie had no notes about his presentation or what he might need. Still, she figured, between her knowledge of the university and Kelly's, they'd manage. In truth, Dulcie wondered why Thorpe had insisted on her presence. All she would be doing was asking Kelly for help anyway. Could Thorpe be trying to sabotage her? Keep her so busy with his petty demands that she had no time to hobnob with the visiting scholars?

'Protocol, Ms Schwartz. Protocol.' She could still

hear Thorpe's injunction, as well as the worry that made his voice sound tight. What he meant was that a media tech might not bow and scrape enough. Well, Dulcie could do that, out of sympathy if nothing else, and silently promised her absent adviser that she'd track down Marco Tesla before trying Paul Barnes again.

If only her assignment was to aid Showalter, she thought with a sigh. Or Barnes. Anyone, really, that she cared about. As it was, she was going to have a hard time recognizing the rising West Coast star. She knew he did something with deconstructivist criticism, but that was all. If only she had spent more time reading up on the other attendees, maybe she'd have been able to identify him by process of elimination. But her own paper had taken up so much time, and she had needed to brush up on Renée Showalter's latest work. Now it was too late.

Fate—or perhaps a certain feline—came to her aid. As soon as she walked back through those glass doors she saw her own California connection. 'Trista!' she called out to the blonde postgrad. 'Thank the goddess you're here.'

Her friend turned and raised one pierced eyebrow. 'Dulcie, of course I am.'

'What?' Dulcie was so relieved to have found someone who might actually recognize the mysterious Tesla, she almost didn't care what Trista was on about. Still, Trista was a friend, so she played along. 'Let me guess, cute guy alert?'

Trista had the grace to smile. 'Always, but what brings you here? Renée Showalter?'

'Not really.' Dulcie shook her head. 'I mean, I've already seen her. I was able to give her a draft of my paper, but she blew me off for lunch.' That hurt less now that she had gotten that call from Paul Barnes. 'The truth is, I've got to find Marco Tesla, and I thought you might know what he looks like.' She looked around. 'I wouldn't mind running into Professor Barnes, though.'

'The old geezer?' Despite her misgivings, Dulcie nodded. 'Dulcie, you should be careful of guys like him.'

'Tris, just because I admire the man…' Enough was enough. 'I mean, you don't think that's why I'm here.' She paused. ELLA did have that reputation. 'Do you?'

'Of course not! But you're about to present a paper.'

And I may have a credit on Paul Barnes's next paper. Dulcie couldn't say that. Not yet. 'Well, I had help,' was all she said.

'Yeah, well.' Trista popped her gum. Dulcie knew her friend was trying to quit smoking, but her substitute habit only added to the shaggy bleached hair and metal adornments to create a decidedly unacademic look. 'Doesn't everyone?'

Another pop. Dulcie put up her hand. 'Hold on, Tris, I'm not following you. And, do you mind? That gum is really distracting.'

Trista grinned. 'I'm going for post-postmodern,' she said, her voice low. 'I love how it confounds the dean.'

'I'm happy for you, Trista. Really.' Now that Dulcie knew that the look was intentional, she was less worried about her friend. 'Especially if you can point out Marco Tesla for me.'

'Not a problem.' Trista paused to remove the gum from her mouth. She looked around for a place to stash it but, catching Dulcie's glare, dug a tissue out of her pocket to wrap it in. 'I wouldn't mind running into him either. He's hot.'

So that, Dulcie thought, was why her friend had

slammed Paul Barnes. Luckily, Trista hadn't waited for a response. 'Anyway, I saw him a while ago down around the media center,' she was saying. 'Down by where Lecture Hall A lets out? I was going to grab him.' Trista wiggled her pierced eyebrows. 'I mean, metaphorically, of course. But he was huddled up close with Showalter.'

'Renée Showalter? You mean they were cuddling?' Could Dulcie have been wrong? Could *this* have been the personal business the professor had told Dulcie about?

'No, not cuddled. *Huddled.*' Trista repeated the word. 'As in, having a very intense, very private discussion in a public place. That's what it looked like to me, anyway.'

'Huh.' Dulcie thought about it. 'Well, she told me she had some private business to see to.'

Trista was shaking her head. 'Oh, I don't think so. I mean, it takes all kinds, but…'

'What?' Dulcie felt a bit affronted. 'Just because Renée Showalter is eighteenth century and Marco Tesla is the new deconstructivist darling, you think they couldn't be a couple? Just look at me and Chris.' She resisted adding that Trista herself was now more or less living with Chris's even geekier friend, Jerry.

'The body chemistry, Dulcie.' Trista looked at her like she was a freshman. 'There was none. Besides, she's about a foot taller than he is.'

Dulcie waved that off. 'So you're saying it was a professional squabble? Like, I don't know, about a publication? They're not scheduled up against each other.' She went back over Nancy's plans in her mind. No, none of the major speakers conflicted with each other. Then it hit her. 'Wait, what does Tesla look like, anyway? I'm supposed to meet him.'

'He's dreamy,' said her friend. Dulcie rolled her eyes. 'Sorry, he's about five-six, slim as a rock star. And he always dresses in these sharp Thom Browne suits.'

'Blue-black hair, all done up in spikes?' Dulcie knew whom she meant. She'd missed him by one of those spiky hairs.

'Yeah, bedhead.' Trista nodded approvingly. 'A dated look on anyone else, but with those piercing blue eyes, he can pull it off.'

'And do you think he's still there?' Dulcie was more or less used to Trista's crushes. Right now, she was running late.

'No, he went back into the lecture hall. I sort of— ah—shadowed him. That's what I was trying to tell you.' Trista must have picked up on her impatience. 'He wanted to keep talking to Big Red, but she tore herself away. I mean, literally, Dulcie. He grabbed her arm and she pulled it away. What I wouldn't do to have him hold on to me like that.'

Dulcie filtered out that last bit. 'So she took off?' That was disappointing. After all, she now had more to discuss with her unofficial mentor.

'Yeah, I'm sorry. That's why, when I saw you, I thought maybe you two were meeting up.'

'No, I've got to meet Tesla. I'm the department liaison.' Dulcie sighed. 'Actually, I'm really glad you're here. I had no idea what he looked like. But now I think I ran into him earlier.'

'Why don't I come with you anyway?' That wicked grin was back. 'Just to make sure you find the right guy.'

Dulcie couldn't help herself. She grinned back. 'Sure.' She hooked her arm through her friend's. 'We'll be the university welcoming committee.'

'Goody.'

Dulcie could barely keep up with Trista as the taller girl skipped through the atrium. But when Dulcie tried to steer her toward the door to the lecture hall stage, her friend pulled her back.

'No, he was around the back—by where the sound board is,' she said.

Dulcie suspected she wanted an excuse to skip for a while longer, but let Trista lead her around the back of the hall to the other door. There, they unlocked arms, and Trista actually took a moment to smooth down her blouse and fluff up her own spiky hair.

'Tris?' Dulcie asked. 'I do have a job to do.'

'Don't we all,' added Trista, and pulled the heavy door open.

They were greeted by a piercing scream. 'No!'

Trista froze, staring into the dark. Dulcie grabbed her, and pushed her aside.

'Hello? What's going on?' Stepping into the hall from the bright atrium, Dulcie found herself momentarily blind. Only the stage, down below, was still lit. On it, she could see a diminutive figure, hunched over the podium. 'Kelly, are you here?' Dulcie called.

'Yes, hang on!' The voice came from her left—in the sound booth. 'Ms Roebuck—Professor—what's wrong?'

Kelly appeared from behind a nearly invisible door and raced past Dulcie, down to the stage. 'Are you okay?'

'Wait, is that—' Trista had joined Dulcie, and seemed about to sprint down the hall. 'Oh, no.'

Dulcie turned toward her friend, but before she could ask for an explanation, the figure on the stage, now bent almost double, screamed again.

'No!' The figure—it was a woman—turned away

from the podium. Still crouched down, she had her hands up around her ears, as if trying to shield herself from her own screams. 'This can't be happening!'

'What?' Kelly had reached the stage by then. Not bothering with the steps at either side, she hoisted herself up right in front of the hysterical woman. 'Are you hurt?'

'I'm dead. Dead!' She'd collapsed on the stage by then. In doing so, she'd moved enough into the spotlight for Dulcie to see black hair, its spikes rumpled further by her desperate gestures. 'He's out to destroy me! Destroy me!'

Dulcie turned to Trista, who stared back. Horrible things happened in academia, and not all rivalries were kept on the bloodless page.

From the stage, Kelly cried out. 'You, back there! Get a doctor! Quick!' She was on her knees now, bending over to examine the woman, who had curled into a fetal position as she wailed.

'No.' The cry changed, becoming lower, more a reprimand than a scream of pain. 'Don't be silly. I don't need a doctor.' Kelly sat back on her heels, and Dulcie and Trista waited, frozen by this latest turn. The woman on the stage—Stella Roebuck—looked up at Kelly and then out at Dulcie and her friend. 'What I need is a witness. You there—who's out there?'

Dulcie stepped forward. She could sense Trista by her side. 'It's me, Dulcie Schwartz,' she said. 'The grad student you met before?'

'You can't help me, then. But, wait—you must have seen him.' She sniffed, audibly. 'If you've been lurking out there.'

Dulcie shook her head, then, realizing that she might not be visible, found her voice again. 'Seen—whom?'

'My ex.' The words dripped venom. 'Paul Barnes. He's sabotaged me. Again. Just like I knew he would. That man won't be happy until I'm utterly destroyed.'

THIRTEEN

'WAIT, WHAT?' DULCIE looked at Tris, who shrugged. Dulcie and Trista were on the stage by now, Dulcie hoping against hope that the distraught Stella was talking about somebody else. 'You don't mean…' A look from the academic let her know that she meant the intent, if not the literal interpretation of her words. Dulcie swallowed, hard, and answered. 'If you're looking for Professor Barnes, I did see him here, but that was a while ago. I thought you two were talking.'

Kelly looked up from Roebuck's laptop. 'He was with you?'

'He was hanging around. I was *not* encouraging him.' Roebuck's grief seemed to have given way to a sullen resignation. It wasn't pleasant, and Dulcie winced as the visiting scholar looked around and settled her gaze on Dulcie. 'You wouldn't know what it's like.'

'What what's like?' Trista sounded more curious than intimidated, and Dulcie was grateful for her friend's presence.

'When you're a woman.' She paused, looking pointedly at Dulcie. 'A certain sort of woman, men see you in a certain way. And they feel they have rights.'

Dulcie bit back her response. Yes, she had picked up on the intimacy between the two. But if anything, she thought Barnes had been the suitor, and the woman before her had been the one with the power.

'Huh, tell me about it.' Trista, clearly, didn't hold the same opinion. Then again, she hadn't seen the two together.

'Tris—' Dulcie tried to draw her friend away.

'Wait, I think I found it.' Kelly was still playing with the keyboard. 'No, no, sorry.'

'What's going on, anyway?' Dulcie was confused. 'What happened, Ms Roebuck? What's Professor Barnes supposed to have done?'

'*Supposed* to?' The academic swooped down on the phrasing, eyes like a hawk. Dulcie swallowed, her mouth suddenly dry. Was this what deconstruction of meaning came to? But the raven-haired Roebuck turned away, releasing her. 'No, you can't know. Not yet.'

Dulcie wasn't going to venture anything more, so it was up to Trista to ask. 'Know what?'

'My presentation,' Stella replied. The anger seemed to drain from her voice as she continued. 'My paper, "The Look of Love". The key to my future—maybe to everything. Everything in our backward-looking discipline anyway. It was on my laptop. I was reading it through a moment ago. Practicing in my mind how to give the opening statement the proper emphasis. I stepped away and now it's gone.'

'Gone?' Dulcie wasn't intimidated any more. The woman sitting on the floor looked tired—and every day of her thirty-plus years. 'How can that be?' Stella just shook her head. Even her hair had gone limp. 'Sabotage? I don't know. I didn't want to think Paul could do something like this.'

Dulcie looked from her up to Kelly. 'Kelly, is this true? Is it really gone?'

The media tech was still typing. 'As far as I can see.' They all heard the disheartened sigh as Stella let her head hang down. 'I mean, I'll take this back to the lab. We can do a search through the hard drive, but as far as I can tell it's gone.'

'You didn't back it up?' Dulcie had learned that lesson the hard way. It helped that Chris had set her up with automatic programs that did the work for her.

Another shake of the head. The voice, when it emerged, sounded like it was coming from a great depth. 'Back up. You say that as if it had no implications. But I know, you see. At Tech, the humanities aren't isolated. The latest technologies have been called back from their exile. From my colleagues' (from the stress she put on the word, Dulcie knew she didn't count as one) 'I have also learned the dangers of your so-called standard back-up. I have disconnected from the Cloud. It was, it *is* too insecure, and I knew—I've long known—that I have enemies.'

Dulcie latched on to that last word. 'So it wasn't necessarily Paul Barnes.'

The eyes that rose to meet hers were ringed and sad. 'Who else?' She shook her tousled locks, as if answering her own question. 'He was here, and he was…well, I hadn't been kind to him. I was angry, I confess. He has a new woman; you've probably seen her. She's been hanging all over him. He should have been happy. I didn't think much of her, but you know men. He couldn't be alone. But I—I have a new man, and what we have is real. I didn't want to hear his sad tale.'

'But why go after your work?' Nothing about her story was making sense.

'He was getting over his new crush. Realizing that it was rebound romance, nothing more. But you know Paul.' She said it with such confidence that Dulcie didn't have the heart to disagree. 'He's soft-hearted. He wants to let her down easy. If she can't have him, he wants her to get her dream job.' A shrug. 'I mean, *he's* not going to get it. So, isn't it obvious? This is all about Renée Showalter.'

FOURTEEN

'WHOA.' DULCIE HEARD Trista's exclamation, soft as it was. 'Paul Barnes and Showalter?'

Stella did, too. She shook her head sadly. 'So I hear. Paul, of course, denied everything.'

Of course he did, thought Dulcie. If what she suspected was true, the two hadn't been closeted for romantic reasons but to talk about her—and her future. But until she confirmed any of it, she couldn't say anything. What she could do was try and save Paul Barnes's reputation. 'Kelly?' She'd start with the basics. 'Could someone really erase all traces of a file that quickly?'

'Erase is the wrong word.' The tech was powering the system down, carefully detaching the cables that linked it to the auditorium's system. 'This looks more like a virus. Someone downloaded something on to her laptop that ate away at the hard drive. In fact,' she disconnected the last cable, 'I'm going to have to check and make sure it didn't get into our system.'

She shook her head sadly. 'This is not good timing.'

Timing! Dulcie jumped up. 'Good goddess, I forgot!' All eyes turned on her, and only Trista was smiling. Dulcie felt the blush rising to her cheeks. Under pressure, she did tend to channel her mother. 'I was supposed to meet Marco Tesla here. He must be outside. He's probably wondering where I am...' If he hadn't wandered off already, she thought. If he complained to Thorpe, there would be hell to pay.

She stood up and turned toward the back of the auditorium. A hand reached out for hers and she turned, thinking it would be Trista.

It was Stella. 'Don't tell him.' She looked more than tired. She looked desperate. 'Please,' she said. 'There's already been too much drama.'

Dulcie opened her mouth and then realized she couldn't say what she was thinking. Any drama here had come from Stella Roebuck. And whatever else the elfin academic might be, she was a guest here—a featured speaker at the conference her department was sponsoring. She nodded, not trusting herself to speak, and, with Trista in tow, headed back to the atrium.

'That was crazy,' said Trista breathlessly, as she struggled to keep up. 'Can you believe we're in the middle of a romantic triangle?'

'There's nothing romantic about it,' Dulcie said as she pushed the back door open. 'I don't know what Stella Roebuck's on about, but I doubt every man she meets is that much in love with her.'

'You're jealous.'

Dulcie stopped short and turned to her friend. Trista looked as surprised by her own words as Dulcie did.

'I'm sorry,' Trista added. 'I didn't know.'

'It's not...' Dulcie shook her head. 'It's not what you think.' She didn't have to explain herself to Trista. Despite her friend's long-term relationship with Jerry, she was always indulging in at least the illusion of other romances.

'But you and Professor Showalter?' Trista sounded a little shocked. 'I mean, I always figured you...'

'No,' Dulcie cut her off, then caught herself, as she looked around the atrium. 'I mean, not like that. I find it hard to believe that Professor Showalter would find herself caught in some trashy romantic comedy.'

'Romantic tragedy is more like it.'

'What? 'Cause Stella Roebuck didn't have the sense to back her work up?' The atrium seemed strangely empty, and the few people who passed by were clearly not the hip professor. Dulcie started walking toward the front of the building. 'Besides, she's just making a fuss. The media tech will find it.'

'You think?' Trista matched her pace to Dulcie's. 'So you think this was all show?'

'I think somebody is used to being the center of attention.' Dulcie paused at the entrance to look back at the white and open space. No, no Marco Tesla here. She went for the big glass doors. 'Blaming Paul Barnes? She reminds me of Esmé. No, even Esmé isn't that desperate for attention. But she also likes to bite to get people to notice her.'

'Then why didn't she want you to say anything to Tesla?' Trista followed her out. 'Word is, they're a couple now.'

Dulcie nodded. The matching wardrobe, even the hair—it made sense. 'Who knows?' She looked around. 'Maybe he's sick of her drama. Sick of having to compete with every past lover, real or imagined.'

'Or maybe she's afraid it was really Marco who sabotaged her presentation and not Barnes.' Trista's voice had gone soft. 'After all, from what you said—he was here earlier, too. And now he's not.'

FIFTEEN

'I CAN'T BELIEVE you lost Marco Tesla.' Thorpe was furious, flushed all the way up to his scalp. 'Lost him!'

'I didn't lose him.' Dulcie knew she'd messed up. Knew she needed to report right away, even though she had wanted to seek out Paul Barnes for his side of the story. But there had been extenuating circumstances. And besides, she hadn't asked to be Thorpe's errand girl. 'He is not *lost*. Simply missing. Maybe he chose not to wait, figuring we'd catch up with him later,' she clarified. 'Maybe he heard Stella Roebuck yelling and thought it best to get out of there.' It would have been, she decided, the sensible reaction.

'And Stella Roebuck…oh, lord.' He had his hands in his hair, pulling at what was left. 'The conference…our reputation. *My reputation*.' Dulcie waited, hoping he'd calm down. He had actually spun around by then, which saved her from having to fake a sympathetic look, and walked toward the back of his office. There, over by the window, she saw a large box of some sort, covered by a blanket. There was something strangely homey about it, a feeling that Thorpe seemed to share. She could see his shoulders lowering to somewhere near normal as he got closer. But before he could reach it he stopped and turned back toward her with a fierce expression.

'That's another thing.' Thorpe glared at her, as if she were supposed to be able to decipher his meaning. 'What happened there?'

Although his meaning was, in fact, clear, Dulcie was tempted to play dumb. Any person who strove to lead the department of English and American Literatures and Language ought to be able to articulate a question better. For a moment, she considered feigning confusion. But beneath his anger, Dulcie knew, lay deep fear. Besides, he had a cat now; the thought suddenly popped into her mind. Everyone who cohabited with a feline was part of a special group. She'd help him out.

'She thinks that someone—' Dulcie was not going to blame Paul Barnes—'erased her paper. Infected her computer with a virus, or something. Though she had the flimsiest rationale for not having backed up.' As she talked, she found herself staring at the box. Almost, she thought, the blanket moved.

Thorpe was waving his hand at her, pulling her attention away from the curious structure. 'Wait—a virus?'

Dulcie nodded. 'Actually, it was Kelly, the media tech, who—'

He didn't wait to hear the end. 'This is great.' His face lit up and, just for a moment, Dulcie thought, he glanced over his shoulder at the box. 'We can salvage this. Maybe make the whole conference! Dulcie, get your boyfriend on the phone.'

'Chris? But why?' Even as she asked, Thorpe's reasoning dawned on her. She'd been too distracted. 'No, Mr Thorpe. Really. Working with damaged hard drives isn't what he does. And Kelly sounded quite confident—' She hadn't, from what Dulcie remembered. Not really. Still, Dulcie didn't want Chris to be dragged into this departmental craziness.

'Dulcie, Kelly is an hourly employee. Chris Sorenson is, by all accounts, one of the rising stars of the department.' Thorpe was standing up straighter and smoothing his hair back, always a bad sign.

'Computer sciences isn't the same as computer repair.' She felt her protest losing steam. Hearing Chris praised like that had taken her by surprise. 'The media department really is more prepared to do more specialized work.'

'Please, Ms Schwartz.' Thorpe's voice had gotten softer too. 'I can't—I can't explain, exactly. But I know this is the right thing to do. For—for Tigger's sake,' he glanced back once more at the box in the corner, 'please call him.'

That did it. The little marmalade tabby bonded her more strongly to the balding academic than any of her studies. It also raised a question.

'Is Tigger here?' She *had* seen a movement.

Thorpe had the grace to look down, momentarily abashed. 'Yes, he is.' He peeked back up. 'I don't like leaving him alone all day at home. And, well…' He blinked. 'I find I concentrate better when the little fellow is in my office.'

'May I?' She motioned toward the blanket-covered box. He nodded, and she approached, kneeling on the floor beside it to lift the edge of the covering.

'Hello, little fellow.' What she'd thought was a box, she could now see, was really a large cat bed, complete with pillow and numerous catnip mice strewn throughout. The blanket, draped over the high sides, allowed the occupant some privacy, but the back was open toward the window, to allow prime bird watching. But even though the afternoon outside was bright, the little orange kitten was curled up on the cushion. He looked up to meet her eye as she peeked in. 'Were you listening to us?'

'He must have been drawn to our voices,' said Thorpe, bending beside her. 'Weren't you, Tigger?'

The little cat turned to his person, batting at his outstretched finger in the approved kitten manner. But after about thirty seconds, he returned his attention to Dulcie. She, too, reached out, if just to feel that soft orange fur. Tigger, however, was having none of it. Ignoring her fingers, he simply sat and stared at her. With, she could not help but feel, some serious intent.

'What is it, Tigger?' She kept her voice low, but still Thorpe turned and looked at her. 'Do you have something to tell me?'

'He does have the most eloquent eyes, doesn't he?' Thorpe couldn't hide the pride in his voice, but Dulcie didn't respond. This cat had something to communicate, she was sure. And if that meant shutting out the person who had taken him in, well, so be it. If she could just tune him out...

'*We do not all choose our teachers.*' The voice, soft and yet clear, startled Dulcie. '*We may choose what we learn.*' She caught herself before she responded out loud, however, and instead found herself staring into the young creature's eyes. '*Keep your eyes open.*' They were blue, so blue that they looked unnatural. Or no, uncanny, like they were really a portal to a different world, a world where nothing was what it seemed...

'Ms Schwartz?' Thorpe's voice broke her out of her reverie. 'Are you feeling ill?'

'What?' She shook off the dizziness that had in truth crept over her. 'No, I'm fine.'

'*Open...*' Was it the voice again, or simply a memory? Resigned, she sat back on the floor and looked up at her adviser.

'I'm sorry. It's just so easy to get caught up in a kitten.' Part of the message was clear. She needed to show more respect. If there was more going on, she was pretty sure she wouldn't get it with Thorpe hovering possessively around the little cat's enclosure. 'Isn't it?' She turned back to the cozy box for one last try. But the kitten had curled up in his bed, pink nose tucked under the edge of the striped orange tail, his loyalty clear.

'I think we should let him rest now, don't you?' Thorpe was already pulling the blanket down to shield the enclosure from prying eyes. 'And, well, you need to call Chris.' The way he was looking, Dulcie knew there was no avoiding it. He'd given her time with Tigger, and the kitten had made her duty clear. She owed Thorpe at least a call to her boyfriend.

With a resigned nod, Dulcie stepped into the relative privacy of the hallway and dialed Chris.

'Dulcie? Can I get back to you?' She had barely begun to explain the situation when her boyfriend cut her off. 'I'm kind of dealing with a situation here.'

'Sure.' Chris was usually the calm one in the relationship. 'Is there anything I can do?'

'No—I...' He paused, and when he started talking again, his voice was tight. 'Things just aren't making sense. It's—well, never mind. What's going on by you?'

'I've got a computer situation. Not my computer.' She felt a bit guilty dragging him into this when he was clearly busy. Not that she had much choice. 'It might be a virus.' She gave him the quick overview, trying to leave out Stella Roebuck's crazier accusations. 'I wouldn't ask if it weren't important. Thorpe is really hoping you can come in.'

'Ah, Thorpe,' was all he said. He and Dulcie had been together long enough that he got it. 'Look, why don't I meet you in about an hour? I'll be in the Square by then and I'll call. Will that be okay?'

'Sure.' He was the one doing the favor. Thorpe would simply have to accept it. 'And one more thing, Chris. I got to see Tigger…' But her boyfriend had already hung up.

When she ducked back into Thorpe's office to report, she saw him on hands and knees in the corner. 'Is everything all right?' Dulcie asked.

'Yes, poor little fellow.' He looked back over his shoulder at her. 'He must be tuckered out.' Rising awkwardly to his knees and then standing, he brushed the dust off his pants and proceeded to pat it into his hair. 'I swear, he was up all night.'

Dulcie paused at that and tried to look past her adviser, hoping to make contact once more with those strange blue eyes. From her vantage point, in the middle of the room, she could see Tigger, lying in his bed by the wall. His eyes were hidden, however, and all she could see were the soft stripes of marmalade and cream, rising and falling as the little beast slept.

SIXTEEN

THORPE HADN'T BEEN thrilled with the delay, but he'd had to accept it. Not only was Chris doing him—and the department—a favor, but Dulcie refused to try to move up her boyfriend's schedule, no matter what the panic.

'Besides, shouldn't I be trying to track down Marco Tesla?' she said by way of peace offering. 'Maybe he went back to the hotel.'

'Or back to San Diego,' Thorpe muttered. Dulcie bit her lip. Some of this was jealousy, she knew. Thorpe had seen the connection she had formed with the kitten. That, she was sure, was why he'd been trying to wake the little creature while she'd been on the phone. 'This is becoming a disaster. Roebuck furious. Tesla gone...'

'He's not gone.' Dulcie tried to keep her tone light. 'And we still have Showalter and Barnes.'

'*Them*.' Thorpe dismissed her favorites and kept talking, almost to himself. 'The department will be disgraced. Our good name...'

If her adviser was going to act like a child, Dulcie felt no qualms about interrupting. 'Tesla's liaison missed him. That doesn't mean the department is at fault. Just, well, me. And I've tried to call him, several times. He doesn't answer.'

'Yes, well...'

Dulcie was never so happy to hear her phone ring. 'Maybe that's Tesla now,' she said brightly. 'Excuse me.' She stepped back out into the hall.

'So what did she think?' The voice, female and excited, threw Dulcie for a moment. 'Did she like it?'

'Mina!' Dulcie snapped back. Of course. The undergrad didn't know that Dulcie hadn't met with the visiting scholar. 'I'm sorry, I didn't get a chance to tell you. Professor Showalter canceled on me.' She could hear the disappointed sigh over the phone. 'But I did give her the paper.'

'Do you think she's read it yet?' Mina's breathlessness reminded Dulcie of how thrilled she had been to get their work into the scholar's hands, only hours before.

'I don't think so.' Dulcie hesitated, wondering how much to share with her younger colleague. If she ended up working with Paul Barnes, would she be able to bring Mina along? He had his own projects—that much was clear from his message, and she had no idea if Mina's research would be relevant. Besides, he had asked her to keep his call confidential. 'I think she had to talk with one of the other visiting professors about a personal matter,' she said instead. That was what Showalter had actually told her, but Dulcie still felt a bit guilty at the partial deception.

'But, you know what? I'm going back to the Science Center,' she added. 'If she's around, I'll corner her, see what I can find out.'

'Oh, you don't have to.' Dulcie could hear the disappointment in the younger woman's voice. 'I'm sure you're crazy busy, what with the conference and all.'

'That's okay,' Dulcie started to explain. In truth, she really would rather be talking with Renée Showalter about her own work—and about Paul Barnes—than tracking down and babysitting some fop who dressed like a schoolboy.

'...big names like Marco Tesla,' she heard Mina say.

'Wait, I'm sorry.' Dulcie had missed what the younger woman was saying. 'Do you know where he is?'

'Of course.' Mina sounded surprised. 'I'll be seeing him in a few hours.'

Dulcie put her hand to her forehead, sure that if she didn't more of her brains would fall out. 'I'm missing something,' was all she said. 'Is there a function tonight?'

'Oh.' Except for that one syllable, there was silence. Dulcie looked at her phone. They were still connected.

'Mina?'

'I was sure you'd have been invited.' The woman on the other end of the line had the grace to sound embarrassed. 'Maybe the invite got lost?'

'Probably.' Dulcie closed her eyes and leaned back against the wall. Right now, she didn't care about the conference. She certainly didn't care about Marco Tesla.

'Hang on.' The sound of typing filled the void. 'Let me dig it up.'

Maybe Chris would call soon, Dulcie told herself. Maybe he would be able to resurrect Stella Roebuck's missing paper. Maybe they'd all go out in a blaze of glory.

'The moonlight eye-opener.' The voice on the phone wasn't making sense. She was too tired. It had already been a very long day.

'Excuse me?' That was the best Dulcie could manage.

'The moonlight eye-opener,' Mina repeated. 'I gather it's an ELLA tradition. Drinks outdoors for all the invited participants.'

'Outdoors?' This was making less and less sense.

'Didn't ELLA start in Southern California?'

Dulcie nodded, more than a little embarrassed that an undergraduate remembered more than she had. 'But they can't have an outdoors party here. It's freezing out.'

'I think it's just going to be a toast.' Mina's voice had taken on a conspiratorial tone. 'Ten o'clock on the patio.' She paused. 'Did you know that ELLA is always scheduled to coincide with the full moon?'

'No,' said Dulcie. 'But nothing would surprise me any more.'

'So you'll come with me? I'm sure you were supposed to get an invite, and I assume I'm allowed to bring a date.'

'I don't know.' Chris had the night off. She was tired. Stella Roebuck wasn't easy company. And if Paul Barnes and Renée Showalter were there, too…

'Please,' Mina was pleading. 'I mean, I know it's going to be chilly…'

'That,' Dulcie replied, 'will be the least of it.'

SEVENTEEN

She waited, breathless, for the Dawn, though e'en its wan light, sickly and pale, could not but fail to illuminate the very Darkness weighing down upon her. Still, she waited, Hope growing feeble in her breast, for, though the light be Dim, the Vista before her could hold no more of Terror than had been witnessed through the dark hours within the nightmare Storm. Then had she Fled into the howling Wind, the lashing Branches so toss'd that each seemed to reach and tear at her ragged garments as she made her desperate way. Then had she come at last to the limits of her strength, and taken Refuge with a Stranger. So soft, his Voice. So calming as he warned her of these very sins. The Unfaithful, the False, the Other-Seeming who might betray her utmost Hopes. Yet she had persisted in her Journey, along that Mountain road, into the very Heart of turmoil, this Castle, this seeming Succor. Thus, here, she waited. Her Chamber, no more a sanctuary but a prison, barr'd by the creeping tendrils of distrust. Dawn would reach her here but barely, bringing nothing of Peace with it, nothing, truly, of Warmth.

'Beware the one who gives you Succor...'

It was closer to an hour and a half before Chris called. Dulcie knew because she kept checking her phone while she read, in the hope that either Paul Barnes or her boyfriend, or even the elusive Marco Tesla, would ring.

None did, and by the time she got to her office, she was tempted to turn her phone off and throw the offending thing away. Somehow, this conference, which she had so looked forward to, had become more of a mess than she'd ever imagined. And somehow, at least some of it was her fault—or her responsibility. And to top it all off, the bothersome thing wouldn't even start officially until the next day at three, when Thorpe would give the opening address.

It was enough to drive her back into research. But, while she could find some solace in her papers, Dulcie knew better than to give in to her fantasy. Chris, she trusted, would get in touch. Barnes, she told herself, probably expected to see her that night. And Tesla, well, at this point she almost didn't care if he'd gone back to California, except for the pain it would cause Thorpe. The phone stayed on.

Still, it was nice to put the conference prep behind her, at least temporarily. And it was with an unexpected feeling of relief that she had made her way to the basement of Memorial Hall, grateful to have some time to herself. Dulcie had promised Thorpe that as soon as Chris came into the Square they'd go meet with Stella Roebuck. In the meantime, she pointed out, she really could be working. In his panic about Tesla, Thorpe seemed to have forgotten about normal deadlines and had wanted her to spend the time looking for the missing scholar. Only grudgingly had he accepted her explanation that she would connect with Tesla that evening. Since he had added his own voicemails to Dulcie's on Tesla's line, apologizing for the Science Center mix-up, there weren't many other options.

'Look, I'll see him at this thing tonight,' she'd said.

Thorpe seemed to take it for granted that she'd be at the party. 'I'll explain what happened, and we'll reschedule.'

Dulcie suspected that it was his desire to be alone with Tigger rather than any sense of resolution that led to him finally letting her go. But after a few more minutes of back and forth, she had gotten free.

Now she sat staring at her laptop, trying to figure out how to work this latest bit into her thesis.

'*Beware the one who gives you Succor.*' She stared at the passage, as if by dint of persistence its place would become clear.

'You okay, Dulcie?' She looked up. Lloyd, her office mate, was standing in the doorway. From the way his brow was furrowed, she suspected he'd been there for some time.

'Yeah, I'm fine.' She managed a smile. 'Do you mind?' Although the two grad students technically shared the space, they tended to take turns with it. Just because two desks could fit into the basement room didn't mean two scholars could necessarily be comfortable working together.

'Not at all.' Lloyd entered, walking over to his desk. 'I really just wanted to retrieve some papers.' With his head in a drawer, his next words were muffled. Dulcie could make out only one word: 'ELLA.'

'I think I've discharged my duties for the day, for good or ill,' Dulcie answered. 'Though I guess there's that unofficial opening thing tonight.'

'The moonlight party?' Lloyd's face popped up again as he placed a handful of folders on his desktop. 'Yeah, time for the thermal underwear, huh? Though I don't know how that will look under formal wear.'

'Formal?' Dulcie sat back. 'Wait, this is formal?'

'Black tie, I gather.' Lloyd shrugged. 'Though I believe we struggling teaching assistants are allowed to wear a suit and tie. The men, of course,' he added. 'You can wear any cocktail-length or evening dress.'

Dulcie opened her mouth, but nothing came out. It wasn't hearing fashion terms from Lloyd. Raleigh, his girlfriend, probably taught him those. Despite being a budding scholar, she did have a penchant for clothes, Dulcie had noticed. It was more that Lloyd also seemed to have known of this party long before Dulcie did—and that she seemed to have unwittingly committed to a fancy do. If it weren't for Mina—and for her promise to do whatever she could to track down the elusive Marco Tesla—she'd have given up on the whole thing. She really should talk to Renée Showalter before she committed to Paul Barnes, anyway.

'I wonder if Mina knows that it's fancy?' She'd have to warn the undergrad.

'She was invited?' Lloyd's eyebrows shot up. 'I thought it was graduate level and up.'

'Well, I wasn't invited.' That came out with more edge than Dulcie intended. 'At least, I don't think I was.'

'Nonsense.' Lloyd ducked back into his drawer. 'The invites went to our homes. I bet Chris got it and didn't tell you.' He looked up, a devilish look on his face. 'Maybe he just didn't want to have to wear a suit.'

Dulcie mulled that one over. 'No, he'd at least *tell* me we'd been invited. I mean, that I had.' She gave it another moment. 'Though with his changing schedule, he's been kind of out of it. He probably just forgot. I wonder if he'd want to go?'

'Tell him he has to.' Lloyd wasn't even trying to hide his grin any more. 'It's not fair to the rest of us if he gets to opt out. And, really, you are presenting at the conference. It is a big deal.'

'Huh.' Dulcie chewed that one over as he reached back into his desk. 'Such a big deal that nobody bothered to see if I had responded.'

'*Dulcie.*' The voice sounded so clear, she whipped around. Lloyd still had his head in the bottom drawer, though. Besides, the voice was deeper than her office mate's.

'Mr Grey?' She mouthed the words rather than speaking them aloud and glanced back at Lloyd. He didn't appear to have heard anything. 'Are you there?'

'*Do you doubt it? Do you doubt all you love?*' The voice had a slight sharpness to it, as opposed to its customary rumbling purr.

'No.' She shook her head. 'Not really. I was just…' She paused. Chris had been distracted, but she herself had noted the effects of the schedule change. Poor guy was sleep-deprived. As for the university? Well, she knew that Thorpe needed her. Relied on her, really, and despite his occasional caviling, she knew that meant that he respected her, too.

'I've just felt left out, Mr Grey.' She focused on the dust motes that caught the light. It felt better to have something to address, even if it wasn't an actual flesh and blood feline. 'And, to be honest, inadequate. Everything I touch has been going wrong. Like everyone else knows what is going on except me.'

The dust motes danced, tossed by some shifting current of air. As she watched, she heard it, the deep rumbling purr that gave her so much joy. '*You must believe in yourself first, Dulcie.*' The rumble was so loud, Dulcie couldn't believe that Lloyd wasn't hearing it too.

Still, he seemed oblivious. '*Trust what you know to be true, Dulcie. Trust yourself.*'

'I bet Chris responded for you,' Lloyd said as he sat up.

Dulcie stared, open-mouthed. Perhaps, to him, no time had passed at all. 'You think?' That was all she could muster.

'I wouldn't be surprised.' Lloyd leaned toward her, as if to share a secret. 'I saw him running around last night in the Square. I bet he's got some surprise planned for you.'

'He was working last night.' Or sleeping.

Lloyd shrugged. 'He must have been on his break. He was running like he had hounds after him, so I bet he had a lot to get done.'

Dulcie was going to protest. Chris was a dear, but he was not the type for romantic surprises. Mr Grey's words stopped her, though. She knew Chris; she loved him. She should trust him. Besides, he'd call soon, and she'd be able to ask him straight out if he had ever received the invitation to the party—and if he had, in fact, responded.

'Anyway, I don't think it's a big deal.' Lloyd had loaded his bag and stood to go. 'If you show up, I'm sure they'll be thrilled you're there. I mean, just in case I'm wrong.'

'So you don't think he was planning something.'

Lloyd took a deep breath. 'He was in a hurry, that I know. And Dulcie, I know he loves you. But we guys can be forgetful. So, just in case...'

'Got it.' She did. 'I won't tell him what you said.'

'See you tonight.' He shouldered his bag. 'It'll be fun.'

With her new resolve, she bit back her immediate response. More like work, she'd been thinking. Only with uncomfortable clothes. But Lloyd was right. A party like this was not only one of the perks of working for the conference; it was a great chance to mingle with the visiting scholars in a relaxed, or at least unprogrammed, setting. Nobody would have their laptop there. Nobody would be arguing about precedence or scheduling, at least not openly. And she'd be with Mina—and maybe, also Chris. They were her friends, and it would feel good to introduce Chris to Renée Showalter, too. Maybe they could even talk about the paper.

If only Chris would call soon. Since he hadn't, Dulcie pulled her laptop toward her with new resolve. '*Beware the one you trust*,' she read. Good thing her mood had improved, she told herself. That could apply to Mina or Professor Showalter. Or even Chris. She read on. '*Beware the one upon whom you would lay every Future hope*.'

She was still staring at the one sentence when her phone rang.

'Chris!' The call had startled her.

'Yeah, where are you?' He did sound tired, poor boy. 'I'm at the Science Center, by the café.'

'Sorry, I thought you were going to call first. I'll be there in three minutes.' Dulcie saved her file and pushed her laptop into her bag. 'Kelly, the media tech, has Stella Roebuck's laptop. She probably still has Stella hanging around, too.'

As she packed up, she explained again about how panicked the academic had been, and how certain that her paper had been lost through sabotage. Chris, who dealt with undergraduate crises every day, sighed loudly.

'And she didn't back up?' He already knew the facts. This was just his way of venting.

'Not everyone has a boyfriend like mine, who sets me up with foolproof programming.' Something about Chris was off, but Dulcie was determined not to let it bother her. He had a right to be tired, and they were both overworked. 'Hey, Chris?' She had intended to wait until she saw him face to face. But if it wasn't a big deal, then she might as well ask him over the phone. 'Did you see an invite for me in the mail recently? For a moonlight party?'

'No...' The way he drew the word out meant he knew there was more coming. Dulcie braced herself. She wasn't going to get mad. 'Should I have?'

'I'm not saying "should", Chris.' She worked to keep her voice light. 'But there is a party tonight that I should, I mean, that I ought to attend. And maybe you'd want to go with me. It's for the conference.' She explained, as best she could, the moonlight ritual and the unusual—for their crowd—dress code. 'So, you didn't see anything in the mail?'

'Well, there was one day...' Dulcie bit her lip. They all made mistakes. This wasn't a question of trust. 'It was the strangest thing. I'd slept late, you know, after one of my night shifts.' Dulcie found herself nodding as she locked the office behind her and headed for the stairs. 'The mail had come through the slot, and Esmé had gotten to it. Dulcie, she'd shredded a few pieces and chewed them up. There was a flyer from the new dumpling place and a cereal sample. I figured it was the smell of that that set her off. And, yeah, maybe there was something with university letterhead in there, too. I'm sorry, Dulcie. For some reason, it completely slipped my mind.'

'Maybe she didn't want me to know about the party.' Dulcie was joking, but stranger things had happened.

'Maybe she just wants us both to stay home with her,' said Chris. 'It is the full moon and all.'

'But that's Tigger…' She left the thought unfinished. 'Anyway, this is work,' she said. 'And I'm on my way.'

EIGHTEEN

DULCIE DIDN'T KNOW if she felt more peeved or relieved when she saw Chris waiting for her. A part of her was annoyed, and rightly so, she told herself. Her boyfriend, a fellow grad student, had not told her about a letter on university letterhead. It had been a party invite, but it could have been about a grant or a grading change. He should have known how important it was.

On the other hand, the idea that she had indeed gotten an invite to the department shindig went a long way toward salving her wounded ego. For a while there, she'd begun to feel like everyone in the world—even, as Lloyd had noted, an undergraduate—had been invited except for her. Besides, she knew how busy Chris was. And how distracting Esmé could be. When she saw him sitting in the café area, a plate of chocolate chip cookies, untouched, before him, she couldn't stay angry. And he did look both tired and sorry.

'Dulcie, I—'

He stood as she approached, but she cut him off with a kiss.

'Don't worry about it, sweetie.' As they sat, he pushed the plate toward her, completing his redemption. 'Where did you get these?'

'They're opening the café again tomorrow.' Chris looked quite pleased with himself as he pointed toward the rolled-down gate. 'I knocked, and they were just coming out with a test batch.'

'We'd better make sure these are okay, then.' Dulcie broke off a piece of a cookie. It was still warm. 'So, you'll come with me tonight. Right?' The melting chocolate was irresistible, and she reached for another piece. 'I guess it's formal, but you can get away with a jacket and tie.'

'If you want me to.'

It wasn't the enthusiastic response she was hoping for, and Dulcie found herself examining him more closely. 'You don't look good, Chris.' In truth, he looked paler than usual, and the rings under his eyes were darker than she'd ever seen. 'It's the schedule change. You're probably running on fumes.'

Her boyfriend nodded. 'I feel—I don't know. Not tired exactly...' He rubbed his hand over his face. 'Just kind of out of it.'

'I hope you're not coming down with something.' Dulcie leaned over the table. Even after the cookie, his forehead felt warm against her palm.

'I don't know.' His voice was listless. 'Maybe.'

That settled it. A departmental function was not as important as Chris, especially one that she hadn't even heard about until today. 'Forget about this party, sweetie,' she told him. 'You should go home tonight. And I should take care of you.'

'No, you should go.' He pushed the plate to the side and took her hand in his. 'This is about the conference, and it's important for you.'

Dulcie looked at him, torn. On one hand, the party was a work function. She'd told Thorpe that she would track down Marco Tesla there. Plus, she wanted a chance to talk to Renée Showalter. Maybe she could even get Showalter and Barnes together.

On the other hand, Chris looked terrible. Even in the

few minutes they'd been sitting in the café, he seemed to have grown paler and his face was now shiny with a thin sheen of sweat.

'It's this weather.' She shook her head. 'It's just not good for anyone.'

''Tis the season.' He mustered a smile.

'You know what Lucy would say about that.' Chris had met her mom and been the recipient of her beyond New Age theories. 'Something about the winter solstice draining your solar energies.'

'I thought the solstice was when the sun started coming back,' he protested. 'And isn't the moon a "source of silver strength" or something?'

'Wow, I think you remembered that perfectly.' Dulcie was cheered. Chris couldn't be that sick if he could poke fun at her mom. 'But I'm sure she'd have a counter argument, too...that Luna needed your essence right now.' He raised his eyebrows at that. 'Or something.'

'Or maybe I just picked up a bug from all the sneezing and wheezing in the computer labs.' His voice had softened. 'I'll be fine at home. I just don't feel like myself today.'

NINETEEN

She tried to get him to go home after that, but he was adamant. 'Look, I trekked down here, and maybe it is something simple that I can fix,' he said. 'Besides, my inner clock is so disorganized that I'm probably going to get a second wind any moment now. But you should go home and change.'

He knew his way around the center, better than she did. And so, with a last kiss and a worried swipe at his brow, she left him to prepare for the party.

'Esmé, are you there?' As she'd walked home, Dulcie had wondered about their young pet. She'd neglected to ask Chris more about the cat's strange behavior, but once she got home she was determined to follow up. 'Esmeralda?'

A small peep greeted her as the round feline bounced down the hall. 'Esmé, why did you tear up my party invitation?' Dulcie scooped her up. 'Why are you being so mean to Chris—and to me?'

'*Mean?*' The question, almost inaudible under the rolling rumble of a purr, was delivered in a voice both soft and innocent. '*Me?*'

'Yes, you.' It was hard to cross-examine something so cuddly, but Dulcie forced herself to hold the cat at arm's length and address those mysterious green eyes directly. 'Chris said you acted afraid of him. Or angry.' She paused; the cat said nothing. 'At any rate, you hissed.'

'No!' With a cat-like wail, Esmé writhed to be put down, but Dulcie kept her hold on her.

'Esmé?' The green eyes blinked. 'You hissed at Chris and you destroyed a very important invitation for me.'

'No!' The same feline wail, but this time another voice, quieter, sounded in Dulcie's mind. '*You should trust me.*'

'So are you saying that Chris was lying?' The cat twisted again in her grip, and Dulcie had to readjust to make sure she held on. 'You do understand what I mean by "lying", don't you?'

'*I know Chris,*' the voice said, with a noticeable emphasis on the last word. '*I know what I know.*'

Out loud, Dulcie heard a more customary version of this protest. 'Naow!' The cat was struggling now, throwing all of her minor bulk into escaping Dulcie's grasp. '*And I know not-Chris, too.*' The voice was clearly riled and, with a final twist, Esmé kicked free of Dulcie's hold and fell to the ground.

'Esmé!' Dulcie needn't have worried. The little tuxedo landed on her feet and scurried away, leaving Dulcie with what seemed to be the harshest insult she could muster.

'*Not-Chris! Not-Chris is evil.*'

'I get it,' Dulcie called after her, looking at the claw marks on her arm. 'I'm a bad person, Esmé. I'm not Chris.'

'No!' One last howl ended the discussion, and Dulcie went to get dressed.

It was fully dark by the time Dulcie was to meet Mina, but the bright party lights cast her shadow in high relief on the frosty ground as she crossed the cold garden in front of the university building.

'Dulcie!' her friend called out. Dulcie shaded her eyes and saw her rise from a bench under a dark holly. 'I'm here.'

'Did I keep you waiting?' Dulcie went to greet her. Mina was agile, even with her cane, but tonight she was holding some sort of shawl tight around her head and neck as well.

'Not long.' Mina smiled back. 'I guess I was excited, I got here early. I haven't seen Professor Showalter yet, though.'

Dulcie grinned. 'Ah, so it wasn't me you were waiting for! Has Marco Tesla shown up yet?'

A quick shake of the head. 'No, I'm sorry. I will keep my eyes open for him, though.'

'Thanks,' said Dulcie. 'Unless he really did leave town in a huff, he'll probably be here. It's early yet. Shall we?'

As they walked toward the entranceway, Dulcie told the younger woman about Esmé destroying her invitation—and about Chris being sick. Her reaction, however, was not what Dulcie would have expected.

'Funny timing, isn't it?' Mina asked as they showed their ID to the guard and stepped into the courtyard. Despite the tradition, the open space was deserted, empty cocktail tables reflecting the blue moonlight, and the two headed toward the other wing of the building. Music, soft and jazzy, could be heard, as well as the sound of laughter, and two rows of French doors—one opening on to the courtyard, the other on to a balcony above—glowed with a warmer illumination.

'What do you mean?' Dulcie paused and turned to her friend. The flagstone paving was a little slick in this weather, and Mina was taking it slowly. Above them, someone had opened one of the ballroom's French doors, and a curtain billowed out, catching the light.

'With the full moon and all.' The ground floor opened, and a lone figure stepped out, lighting a cigarette. Dulcie reached for the door, and the two passed into the reception area. The music was louder here, beckoning guests up the stairs, but Dulcie and Mina joined the queue for the coat check first, before moving over to where a student bartender was offering refreshments. 'It makes you wonder.'

Dulcie accepted a glass of dubious-looking punch and thought about her friend's words. The month before, she'd gotten worked up about the possibility of a werewolf on the campus after Mina had been attacked. The culprit, it had turned out, was of a much more mundane variety, but Dulcie had never successfully answered some of the questions raised during those few days. There had been a mysterious howling, she recalled. It had been such an eerie sound that it still haunted her dreams. If, that is, she had been dreaming.

'Why did you say that?' Mina had settled on the cider and a cookie and looked for a moment as if she didn't understand Dulcie's question. 'About the moon?' Dulcie elaborated.

'I'm not really sure.' Mina sipped her cider and grimaced. She hadn't, Dulcie realized, known it would be spiked. 'Maybe I was thinking of seasonal affective disorder or something?' The younger woman took another sip, then went on. 'It is funny, though,' she said. 'I'm not sure *why* I thought of it. Does that ever happen to you?'

Dulcie nodded. 'All the time. In fact…' She paused. She and Mina had grown close and at times like this, Dulcie sometimes wondered if Mina could also, well, occasionally hear things. Or if she got the occasional message from a feline.

'I can't ask,' she muttered to herself now. 'I'd sound like Lucy.'

'Excuse me?' Mina had been looking out at the courtyard but now looked up.

'Nothing.' Dulcie shook her head. There were some familial connections she did not want to evoke. 'Do you want to go up?'

Mina reached to put down her cup, and Dulcie realized her mistake. Because the younger woman walked with a cane, she couldn't proceed with both her hands full.

'I'm sorry.' Dulcie stopped her. 'We can wait down here.'

'No, it's fine.' Mina pushed the glass back on to the table. 'It's too strong for me. But I will grab one more of these.' She held up an iced cookie. 'Want one?'

'Sure.' Dulcie abandoned her own punch glass to take the proffered treat, and waited while Mina reached for another for herself. 'Maybe we are related.'

'I don't know about that cider.' Mina led the way to the staircase. 'It's even stronger than the punch, and with this crowd...'

Dulcie nodded her understanding. For all their staid reputation, academics were fond of their booze. 'This could be interesting.'

The sound of loud laughter could be heard from above. Laughter and the kind of boisterous conversation that made both the women shrink back.

'Maybe we should stay down here.' Mina made a joke out of it, but Dulcie was grateful. In truth, the entrance hall was getting crowded and hot. Dulcie thought of that open door on the balcony. The ballroom was undoubtedly overheated to start with.

'I'd even go out on the patio again,' she offered. 'Check out that moon.'

'Let's,' Mina said. 'I could use some air.'

A lull in arrivals allowed them to retrieve their coats quickly, and they stepped into the cold.

TWENTY

THE NIGHT HADN'T gotten any less frosty, but after their brief spell inside, Dulcie relished the crisp cold. Besides, she could actually hear the music from here, the party noise fading into the background. Mina, beside her, was humming along softly, when she heard footsteps approaching.

'Ms Schwartz.' Dulcie turned to find herself face to face with Martin Thorpe.

'Mr Thorpe.' He was, she saw, holding a glass of the punch and already looked a little the worse for wear. 'Have you met Mina Love?'

'Of course, Ms Love.' Thorpe reached forward to take her hand, only to find himself holding on to her cookie. 'You're the undergrad who…who…' He let go and stepped back, swaying a bit.

'Mina worked with me on the paper I'm presenting.' Dulcie wasn't sure what Thorpe had been about to say, but she didn't want him referencing the brutal attack of a month earlier. 'Have you been here long?'

'Yes, yes.' He gestured with the glass, slopping some over the side. 'I wanted to oversee the set-up. Make sure everything was in place.'

Mina and Dulcie exchanged a look. 'I'd say you did a good job,' said Dulcie, reaching for the glass. 'I'm sure they appreciate it. And as soon as I find Marco Tesla, I'll smooth over—'

She didn't get a chance to finish—or to remove his

drink: Thorpe had turned away and out of her grasp.
'Look at them all.' He gestured back toward the lit windows, more of his drink spilling in the process. 'Do you
think any of them know how much work went into this?'
His voice would have been bullhorn loud had they been
indoors. Out here in the crisp cold, it was simply loud.

'Well, some of them have hosted the ELLA in other
years.' Dulcie wanted to be circumspect. 'But I'm sure
that just makes them appreciate your efforts even more.'

'Huh.' The rest of the punch went into a shrub. It
probably wouldn't hurt the bush much, Dulcie decided.
'Like they care.' Thorpe certainly didn't need it. 'Stella
Roebuck has left already. Said she had to check on
something, but I doubt we'll see her again.'

That was Dulcie's cue. 'Maybe she's checking on
her laptop? Chris went over there to work on it. He's
probably done by now.' And home asleep, she thought.

Thorpe turned to her, his face bright with hope—
or alcohol.

'I don't know if he managed to find her paper,
though,' Dulcie felt compelled to admit. 'But if anyone can, he will.'

'Exactly.' Thorpe was addressing the patio again.
'Why I wanted him. He's the best.'

Dulcie had painted herself into a corner with that,
but Mina seemed to sense her predicament. 'Look! Is
that Paul Barnes over there?' She pointed over to the
far side of the terrace.

It wasn't the distraction Dulcie would have chosen,
but it did serve to get Thorpe's attention.

'Where?' Thorpe was peering into the shadows, his
voice a little too loud for discretion.

'Never mind.' Dulcie grabbed his hand and pulled
him around to face her. Too late, she had seen that

Barnes was deep in conversation with a certain red-haired professor. He was leaning in, one hand on her arm, but she shook him off, nearly spilling the punch glass he had pressed into her hand. It looked heated and personal. And as much as she wanted to speak with both of them, she didn't want to interrupt. She certainly didn't want to do so with Thorpe as a witness. 'So tell me what made Marco Tesla change his mind and decide to attend?'

'Sorry,' Mina whispered. She might not know about that phone call from Barnes, but she was well aware of the tensions between Thorpe and Showalter.

'I gather he's got some personal reason, and he thinks he's a big enough deal…' Thorpe broke off, slightly unbalanced by his own dramatic gestures. 'Well, look who's over there.' He righted himself and was peering over Dulcie's shoulder. 'If it isn't the Canadian interloper.'

Dulcie spun around. Sure enough, Showalter was behind her, arms crossed as she made her way back toward the French doors. Dulcie bit her lip. As much as she would love to grab the red-haired academic, she couldn't abandon Thorpe, not in this condition.

Mina saw her frustration. 'I'll go after her,' she said softly. 'Pleasure to see you again, Mr Thorpe.' She headed back into the dining hall, on the heels of the visiting scholar.

'Chasing a dream, that one.' Thorpe was slurring his words, and Dulcie was looking around for relief. Surely she could hail one of her colleagues to take a turn with their interim chair.

'Mr Thorpe, look! There's Lloyd!' She waved. Her office mate waved back from inside the entrance hall and then turned away, back to what seemed to be a discussion with several postgrads.

'She's not going to get what she wants, you know.'

Dulcie turned back to Thorpe. This was getting annoying. 'Who, Mina? She's only an undergrad, and she's already getting recognition. I was lucky to have her input on my paper.'

'Not her.' Thorpe shook his head, then seemed to think better of it. 'The other one. Redheads!'

That could have referred to Dulcie herself, but she knew he meant Showalter. Well, the Canadian professor was a front runner for the job he had effectively held for more than a year now. He had reason to be bitter.

'And there's Professor Barnes.' Dulcie smiled and waved, hoping the silver-haired academic would know enough not to say anything too obvious in front of Thorpe. He nodded back, his hands full with discarded dishes.

'He doesn't matter.' Thorpe shrugged, an eloquent if overdone gesture. 'He's not going to get it.'

'Excuse me?' Dulcie had never heard her adviser speak so openly about the chairmanship.

'She doesn't have it.' Thorpe delivered this apparent non sequitur with a dismissive snort, as he raised his now-empty glass. 'I need a refill.'

'Are you sure that's wise?' Dulcie did not want to be in the position of monitoring Thorpe's drinking. Then again, she didn't want to think what might happen if he imbibed more. As much to distract him as for her own curiosity, she asked the question that popped into her mind. 'So, you think Professor Showalter and Professor Barnes are having some kind of a disagreement, and that she wants him to go after her?' Voiced out loud, it sounded ridiculous. 'I'm sorry,' she added. 'That was silly of me.'

'Not silly at all.' Thorpe leaned forward and Dulcie got a strong whiff of rum. He must have started with the cider. 'She's got something he wants, but not...'

It was the leaning that did it. Thorpe was not the most physically adept man at the best of times. Three sheets to the wind, he was as unstable as a rotten pine. With a whoop, he fell forward, causing Dulcie to stagger backwards under his weight.

'Sorry! Sorry!' He overcorrected and started to tilt back.

'Mr Thorpe!' Dulcie grabbed for him. The terrace was stone, and in this condition he could crack his head open.

'Got him!' A burly post doc jumped out of the doorway, righting the tipsy scholar with an arm around his waist. 'Shall we go inside and find a seat?'

'Nonsense,' said Thorpe, who seemed amused by the small crowd that had gathered, silhouetted in the doorway.

'I'll take him from here.' Dulcie turned to see Lloyd and Raleigh emerging from the building. They had seen her predicament.

'Thank you,' she mouthed the words as Lloyd stepped by her to guide the weaving Thorpe through the smirking partygoers and back inside the busy entrance hall. The post doc closed the doors behind them, the moonlight making the sheer drapes shimmer as they fell into place.

Inside the reception room the crowd had grown, and Dulcie let Lloyd move ahead, clearing a path. Thorpe seemed to be heading toward the stairs, and Lloyd let him. It was a smart move, Dulcie realized. There were chairs over by the stairwell, and it would be quieter once they had passed to the other side of the bar.

Hanging back, Dulcie watched them go. Chris was not going to believe this. Thinking of her boyfriend, she decided to check in. 'Chris? It's me.' His voicemail had picked up. 'You wouldn't believe what Thorpe did.' She paused. It was foolish to hope he'd pick up. He was probably fast asleep, as she had wanted him to be. 'I hope you're feeling better, sweetie. I won't be out too late.' She would have felt better if he had answered, but knowing that he was home would have to be good enough.

'Chris?' Raleigh waited till she had pocketed her phone.

'Sick.' Dulcie nodded. 'Not self-induced.'

'Poor guy.' Raleigh's eyes were also following the path Lloyd and Thorpe had taken. 'The pressure must be unbearable. Is he going to be okay?' This was to Lloyd, who had emerged from the scrum, alone.

Lloyd shrugged. 'He's going to have a bad head tomorrow. That's for sure.' Dulcie was about to question him, when he continued. 'He said he was going to go upstairs to the Men's room. I did not think I had to follow.' He paused. 'Unless you think I should?'

'No, I'm sure he'll be fine.' Dulcie wasn't, but there were limits to their loyalty. 'Did you happen to see either Renée Showalter or Paul Barnes?'

'Yeah, both of them.' Lloyd had his arm around Raleigh and was guiding her back to the bar. Dulcie, who had begun to follow, stopped.

'Lloyd?'

'Sorry.' Her friend turned. 'You'd think after that I wouldn't want a drink, but...' He shrugged. 'Showalter was on the stairs when I was trying to get Thorpe to take a seat. I think she'd been talking with Barnes, 'cause I saw him—up the first flight. He was saying something, though the music was so loud I don't know that she heard. Or that she wanted to.'

Dulcie could feel her pulse speed up. 'Why? What did he say?'

Lloyd shook his head. 'I'm not positive. It was very loud, and they were on the landing. But she had a face like thunder, and he sounded, well, not angry. Maybe a little desperate.

'He wasn't yelling, but he kept repeating himself. "You're wrong, you know. It's not like that. I wouldn't do that to her."'

'Huh.' Dulcie thought that one over as Lloyd turned again for the bar. Raleigh stopped him, taking his hand, and turned him back toward Dulcie.

'Dulcie, what's going on? What does this mean?'

Dulcie shook her head. 'I'm not sure.' She paused, wondering how much she could—or should—tell her friends. Besides, Mina had just appeared, and if Dulcie was going to leave their project to go work with Barnes, she should tell the undergrad first.

'Mina, did you find Professor Showalter?' Dulcie kept her voice low. 'Lloyd said she was upstairs. I really need to talk to her—and to you.'

'This party, I don't know, Dulcie. Maybe there is something to the whole full moon thing.' Mina was speaking softly too.

'What do you mean?'

'Well, I went after her. I thought, you know, maybe she was simply going to the Ladies. And besides, I knew you wanted me to keep my eyes open for Marco Tesla, too.' Mina stopped and looked around. 'I mean, I saw her go up to the ballroom, so I figured I'd follow.

I thought I'd lost her, but she was just standing by those big windows, pacing. Then Professor Barnes came by and it was clear he'd been looking for her. And they started whispering to each other.'

Dulcie nodded in confirmation. 'That's what Lloyd said. I gather they were—ah—having a discussion.'

'Yeah, I think they were talking about Stella Roebuck. I couldn't get too close without being obvious.' She held up her cane. 'But I swear I heard them talking about a paper—Showalter said "*her* paper".'

This was interesting. 'I should tell you, Mina, I've got to talk to both of them, but—'

'And there's—oh, never mind.' Mina had grabbed her arm, pointing. Dulcie turned. She immediately saw why: Stella Roebuck was standing in the doorway, about to make an entrance. In her man-tailored frock coat and pants, she looked a lot like Marco Tesla had that afternoon. It must have been intentional, Dulcie thought, and mistakes like Mina's only one of the desired effects. Once again, Dulcie was struck by the petite academic's sense of drama.

Frozen in place, her face a bloodless white under those peaks of blue-black hair, Stella Roebuck looked like a statue. With Marco Tesla beside her, she'd have been even more striking. If they had been civilians, their nearly identical look would have been some kind of statement about them as a couple. Maybe, Dulcie pondered, it was a uniform: what the well-dressed deconstructivist was wearing. No, she dismissed the thought. Considering who they were and what they were both known for, it couldn't be that simple. It had to be a statement about gender roles and identification in a postmodern context.

'Do you think,' Dulcie said, turning toward Mina, 'that she's riffing on fashion as a—'

Again, she was cut off. This time by Roebuck, as the frozen figure opened her mouth and let loose a blood-curdling shriek, before collapsing to her knees.

TWENTY-ONE

THE FUNNY THING WAS, there didn't seem to be anything wrong. At least, nothing that Stella Roebuck wasn't doing to herself.

Dulcie and Mina were the first ones over. Kneeling there, eyes staring straight ahead, Stella was still screaming, like some kind of nightmare automaton, pausing only to draw in another breath. But by the time they reached her, she had also started clawing at her face, drawing the black-lacquered nails of both hands down her pale cheeks again and again, as if to release even more of the piercing sound within.

Dulcie had been flustered for a moment. This was, after all, a visiting scholar. A dignitary, of sorts. And a rather formidable woman in her own right. But after a split second delay she reached up, taking the arched and rigid hands in her own and drawing them down. The woman didn't resist, but neither did she respond, except to take another breath and start screaming again.

'Ms Roebuck, please!' Dulcie was right in the visiting scholar's face where she could see the angry red welts left by those dark nails. Stella seemed not to see her and tried to lift her hands, still held in a raking pose. 'No, Ms Roebuck. No!' Dulcie held tight, determined to stop the self-destructive scratching, even if the screaming continued.

'Ms Roebuck!' Mina had grabbed her shoulder and

was shaking her. 'What happened? What's wrong? Are you hurt?'

For a split second, Dulcie thought she saw a response. Those dark eyes shifted ever so slightly, though whether in response to Mina or to something else, she couldn't say. Because in that split second, she heard another voice. The student bartender, and soon after the confused noise of a dozen or more partygoers, all rushing down the stairs.

'Oh my God!' 'What?' The noise was cut by another scream, and for a moment Dulcie wondered if she was witnessing a case of contagious hysteria. After all, the new person screaming had been downing some of that spiked cider only seconds before.

'Oh, hell.' It was Mina. She'd let go of Stella Roebuck's arm and taken Dulcie's. She pulled at it, till Dulcie turned. She was pointing. There were about fifteen people behind Stella now, piled into the space between the screaming academic and the French doors. It was the press of them, she thought at first, that opened the doors. Too many people in too small a space, the air thick with noise and booze.

But as the cold air rushed in and some of the revelers stepped out, the crowd thinned just enough for Dulcie to see past Stella Roebuck and out into the courtyard. Five people, maybe six, had stepped into the stone patio without their coats and stood there frozen. But not, apparently, by the cold.

They were staring, and from inside, Dulcie followed their eyes to see, lying sideways on the frosted stone, a shoe. A man's shoe, lace-up, its dark leather glinting with the moonlight. Even as Mina tried to hold her, Dulcie left Stella and walked toward the shoe. Just then one of the partygoers turned away to vomit noisily against the wall. And Dulcie saw why: the shoe was attached to a leg that belonged to Marco Tesla. The visiting academic was lying on his back on the cold flagstone. His face was as pale as ever, and his dark eyes seemed to be staring straight at Dulcie. But after her initial intake of breath, Dulcie realized that the foppish scholar was not, in fact, seeing her. Or anyone else for that matter. Because the rakishly coiffed head was bent at an angle not found in nature. Something—or someone—had broken Marco Tesla's neck.

TWENTY-TWO

'I DIDN'T HAVE anything to do with this,' Dulcie said, resisting the temptation to add 'this time'. She didn't need to. Detective Rogovoy hadn't even asked her if she did. The campus detective was simply taking her statement, much as he and his colleagues were taking down the basic information of everyone there: partygoers, waiters, that poor student bartender. He'd been the one to lose his dinner at the sight of Marco Tesla, and Dulcie saw him now, sitting with his head between his legs. Someone was trying to get him to take a paper cup of water, but he wasn't having any of it.

Dulcie knew how he felt. 'You know I didn't,' she said, turning back to the big detective. Rogovoy was a large man, and ugly, with a nose like a growth on the potato of his face. He wasn't unkind, however, and he only nodded as Dulcie protested.

'This isn't like…' Dulcie stopped herself, the adrenalin that had driven her finally draining off. She and the detective had become acquainted in the past, when various misadventures had thrown her into the hot seat. Surely he could understand that as fond as she had actually grown of the ogre-like man, she didn't want to go through all the rigmarole of a police investigation again. 'Well,' she said, suddenly deflated. 'It isn't.'

Rogovoy looked equally exhausted, his face a topographic map of grief. 'Why don't we start at the beginning, Ms Schwartz?' His voice, rumbly deep, was kind. 'Let's just start with how you know this young man.'

'He wasn't…' She paused. It was funny, in a way. Dulcie didn't think of him as a young man. A scholar. A guest of the university. One of the rising luminaries of her field. But the detective was right: Marco Tesla was a young man. A handsome young man. And he was, she knew, dead. Mina had dragged her back, away from the scene on the steps, before the ambulance had arrived. It didn't matter. One look at Tesla, at the unnatural angle of his head, and she had known. Everyone had. There was no emergency treatment that could put that right. She turned toward the cop. 'What happened?'

Rogovoy looked at her, eyebrows raised.

'I mean, I know he's dead.' She felt foolish under that gaze. 'I mean, he is, right?'

'Let's go back to my question, first, shall we?' For a big man, Rogovoy's voice was soft.

'But why? You know who he is, right?' She looked up at him. His lack of response seemed to confirm her supposition. 'And it was an accident, right?'

Nothing. Dulcie began running through the facts out loud. 'That balcony. Everyone talks about how dangerous it is. The railing is really low, and people sit on it all the time. I mean, it's not that high, but the patio below is stone, so if you fell…' She stopped, the memory of the broken man suddenly filling her vision. 'Oh, God.'

Rogovoy was around the desk in a minute. 'Ms Schwartz, are you all right? Do you feel faint?' For a big man, he was fast. And gentle. She felt his hand on her back pushing her forward, so that her head was down and the wave of dizziness passed.

'I'm fine,' she said, but held the position. 'I was just remembering.'

'Why don't you tell me what you remember?' His voice was still soft, but Dulcie paused.

'You asked me that already.' She could think again, and she didn't like what her brain was putting together. 'It was an accident, wasn't it?'

Silence. She looked up at Rogovoy. The big detective looked back, his eyes sad.

'It wasn't?' She swallowed. 'No, of course not. That's why you're asking.'

'Whatever we think we know, Ms Schwartz, we have to confirm. Isn't that the scientific way?' He sat back, the ghost of a smile edging into his cheeks. 'Now, if we can get back to my questions…'

She nodded. It was going to take a while to absorb this. Having something else to think about helped. 'What did you want to know again?'

'What can you tell me about Marco Tesla?' It was an open question, but Dulcie was grateful for it.

'He was here for ELLA.' Dulcie paused, but Rogovoy didn't ask for details. Of course not, she realized. His department was probably aware of such a momentous happening. 'Oh, Mr Thorpe is going to have a heart attack.'

'Is he related to this Ella somehow?' So much for the cop's omniscience.

'It's a conference,' Dulcie explained, as quickly as she could. Now that she was away from the scene, the energy seemed to be sifting out of her like, well, like sifting sand. 'We have scholars from all over the country. Canada, too.' She thought of Renée Showalter. At least she had left before this had happened. 'He— Marco Tesla—was in from California. He's a big deal.' It sounded lame, even to her. 'He was, I mean.'

Rogovoy nodded. 'And you saw him at this party?'

She shook her head. 'No, I'm helping with the conference. I actually met him earlier today, but...just in passing.' She flashed back to the scene in the Science Center. Tesla had been there for Stella, but Paul Barnes had been there, too. It was clear the pixie-like brunette preferred the younger man, but that didn't mean there hadn't been tension.

'What is it?' Rogovoy's voice was soft, but his eyes were bright.

'There was...' Dulcie paused. She wasn't the sort to tell tales. Besides, she knew herself well enough to understand that half of what she assumed was reality might well be a fiction, embroidered on to a few scraps of observed behavior. 'I kind of met him in the Science Center this afternoon.' She settled on a few hard facts. 'That's where the big talks are going to be given. Were, anyway.' What would this mean for the conference? She couldn't think about that now. 'Stella Roebuck—the lady who was taken away? She was doing a soundcheck.'

The eyebrows went up again. 'Like for a concert?'

'Kind of.' Dulcie had to smile. He didn't understand. In her world, these people were rock stars. 'Some of these presentations are very big deals. There are graphics and charts and, well...they're just big deals.' She didn't have the energy to explain. 'Anyway, Tesla showed up. I think he and Stella were, um, a couple.'

Rogovoy nodded again, and Dulcie had the sense that this wasn't news. 'And then?'

'Then, nothing.' She shrugged. 'I was supposed to meet him after. He was the next speaker up, and I am the departmental liaison and all.' Rogovoy pursed his lips. Dulcie thought, for a moment, that he was impressed.

That was quickly followed by the suspicion that he was suppressing a smile.

'Well, I am.' It was the best she could do, and she found herself talking faster. The sooner she could get through this all, the sooner she could go home. Chris, and Esmé, both beckoned. 'But with all the fuss about Stella Roebuck's presentation, I missed him. And Thorpe was really mad about that, and so I was hoping to catch up with him here. Tesla, that is, not Thorpe. Thorpe left, and then—'

'Hang on a minute.' Rogovoy had raised his hand. 'Back up, Ms Schwartz. Let's back up a bit. There was a "fuss" in the Science Center this afternoon?'

'Her paper, the one she was going to deliver. It got lost somehow.' Dulcie didn't see what this had to do with anything.

'Like, she put it down somewhere and forgot about it? Or someone stole it?'

Dulcie shook her head. 'Not a paper, literally. It was a presentation. Some kind of multimedia presentation. She had it on her computer.'

'Ah.' Rogovoy sounded like he understood. 'And it got erased?'

'Not exactly.' If only Chris were here. He could have explained. 'We were working with one of the media techs. I mean, if you just erase things, sometimes you can get them back. This was worse.' She flashed back to the scene with Stella Roebuck. 'She thought—well, it doesn't make sense, but she thought maybe someone had sabotaged her. You know, gotten a virus into her computer or something.'

'Did she blame this Mr Tesla, by any chance?' Dulcie looked up into the detective's deep-set eyes. His tone was light, and for a moment she wondered if he was joking. But those eyes were sad. A man had died.

'No.' She shook her head. 'She blamed her ex, Paul Barnes. But that didn't make any sense.'

'Because this other dude, Paul Barnes, he wasn't there?' Somehow, Dulcie got the feeling that he knew a lot of this. That he was simply trying to find out if she, Dulcie, was telling the truth.

'No, he was.' She stopped and looked at him. 'You know this, don't you?'

'Never mind what I know, Ms Schwartz.' His voice was as even as ever, low and grumbly, like something from deep below the earth. 'All you need to do is answer my questions. So Paul Barnes was there. Had he been talking to this Marco Tesla?'

'I don't think so.' She shook her head and tried to think back. It had been a very long day. 'No, he spoke to Stella Roebuck, but that was before she started freaking out about her computer. Then they went off together.'

'They—he and Stella?' The voice was low but warm, gentle.

'No, Barnes was with Renée Showalter. They had been talking earlier. There's a chance I might be—no, never mind. That really doesn't have anything to do with any of this. But they left together, at least I think they did.'

'And this Showalter, this other professor,' Rogovoy's voice had gone even quieter. 'Is she a big, strong woman, would you say?'

TWENTY-THREE

'PROFESSOR SHOWALTER DID not kill Marco Tesla.' Dulcie's vehemence was, perhaps, undercut by her follow-up question. 'I mean, why would she?'

Trista opened her mouth as if to answer, then closed it when Lloyd elbowed her. They were squeezed in so tight at the diner's booth that it could have been an accident. Dulcie didn't think so, and the look Trista gave Lloyd confirmed it.

'Seriously.' Dulcie turned to her blonde friend.

With a sidelong glance at Lloyd, Trista responded. 'I'm not saying she did. But she was upstairs. And even though he was only recently added to the conference line-up, Marco would have been considered a serious contender for the chairmanship. And, well, we know how high tensions can run.'

Dulcie shook her head and considered her coffee. The friends had all felt the need to go out after the police released them, and a bar hadn't felt right. Looking at the stale brew now, however, Dulcie regretted the choice. 'I don't know. I mean, Tesla's a big name and all, but I would have thought Stella was a greater threat. Or Paul Barnes.'

She caught the look Trista and Lloyd shared. 'What?'

'I know you like him, but Barnes hasn't published anything in years.' At least Trista sounded apologetic.

'And Stella's work has been sabotaged.' Lloyd cut in,

before Dulcie could explain about Barnes's upcoming work. 'That's kind of thrown her.'

'Wait, why would that matter?' Dulcie didn't understand. 'Chris will probably get her paper back for her.'

'Doesn't matter. She still blew up.' Trista chimed in. 'I heard people were talking about her little temper tantrum, and the powers that be were not impressed. Unprofessional and all that.'

'You heard people were talking?' Dulcie raised an eyebrow. Trista shrugged. 'And why are you assuming that Paul Barnes is not in the running? What is it with this place anyway? Or is it simply academia?'

As she spoke, she realized she hadn't exactly made the clearest argument. It didn't matter. Her friends were all on the same wavelength.

'I mean, how could something like this happen and nobody see anything?' Dulcie looked around at her friends. Not that any of them had the answer.

'All anyone saw were those damned drapes,' added Trista, echoing what they had all heard. Lloyd, Raleigh, and Mina had nothing else to contribute, and sat there shaking their heads. That motion, combined with the acidic coffee and the bad fluorescent lighting, was making Dulcie a bit nauseous, and she closed her eyes.

'You okay?' She opened them to looks of concern.

'Yeah.' She nodded. That was a mistake. 'Chris has some kind of virus. Maybe I'm getting it. I should go home.'

'We're walking you.' This from Raleigh, although Lloyd nodded his agreement.

'No, really, I'll be fine.' Dulcie knew her friends cared about her, but she didn't want to be a burden.

'Dulcie.' Now it was Trista giving her a look.

'Really.' Dulcie gestured to the grimy window. 'It's

as light as day out there. Look, I'll walk Mina to her dorm. If that's okay?' Mina nodded. 'Then I'll call a cab.'

She could tell from Trista's face that her friend doubted that she'd follow through. But really, what could they say? At any rate, Dulcie knew she had to get home. This night had just been a horror from beginning to end.

'At least Thorpe wasn't involved,' she said as the friends donned their coats.

'As far as we know,' Lloyd said, his voice grim.

'Oh, come on.' Dulcie felt cheerier now that they were leaving. 'How could he? You saw how drunk he was.'

'Unless it was an act.' Lloyd looked over at Raleigh, and Dulcie realized that the two had been discussing just such a possibility.

'You don't really think that Thorpe…' She glanced from one to the other.

'I don't know,' said Raleigh. 'That's the problem.'

'Maybe it was an accident after all.' Dulcie really wanted to look on the bright side.

'Whatever it was, we're not involved.' Lloyd sounded relieved, and Dulcie wanted very much to believe him.

The night had turned frigid, but the fresh air did Dulcie good. Because of her cane, Mina was one of the few of Dulcie's colleagues who actually walked as slowly as she did, and Dulcie found this relaxing. Even as she shivered, she felt invigorated by the clear, cold air.

'Isn't it beautiful?' With the trees bare, Dulcie could see the moon. It made a welcome distraction.

'I guess.' Mina didn't sound distracted. 'Me, I'll be happy for spring to come around.'

'Maybe I'm just relieved.' Dulcie was talking to herself as much as anything.

'Because it's just a moon?' Mina filled in the rest of the thought. A month before, Dulcie had been convinced that there was something…unnatural stalking under the full moon.

'Yeah, I guess so.' Dulcie nodded. 'Though it is kind of cool to think that maybe it is magical somehow. That maybe…' She paused. Now that she had Mina alone, she ought to tell her about the call from Paul Barnes. If only she'd had a chance actually to talk to the scholar. 'Mina, I'm really glad we got a chance to work on this paper together.'

'Thanks, Dulcie,' Mina said, her voice a little sad. 'Do you think you'll still get to present it?'

'I hope so.' At the diner, the friends had avoided talking about the repercussions of Tesla's death. Only now did it hit Dulcie that the conference might be suspended. However, it did give her an opening. 'I didn't get a chance to tell you earlier,' she began. 'But I spoke to Paul Barnes a little about my work—about *our* work.'

'Oh, Dulcie, you didn't?' Mina's voice was breathless. 'Professor Barnes?'

'Well, I know he's a star and all, but he was the one who brought it up.' Dulcie couldn't help feeling a bit proud. 'He's very interested in it.'

'But… Professor Showalter.' Mina was sputtering.

'Oh, I'll talk to her first,' Dulcie reassured her. 'I've been meaning to, just with everything that's happened…'

'It's not that, Dulcie.' They'd reached Mina's dorm, and the younger woman turned to face her friend. 'It's— do you remember what we were talking about before?'

'Marco Tesla was not killed by a werewolf.' Of that, Dulcie was sure. 'Or a were-anything, Mina.'

'No,' Mina said. 'Not that—I mean, what I heard Professor Showalter say to Professor Barnes about Stella's paper. It's been bothering me. Maybe the whole thing with Marco Tesla…maybe it wasn't academic jealousy. I mean, wasn't Tesla involved with Stella Roebuck?'

Dulcie stopped short, remembering what Roebuck herself had said. 'Do you think Paul Barnes erased the paper? Out of jealousy?' The idea of one of her heroes hurting someone was bad enough. But for Stella Roebuck? The striking scholar's accusations leaped back into her mind: she had accused Barnes of sabotage, too.

Mina had kept walking. 'Could be,' she said, pausing as Dulcie caught up. 'I mean, I guess she left him after she met Tesla at the "New Paradigm" conference.'

'New paradigm? You may as well just say there are no rules.' No, she stopped herself. 'You might as well say Renée Showalter did it.' Dulcie didn't buy that, either.

'That's a possibility, too.' Mina's voice was soft, but level.

'Wait—how do you figure that?' Dulcie asked. 'I mean, why would Renée Showalter want to hurt—' she couldn't bring herself to say 'kill'—'Marco Tesla?'

'I'm not saying it's logical.' Mina shrugged. 'But if Professor Showalter, you know, likes Professor Barnes… Stella Roebuck and Marco Tesla looked a lot alike. At night, even with the moon, if someone had been drinking…' She looked over at her friend, holding her eyes. 'Maybe Tesla was killed by mistake. Someone pushed him, sure. But maybe he—or she—thought they were pushing Stella.'

After that, not even the moon could distract Dulcie. She declined Mina's offer to come in and use the phone, promising instead to call if she couldn't find a cab in the Square. In truth, she just wanted to walk. That idea—that someone had killed Marco Tesla— was too upsetting. Probably, she admitted to herself, because it was possible. Not likely, but possible. And she knew who.

Stella herself had accused Paul Barnes of sabotaging her work. And from what Dulcie had learned tonight—from what both Lloyd and Mina had overheard—it sounded like maybe Renée Showalter had, too. If Paul Barnes had been indulging in that punch... No, it didn't make sense.

'*We are not what we seem...*' Mr Grey's words came back to her, as chilling as the wind.

'That's not what you meant,' she asked that same wind, 'is it? Mr Grey?' It was hopeless. Her spectral pet rarely came when summoned.

She was three blocks past the Square by the time she settled down. By then, the streets were empty, and Dulcie remembered her promise to her friend. She had her phone in her hand before she realized how ridiculous it was, however. What was she going to do: call a cab and stand here, freezing, as she waited? Better just to head for home. As a compromise, she'd text Chris. He was probably asleep, but if not...

'Hey sweetie,' she typed. 'Walking home from Sq. Meet me if up?' She sent it. She was perfectly capable of getting home alone. Still, the idea that at the next corner, or the one after that, she might see her boyfriend coming to meet her made the night a little less lonely. At least, she thought, it wasn't too dark.

'It had to have been an accident,' she said, speaking aloud. 'Paul Barnes couldn't be a killer. Could he, Mr Grey?'

The moon, like the streets around her, remained silent.

TWENTY-FOUR

'MEW!' ESMÉ GREETED Dulcie with an affronted cry and began headbutting her before she could even get her coat off. 'Meh!' the small cat said.

'What is it, Esmé?' Dulcie couldn't help but be somewhat cheered. The little creature sounded so purposeful—and yet so incoherent—she distracted Dulcie from the horrors of the night. 'You can talk to me, you know.'

'Wow.' Esmé twined around her ankles, nearly tripping her.

'Hang on.' Dropping her coat on the ground, Dulcie picked up the cat. 'Let's get to the bottom of this. Chris?'

She hadn't seen her boyfriend on the way home. By the time she turned off Mass Ave, she had even found herself hoping she wouldn't run into him. If he was sick, he should be at home. Even if he was simply exhausted, bed was the place for him. And really, the thought of her boyfriend, warm and sleepy, was more of a comfort than having him come to meet her would have been. 'Chris?'

'Meh!' Esmé pushed against her chest and Dulcie found herself looking down into her green eyes.

'Did he go out and I missed him? Is that what you were trying to tell me?' Dulcie said to the affronted kitty. 'I guess I should text him again.'

She put the cat down and retrieved her phone. It didn't seem likely she and her boyfriend would have missed each other. They both walked into the Square often enough to have a fairly set route, and Dulcie had seen only a few other pedestrians out in the night. It was true that she'd *heard* other creatures. Someone's party had not been as rudely interrupted as her own, and loud music had filtered down from a window. And, as much as she didn't like to think of it, she had also heard *something*... Not a howl, exactly, but some kind of animal noise. Only that had been far off. Down by the river, possibly, if not farther away. Not anything for her to worry about, and she had only picked up her speed a little at that point, telling herself that it was the cold more than the long, high wail that made her step faster along the lonely sidewalk.

'I'm home,' she typed. 'Did we miss?' She sent the text. But before she hung her coat up, she paused. Maybe she should go back out. He had gone out looking for her. He was sick, or at least tired. And if there was something out there...

'Dulcie?' At the sound of her name, she turned. Chris was coming in the door.

'Oh, Chris!' She threw herself on him with the vehemence of a kitten. 'I'm so glad.'

'When did you get back?' He smiled, a little flustered. 'Have you been home long?'

'I just got in.' She'd dropped her coat again, but now she took his. 'We must have just missed each other.'

'I guess.' He rubbed his hands to warm them. Dulcie was glad to see there was some color in his cheeks again. 'I just needed some air.'

'Oh.' She paused, coats in hand. 'So you didn't come to meet me?'

He shook his head, clearly confused.

'You didn't get my text?'

'No, I'm sorry.' He walked by her into the kitchen. 'I must have forgot my phone. How was the party?'

'It…' Dulcie didn't know where to begin. She'd left a long message before the friends had gone out to the diner, explaining everything that had happened, and telling him not to worry. 'How long have you been out?'

'I'm not sure.' He'd taken the sliced turkey out and was eating it in front of the open fridge. 'You want some?'

'No.' She shook her head and plopped into a kitchen chair. 'Chris, I called you, must have been an hour ago.'

'Guess I've been out longer than that,' he said, rummaging around in the meat compartment. 'Do we have any of those meatballs left?'

'You finished them.' She watched her boyfriend devour the rest of the sandwich meat. 'I gather you're feeling better?'

'What?' He turned to face her, a slice of turkey in his mouth. 'Oh, yeah. 'Scuse me.' He chewed and swallowed. 'Sorry, I'm just famished.'

'That's good, I guess. You must have walked a lot.' He shrugged, and she felt the weight of the evening on her. 'Look, it's been a long night. I left you a message. You should—you should just listen to it.' It was all she could do to push herself out of her seat. 'I'm going to bed.'

'*Don't.*' The single word stopped her. She turned. Chris was back in the fridge, this time pawing open an old Chinese food container. It didn't matter. Dulcie knew that voice.

'Mr Grey?' she whispered, although she couldn't have said why.

'*Don't leave,*' the voice continued, and as she turned

again toward her boyfriend, she realized that the quiet command had been for her ears only. '*Chris*...'

'Got it,' she whispered to the air. 'Chris?'

He turned, mouth full.

'Can we talk?'

He nodded and came over, that leftover Chinese container in his hands.

'Chris, I don't know when that's from.' Dulcie shook her head.

'It smells fine.' He stuck his face between the cardboard wings as if to demonstrate. 'If that's what you were worried about...'

'No.' She sat and reached for his hand, forcing him to put the container on the table and revealing those long, deep scratches. 'You still don't remember how you got these?'

'Oh, this?' He seemed to be seeing it for the first time. 'I don't know. That must have been when Esmé went for me. I told you she was acting weird, right?'

'Yeah.' Dulcie remained sceptical. Since her boyfriend had come in, she hadn't seen the cat. 'Chris, what's going on?'

He shook his head. 'Nothing. I went for a walk, I guess. And I forgot my phone. Why?'

'You were feeling awful when I left for the party. You looked pale and I swear you had a fever. I go out for a few hours, and you suddenly recover? Chris, I called you over an hour ago, and you didn't pick up. You must have been out all this time. It's cold out. It's the middle of the night. And you're acting like you just got back from a run or something.' She paused to look at him. It wasn't just the cold that had made his cheeks red, she decided. In the moonlight that streamed in the window, she could see that his cheeks were still flushed. The high color hadn't faded in the warmth of their kitchen, nor had the unnatural gleam of his eyes that reflected that bright blue-white light. And something he had just said... 'Wait, Chris, why did you say, "I went for a walk, *I guess*"?'

Like a cloud across the moon, a spasm of pain seemed to pass over his face. Finally he stopped eating. Even the light seemed to dim, as the two sat in the kitchen. Dulcie reached to take that bloodied hand. It didn't *look* infected. 'Chris? What is it?'

'I don't know, Dulce. It's the weirdest thing.' The color that had seemed so unnatural was receding now. 'I mean, I must have been out walking for hours. I feel so drained. But all I can remember is coming up our street maybe ten minutes ago. I have no recollection of how I got there—or where I've been.'

TWENTY-FIVE

THIS, SHE WAS SURE, was what Mr Grey had wanted her to hear. When Chris's unnatural—Dulcie immediately labeled it 'feverish'—energy had abated, she hustled him off to bed, running off only to get a thermometer.

'But…' he started to protest.

'Mouth shut,' she said. Sitting on the bed, she stared down at him, as if the force of her eyes could keep him still. When Esmé landed, with a soft thud, behind her, and made her way up to Chris's pillow, she felt a little easier. The cat looked as concerned as she was. And although Chris hid his hands under the blanket, the little creature seemed quite calm.

While she waited, Dulcie pondered what to tell her boyfriend. He'd hear about it all eventually, but if he was sick, she thought, maybe she should let him rest. It wasn't like he could do anything for poor Marco Tesla anyway.

'Wait for the beep,' she cautioned, then went ahead anyway. 'But then, I want to know, did you find anything on Stella Roebuck's computer? I mean, anything that would explain what happened?'

That he could talk about, she figured, without undue excitation.

'Yah,' he started, and she put her fingers on his mouth. As if to distract them both, Esmé extended one hind leg, drumstick style, and started washing. Maybe it was the crowd on the bed or the slant of the pillow, but she promptly fell over, provoking a smile from Dulcie.

'Esmé,' she said. 'You haven't done that since you were a kitten.'

The thermometer beeped then, and Dulcie checked. 'No, you're healthy.' She paused to re-evaluate. 'At least, you don't have a temperature.'

'I'm telling you, I feel great,' Chris said. 'Tired, that's all. Maybe it was some kind of fast-moving virus.'

'Speaking of viruses—' Dulcie lay down, stroking the kitten who now curled up between them—'Stella Roebuck's computer?'

He shook his head, which must have been why Esmé looked up at him. 'Nothing. There was nothing left.'

'Was it a virus?' Even Esmé wanted to know.

'No. If it had been, I'd have been able to find parts of it, most likely. The way most viruses work...'

Dulcie let him talk, even though she didn't understand half of what he was saying. After the strange eating frenzy, he was himself again. He was even using his hands to explain, unfazed by his wounds, and while Esmé was looking up at his long fingers, she was, for now, resisting the urge to attack again.

'Someone must have been really angry at her,' he concluded, and Dulcie realized she'd missed something.

'Angry?' From Chris's smile, she knew she'd been caught out.

'Sorry, sweetie. I tend to go on about this stuff, I know.' He put his hands on top of the coverlet, and Esmé curled up again, tucking her pink nose into her long black tail. 'Basically, I don't think it was malware. It really looks like someone got on to her computer and systematically erased whatever was there. I mean, every copy, from everywhere.' He paused, and when he started speaking again, there was a note of admiration in his voice. 'It's quite hard to do, actually.'

'Would it have taken long?' Dulcie tried to remember how long Stella's laptop had been unattended.

'A little while.' Chris considered the question. 'Some of it would depend on whether you knew what the file was called, and if you knew her system. Why, who was there when it went missing? Kelly didn't want to say.'

Dulcie nodded. 'Stella Roebuck was making all kinds of accusations.' She thought back to the afternoon. 'Paul Barnes—he's one of the visiting bigwigs and, I guess, her old boyfriend—was there briefly. And, well, Renée Showalter was in the area, too.' Chris knew of Dulcie's connections with the Canadian. 'But she wouldn't…' Her voice trailed off, as another idea hit her.

'Chris, you don't think Kelly somehow…you know, by accident? When she was hooking Roebuck up to the audio-visual stuff?'

'No.' He was shaking his head. 'This wasn't an accident. And she said the paper had been there when she left the hotel, so it had to have happened at the Science Center. Wasn't there anyone else there this afternoon?'

'Marco Tesla,' she said. 'But he was…'

'Her boyfriend?' Chris emphasized the word. 'I think we have our answer. Kelly said Roebuck was talking to that other guy, Barnes. Maybe Tesla got jealous. Maybe she was planning on dumping him. Maybe he wanted to sabotage her so she'd have to stay with him.'

He paused, watching Dulcie's face. 'It's your fault, Dulcie,' he said, his voice growing more gentle. 'You've been telling me about these Gothic novels for so long, can you blame me if I see some kind of convoluted plot here? A romance gone bad, or something?'

'It's not that, Chris.' She lay back on the pillow. Es-

mé's fur was soft against her cheek, and she closed her
eyes. The night outside was dark again, the bright moon
still firmly covered by the clouds. If she could just close
her eyes and go to sleep, she could believe that everything was fine. For just a little while. Just until morning.

'Dulcie?' Her boyfriend's voice was quiet, but questioning. 'What's going on, sweetie?'

'Oh, Chris.' Dulcie felt her eyes filling with tears.
The night had just been too long. 'I didn't want to tell
you until the morning. There's been a horrible accident. At least, it must have been an accident. Marco
Tesla is dead.'

TWENTY-SIX

'AND THE CONFERENCE is still going to happen?' Of all the questions Chris had for Dulcie, this was the one that most stumped her. Her best intentions of letting him sleep—and keeping the night's tragedy to herself until morning—had been blown sky high by her bombshell revelation. He had sat up at that point, provoking a squeak of dismay from the cat, and Dulcie had finally revealed all, from Thorpe's unfortunate inebriation to the tragic discovery of Marco Tesla.

'I don't know, Chris.' Dulcie shook her head. She'd tucked her feet under her by then, and was leaning against the wall. Esmé had settled back down, tucking her nose under her tail, and with both of them beside her it should have been quite cozy. If only they hadn't been discussing the death of a fellow human being—and the possible disruption of what should have been the crowning achievement thus far of Dulcie's academic career. 'I don't really see how they can cancel it.'

She could tell he was about to say something, when she continued. 'It's not my paper. Really, Chris.' It wasn't, although she knew she would be sad if her presentation were to be canceled. 'I'll get it published. But just think of all the people who have traveled here. Poor Thorpe.' It might sound like a non sequitur, but she knew Chris would understand. 'He's going to be such a mess tomorrow.'

'Dulcie, can I do anything to help?' Her boyfriend

reached around her. It was awkward to snuggle with Esmé between them, but it was possible. 'Not Thorpe, I mean. For you?'

'I think you already have.' She leaned into him. 'Just to be able to tell you about all this. I hope you don't have bad dreams, now.'

'Don't worry about it, sweetie,' he said, nuzzling the top of her head, before lying down again. 'I'm glad you shared.'

'And no matter what,' she mused, lying beside him. As she began to drift off to sleep a happy thought had hit her. 'I know it's awful,' she said to her boyfriend. 'But it hasn't been a total loss. I mean, because of the conference, I may end up working with Professor Barnes.'

'What?' The speed with which Chris sat up again almost sent Dulcie toppling off the bed. 'What are you talking about?'

'Paul Barnes.' Dulcie turned to face her boyfriend. 'From San Francisco?'

'No,' said Chris, shaking his head.

'You know, the author of *So Many Cities, So Many Hills*?'

'No, Dulcie—wait.' He raised a hand to stop her before she listed more credits. 'It's not what he's written that I'm interested in.'

'That's the point.' Dulcie rushed in to explain. 'I know he hasn't published in a while. But he's working on something now. He told me! And Chris, he said he wants me to work with him.'

'You can't.' He reached for her hand. 'Dulcie, stop. Listen to me.'

'No, I can, Chris. I know I can.' She was fully awake now. 'I know I have to finish my thesis—and I will. But this paper is basically done, and working with Barnes would be huge. I mean, I might have to spend some time out in San Francisco. But, well, maybe he'll end up getting the job here.'

'Dulcie!' Chris rarely raised his voice. He did now, and even Esmé seemed to be paying attention. 'You're not listening. You can't work with Paul Barnes. Not because of whatever it is that he's written or not written, or whatever. Not because he's in San Francisco.

'Dulcie, you can't work with Paul Barnes because he's a suspect. Paul Barnes may have murdered someone at your conference.'

TWENTY-SEVEN

She knew not at first what had awakened her, whether 'twas the storm that split the night, with Lightning that Sear'd its ragged Fissures through the clouds, or the roar of Thunder, rolling o'er the Storm-toss'd clouds. Then she heard Them, their Hellish voices riven by demonic rage. The howls, the howls of the damned, rising up to meet those white-hot shards of fury. 'Twas those that called her forth from her bed. The very shriek of the damned, cast in hellhound form, baying for their Mistress, the Moon, hidden as she was by the storm. Almost, from her window, she could see them, sense their glowing Eyes, red like the infernal flames that tormented and drove them. Almost, she was sure, she could plot their bloody steps as they tore through the forest below, scrambling up rock and river bank, stretching out upon the roadway below. Panting as their claws dug into living Rock and driven by the twin demons of their damnation—appetite and despair—as they made their last desperate push upward. They were coming, she could sense, for her only treasure—for her very life, and for that of her Child, innocent as Spring, who lay peaceful in Slumber, still, upon the unmade bed.

Dulcie woke with a start that caused Esmé, still sleeping beside her, to mew in protest. Extricating herself from the sheets, and Chris's arm, she slipped out of bed and walked to the kitchen. The howls, what was it with the howls? The dream, she understood. It had been a harrowing night, and while telling Chris about it may have made it possible for her to fall asleep, what she had seen was bound to haunt her. His suspicions about Paul Barnes had shaken her further, and that diner coffee hadn't helped either, she realized, swallowing the acid taste that had filled her mouth. Something soothing. Warm milk, or maybe cocoa, was in order.

Moving as quietly as she could, she put the kettle on. Instant hot chocolate was easy, and as she pulled the box from the cabinet, she heard soft footsteps approaching her.

'*What do you most fear, little one?*' The voice was as calming as any warm drink would be, but Dulcie retrieved the envelope anyway. Too often, if she turned to see Mr Grey, even his voice would disappear.

'Thanks for coming, Mr Grey.' She poured the powder into a mug, just as a formality. A low purr greeted her, but at the same time she felt the slight rake of claws across her bare feet. She'd been asked a question. 'I guess I'm afraid of a couple of things.' While the water boiled, she tried to articulate her feelings. 'Okay, this sounds bad, and I know it, but I'm afraid that Tesla's death is going to ruin everything.' Another scrape, harder this time. 'Hurt the conference,' she explained. 'Or, no, hurt someone I care about.' She paused to consider her own words. 'I don't think that Renée Showalter can really be involved, but, well, she was there. And Paul Barnes was too. And I—well, I really want the chance to work with him.' She paused, hearing how selfish her words sounded. 'It's not just that, Mr Grey. He's kind of a hero to me.' No, that wasn't it either. 'I like him.'

She dug a spoon out of the drawer and idly stirred

the powdered cocoa. 'I guess I'm afraid that this will be more than just a horrible accident, and that it will bring down the people I care about.'

A low rumble with a distinctly questioning tone seemed to fill the kitchen.

'Even Thorpe,' she answered it. 'I know he's a pain, but he means well.'

The purr came back, and with it, a sense of peace. 'He has Tigger now, though, right? Won't Tigger look after him?'

The purr grew, but Dulcie wasn't entirely satisfied. Even after all this time with Mr Grey, she had no idea how these ghostly visitations worked. 'Well, I hope he will,' she concluded. The kettle had started to whistle, and she grabbed it. The generous part of her wanted not to disturb Chris. The selfish side wanted Mr Grey to herself.

'*Now, now, little one.*' The purr was gone, and Dulcie felt a stab of guilt.

'I'm sorry, Mr Grey.' She stared down into her cup. The steam was rising in lazy curls, each turn looking just a bit like a graceful tail. 'I know you love him, too. I know you're big enough for us both.' The silence that followed made her afraid she had lost him, and she felt the tears start to gather. 'I just wanted you all to myself, like the old days.'

Nothing, and as she swallowed, she felt a tear fall on to her hand. Then she felt it, the brush of fur. A cat—a larger one than Esmé—was twining around her ankles. A wet nose brushed her calf, and whiskers tickled her knee. She wanted, more than anything, to reach down and pick up the friend she knew was not there, and as she felt him circle again, she gave in. Closing her eyes, lest she dispel the magic, she reached for him. His long fur, silkier than Esmé's, rubbed against her cheek as she buried her face where his ruff would be. His scent, like baby powder, overwhelmed the aroma of the hot chocolate, and she let the tears flow.

'I didn't think it would be this hard, Mr Grey,' she said, her words barely audible as she buried her face in his unseen fur.

'*Mrrup?*' Cat-like, the question seemed to hold multiple possibilities.

'My thesis. The conference.' She drew in a breath. '*Living with Chris. Everything.*'

Rather than explain it all, she let the memories go through her. Living with someone who was out every night had been bad enough. Now that he was around more, she found she missed her solitary time. 'I almost feel like I knew him better when he wasn't around,' she said to her one-time pet. 'Like, these last few days, I've seen him a lot, but he's different somehow.'

'*Mrrrr...*' The purr started up again, soothing the raw feelings she had just exposed. '*Seeing is not everything, is it, little one?*'

She had to smile as she shook her head. 'No, Mr Grey. I've learned that.'

'*What*—' the voice grew lower and, Dulcie felt, more serious—'*do you fear?*'

'I wish I—' She stopped herself. Something in his voice, or the way the small body seemed to tense in her arms, had warned her. This was not a question to answer lightly. She had to think.

Maybe she was worried about him? His strange sickness—even his sudden recovery seemed unusual and unlike the man she loved. Then there were his hands, the bloody lines that ran from the back of his fingers up past his wrists. Even if they had come from Esmé, the little cat would not have attacked him unprovoked, would she? As Dulcie thought it through, a dozen other memories came flooding in. The undergraduates, talking in the café. Kelly's tale of the unlatched door to the Science Center—and the damaged lock. Her nightmare. The howls she had heard, out in the moonlight. Those howls that she had heard before, also at the time of the full moon.

Marco Tesla's body, his skin so pale under that hideous moon.

'I'm afraid…' She paused, unsure even how to phrase what was in her mind. 'I'm afraid something has happened—is happening to—Chris,' she said finally. 'I'm afraid he's changing. I'm afraid he's—'

'Dulcie, you're up.' She opened her eyes and realized her arms were empty. She was standing in the dark kitchen, her cup of cocoa cooling on the counter. And her boyfriend was standing before her, pale in the fading moonlight.

'What is it, Dulcie?' He came toward her, a look of alarm on his face.

She blinked and shook her head. The nightmare, it had gotten to her. 'It's nothing,' she said, smiling up at her boyfriend. 'I had one of those dreams.' He knew her well enough to understand: Gothic novels were spooky enough often to haunt her sleep. And if sometimes they had other, deeper messages for Dulcie, well, that was something she hadn't been entirely candid with Chris about. For now, she'd let it be a nightmare.

'It's okay, though,' she tied up her brief summary of the fearful vision. 'Mr Grey was comforting me.'

'In the dream?' He didn't wait for an answer. 'That's nice.' He gave her a half-hearted hug and turned the stove back on. 'I guess it makes sense though. The night you've had. Is there any more of that hot chocolate?' He started rummaging in the cabinet, and she pushed the box toward him.

This was crazy, she told herself. This was *Chris*, her boyfriend, waking up in the middle of the night to take care of her.

'I guess,' she said. What he was saying made sense. The only thing that didn't was her gut. Even as he had hugged her, she had felt the hairs on the back of her neck stand up, as if...'Is Esmé still in the bed?'

'No.' He fixed his mug. 'She bolted. I guess my waking scared her.'

'Nothing scares Esmé.' She meant it as a joke, but her own words gave her pause. 'Chris?'

'What?' He turned toward her, but something about the light—the shadows from the trees outside—obscured his face.

'Never mind,' she said, suddenly chilled. 'That nightmare shook me. I'm going to try to get back to sleep.'

'Good idea.' He sipped his cocoa. 'I'll be in soon.'

But although Dulcie lay awake and wide-eyed for hours, watching the shadows creep across the ceiling as the moon faded away, she did not hear him come back to bed.

TWENTY-EIGHT

THE MORNING LIGHT woke her. That and the sound of Chris rumbling in the kitchen. It was such a familiar clatter—the coffee maker, cereal bowls—that for a moment Dulcie was utterly content. Then she remembered the nightmare, and her own strange apprehensions about the man who even now was probably scooping out French roast. Not to mention the mess of a conference, and the man who had died at its launch party.

'Morning, sweetie.' The man who looked up from the silverware drawer when she came in was undeniably Chris. 'I know you have to get an early start today, but I wanted to let you sleep as late as possible.'

'Thanks.' She accepted a mug with gratitude. Chris made the coffee stronger than she did. Today she needed it. 'I should go see Thorpe first thing.'

'He'll be a ray of sunshine.' He handed her the milk. 'And Dulcie?'

She doctored her coffee, waiting for what she knew was coming.

'About that other professor—Barnes?'

Taking a deep breath, she dove in. 'Chris, I'm not committed to anything. We haven't even spoken. He simply left me a message.' She knew this sounded like a concession, and she didn't want to give him false hope. 'But I have to follow up on this. I have to.'

He looked at her in wordless misery.

'Chris, this is just too good a chance to miss.' She felt

awful. But what could she do? 'I'll be careful, sweetie. I'll talk to Professor Showalter before I do anything.'

'And that detective?' Chris had met Rogovoy and, Dulcie suspected, talked to him about Dulcie's tendency to get involved in things.

'I'll tell him, Chris. I promise.' She paused, trying to weigh her feelings. 'I just can't see him as, well, as a killer. And besides, Chris, we don't know what happened yet. It could have been an accident. Everyone was drinking.'

'You're right.' He reached for the pot and refilled his cup. 'I'm sorry for making such a fuss. Is there anything I can do?'

'You can refill me.' She held her mug out. The coffee was good, and Dulcie could feel her brain waking up. 'Beyond that, does it make any sense to take a second pass at that computer?' Before Chris could argue the negative, she went on. 'I mean, at least to buy us some time?'

'Got it.' He nodded. 'I could definitely take another look at it. I believe Kelly still has it down at tech services. Do you want me to talk to that professor?'

Dulcie shook her head. 'No, I couldn't ask that of you. I'll tell Thorpe that you're working on it—and he'll let Stella Roebuck know. Maybe she won't care, but it couldn't hurt.'

'Who knows?' Her boyfriend stared down into his mug. 'Maybe that's what Mr Grey was talking about.'

His voice was soft, but Dulcie sat up. 'Mr Grey?'

Her boyfriend shrugged. 'I think so. I mean, maybe it was a dream.' She waited, curiosity battling with a twinge of jealousy.

'It probably wasn't even him, Dulcie.' He must have seen the latter emotion on her face. 'Probably my own sense of competence—or lack thereof.' He tried to smile. 'It's just that I woke up thinking that I had to keep looking. That there was something there, or a trace of something—something about authorship.'

'Authorship?' That sounded so much like some of Dulcie's dreams that she didn't know how to respond.

'I'm sorry, I wish I could be sure.' Chris poured the rest of the coffee. 'I thought he said something about "an author". But maybe it was "another". Another author? Who knows what it meant, what *he* meant,' he said, as he retreated to the bedroom to dress. 'But I've got to keep looking. Maybe I'll even find something.'

TWENTY-NINE

FULLY CAFFEINATED AND with a renewed sense of purpose, Dulcie headed toward the little clapboard that housed the departmental headquarters. Today was going to be awful, there was no way around it. But the knowledge that Chris was on her side—that Chris was Chris again—made her optimistic. No, he didn't like the idea of her working with Paul Barnes, but he seemed to accept her plan. And he was going to have another whack at Stella Roebuck's computer.

Even the weather seemed to be obliging. It was cold, something would be seriously wrong if New England weren't cold in December, but the stray clouds of the night before had cleared away, leaving the day as clear and fresh as a mint. Wintergreen, Dulcie thought to herself. Or, more accurately, winter blue.

Blue certainly described the mood at the English department headquarters, although peacefulness had no place in it. Dulcie felt the atmosphere the moment she walked in, perhaps because of the look on Nancy's face.

'You heard?' she asked the kindly secretary, her voice low. Suddenly her own relative optimism seemed out of place.

Nancy nodded. 'The police have been here, and the phone has been ringing constantly.' She was talking softly too, and paused to look up toward the stairs, where Martin Thorpe had his office. 'I'm hoping he can have a little time now to get himself together.'

'He must be a wreck.' It wasn't always easy to sympathize with her adviser. Today was an exception.

'To be honest, I'm a little worried about him.' Nancy leaned in for her confidence. 'He's positively sick.'

'I'm not surprised.' Dulcie responded, thinking of the last time she had seen Thorpe. 'But, you know, to some extent he did it to himself.'

Nancy's head jerked back, and Dulcie realized that the secretary had misunderstood.

'I don't mean—' She'd started off wrong. 'I mean, he's probably got the hangover from hell,' Dulcie hurriedly explained. 'I understand the pressure had been enormous. But, Nancy, even before Tesla—even before the accident—Thorpe was three sheets to the wind.'

'Excuse me?' Nancy was clearly taken aback, and Dulcie immediately felt guilty.

'I'm sorry. I don't mean to be rude,' she said. 'But he was awfully drunk last night.'

'That's not possible.' Nancy was shaking her head. 'Mr Thorpe doesn't drink.'

Dulcie started to protest, but decided against it. Nancy hadn't seen her boss the night before, and maybe it was just as well if she kept a few illusions. Besides, they had bigger problems today, like the phone that had never stopped ringing.

'English and American Literatures and Language.' Nancy was nothing if not professional. Still, Dulcie could tell the call wasn't business as usual by the way the secretary slumped after her perky greeting. 'Yes, I know. We're doing—we're doing everything we can to help.' She paused. 'An awful tragedy.' Another pause. 'Yes, that's true.' An even longer pause. 'We are planning to proceed, with an opening address by Martin

Thorpe.' From the look of her face immediately after that, Dulcie deduced that the caller had hung up.

'Are they all like that?' Dulcie asked.

Nancy nodded, then stopped herself. 'No, not all of them. Too many though.' She leaned back against her desk. It wasn't yet ten a.m., but she looked as tired as Dulcie had ever seen her. 'People don't seem to understand why we're going on with the conference.' She shook her head. 'Marco Tesla's death is a tragedy, nothing less. But we have people from all over the world here for the weekend. Are we just going to send them home?'

'Not before Detective Rogovoy speaks to them.' Too late, Dulcie realized that Nancy had been speaking metaphorically. Seeing the color drain out of Nancy's face, Dulcie hurried to cover up. 'I mean, just to get information. To find out what happened, and everything.'

'I thought—I thought...' Nancy looked positively grey.

'Nancy, please, sit down.' Dulcie pulled her desk chair out and maneuvered the plump secretary into it. 'Put your head down, between your knees. May I get you some water?'

'How will I drink with my head down like this?' The face that turned to look up at Dulcie had a bit of pink in it.

'Sorry, I wasn't thinking.' A wave of relief swept over Dulcie; Nancy wasn't the fainting sort.

'No, it was I who didn't think.' Nancy sat up but stayed seated. 'I'd heard that Professor Tesla had fallen. I just assumed, well, the worst.'

'That he'd been drinking?' Dulcie was still hoping that the fall would be deemed an accident. That would be bad enough. But Nancy was shaking her head.

'No, though I wouldn't blame the poor man.' She looked up at Dulcie. 'Considering what he was going through.'

'Nancy, what are you talking about?' Dulcie felt like they'd jumped into a different conversation. 'What was Marco Tesla going through?'

Nancy looked down at her hands. 'It's not for me to say, really. And it certainly isn't for me to judge.'

'Nancy?' Dulcie was getting an idea, but that idea didn't make sense. 'What are you saying?'

'Well, that the poor man simply couldn't stand it any more,' Nancy said, her voice both soft and gentle. 'That Marco Tesla committed suicide.'

THIRTY

DULCIE STARED AT the departmental secretary open-mouthed. That was an option she hadn't even considered. 'Suicide?' The word sounded foreign in her mouth.

'I'm sorry, I shouldn't have said anything.' Nancy's eyes darted toward the stairway.

'Nancy, you can't just leave it like that.' Dulcie leaned in. 'Why did you say that? Do you know something?' She paused. 'You have to tell me.'

Nancy only shook her head. 'I never should have mentioned it,' she said. 'It's just that, being here, sometimes I hear things.' Dulcie knew what she was talking about. Among the grad students and much of the faculty, Nancy was such a benign constant that it was easy to forget she was there.

'Who said it was suicide?' She stopped herself. She didn't think there'd been time for anyone to come by this morning. 'I mean, who suggested that Tesla might be considering it?'

It was too late. Nancy only shook her head. 'I really don't think I should talk about it. It was gossip, pure speculation at best, and I probably misheard it, anyway, what with everything going on...' She waved her hand in a gesture that could have encompassed the totality of university politics, as well as the recent tragedy. 'And really, everybody complains about that balcony, with its low railing and all.'

'Fair enough.' Dulcie knew Nancy well enough to

know that, as soft-spoken as the departmental secretary might be, she could also be stubborn, when her principles were engaged. 'Still,' she couldn't help musing, 'suicide…that would be so wonderful.' Even as the relief flowed into her, Dulcie felt Nancy tense. 'I'm sorry,' Dulcie back-pedaled. 'I just mean, as opposed to the alternative.'

That wasn't much better. The kindly secretary was staring at her, mouth agape.

'Nancy,' Dulcie rushed to explain. 'I'm afraid—no, I've *been* afraid that it wasn't an accident, but that it was, you know, someone pushed—'

'You mean murder?' Nancy's pitch rose and for a moment Dulcie was afraid that the poor woman would start yelling. Before she could explain, another voice broke in.

'Who is calling it murder?' Thorpe, coming down the stairs, was peering into the room. 'I wasn't told there was a ruling yet.'

'I'm sorry.' Nancy was on her feet. Dulcie reached for her, to urge her to sit, but the older woman had already stepped toward Thorpe. 'We weren't gossiping,' she added. Thorpe didn't seem convinced. 'Ms Schwartz was simply telling me what she knew.'

'And that's not gossiping.' Thorpe shook his head, and then seemed to regret it, reaching out to steady himself against the door jamb.

'Are you all right, Mr Thorpe?' Nancy took his arm. Even Dulcie had come forward.

'Yes, yes.' He nodded. His closed eyes and the sweat that had broken out on his brow seemed to belie his assertion, but he pulled himself upright. 'I am simply a bit ill.' He pulled a handkerchief from his pants pocket and dabbed at his brow. 'However, that doesn't mean that I have lost the ability to hear.'

'I'm sorry.' Dulcie stepped up. Nancy shouldn't have to take the rap. 'I was telling Nancy that Detective Rogovoy—he's the cop who questioned me—was implying that someone, well, that someone may have helped Marco Tesla to fall.'

Thorpe's brow wrinkled, sweat popping out again. 'But I thought I heard…'

'You did.' Nancy took his arm and led him toward her chair. 'I'm afraid that's what I may have said, when I heard about what had happened. Because of what happened with his paper and all. Here.' She quickly filled a cup of water. 'Please drink this, Mr Thorpe. You appear unwell.'

He nodded and took a sip. 'It is the strangest thing,' he said finally. 'I don't feel like myself this morning.'

'Paper?' Dulcie looked over at Nancy, hoping to catch the secretary's eye. She did, but the older woman simply shook her head in a censorious manner.

'I wonder if I ate or drank something that was off?' He wiped his brow again. Dulcie opened her mouth, but one look from Nancy shut her down.

'Could it have been the punch, sir?' Her tone was solicitous. 'Perhaps, with all the distractions, you might have overindulged?'

Dulcie had to hand it to her. The way Nancy was asking, tying one on was a logical move.

'No.' With a shake of his head, Thorpe rejected the possibility. 'I know about those punches. I didn't…' He paused, his hand to his forehead. 'Oh, my head.'

Dulcie looked at the man. It was possible that he was innocent. The cider, for example, had been just as deadly as the punch. Of course, there was another option, one that now sprang into her thoughts.

'Mr Thorpe, why don't you tell us about how you ended up leaving the party last night? And when?' She was watching her adviser, but the quick movement of Nancy's head made her turn. The secretary was scowling, as much as she could, and mouthing the word 'no'.

'I don't mean to imply anything,' Dulcie said, as much to Nancy as to the man seated before her. 'Nothing of the kind. It's only, well, I could be wrong, but I definitely got the impression from Detective Rogovoy that he suspected some kind of foul play.' She paused, trying to figure out a wording that wouldn't upset her adviser even more. 'And I don't believe you were one of the partygoers who stayed around to be questioned.'

'Well, I know I felt unwell.' Thorpe looked up at her, his face pale as paste. 'That's why I left when I did. I'm sure I left before all of…all of this happened. I must have. But before that…it's strange. It's all a bit unclear now.' He mopped at his temples.

'Unclear?' Dulcie paused to consider her phrasing. 'Then, how do you know when you left?'

Thorpe shook his head. 'I know I saw Paul Barnes and that woman—'

'Stella Roebuck?' Dulcie broke in, but Thorpe kept on talking.

'No, no,' he said. 'The redhead. Big woman. The one you—' He paused.

'Renée Showalter.' She finished his sentence.

'Yes, they were talking. Arguing, I think, and they left. I thought I saw her go upstairs. Maybe they both did? I'm not sure. But I know I meant to follow, when I—when I was taken ill.'

'Dulcie, I don't think we should be questioning Mr Thorpe right now.' Nancy had her stern voice on. 'The conference doesn't start until three, and I think it would be best if Mr Thorpe was allowed to have a nap before then. I think it's time to call a cab and get him home. He—and maybe his friend.' She looked up meaningfully at the ceiling, and Dulcie remembered Tigger.

'Okay. I'll go put the little fellow in his carrier.' She wasn't getting anything from Thorpe. She might have better luck with the kitten who, she noticed, they all refrained from mentioning directly. So much for Thorpe's secret.

But as she turned, her adviser grabbed her wrist. 'Ms Schwartz, wait.' She turned, ready to promise him that she'd be gentle. That she knew about loading cats—even unwilling ones—into carriers. That she wouldn't let the little fellow come to harm.

'No, no, I trust you,' he interrupted her protests. 'But, please, leave him be. I'll be back this afternoon. And Dulcie?' He looked up at her, his eyes sharp beneath his sweaty brow. 'I believe he likes it here. I think he should stay.'

She smiled. The kitten did add warmth to both his office and its occupant. 'We'll just let him be, then.'

He nodded, his mind clearly elsewhere. 'You were asking about the party. About what I was doing,' he said. 'Before the—the event. Are you postulating a theory, Ms Schwartz?'

'I don't know if I'd go that far.' She looked at his shiny face, his pallor. 'But, well, it is a possibility, isn't it?'

He shook his head, which made him go even paler—
with a slight overtone of green.

'I'm thinking someone wanted you out of the way, Mr
Thorpe,' Dulcie said. 'I'm thinking you were poisoned.'

THIRTY-ONE

'THAT'S CRAZY.' THORPE waved off the idea, then immediately seemed to regret it. Shaking his head, Dulcie could see, had brought some of the nausea back. 'Why would anyone…' He paused and swallowed, bringing Nancy in a rush.

'Here you go, Mr Thorpe.' She held a cup up to his lips. 'Please, try to take a little water.'

He sipped, his eyes closed. 'Thank you, Nancy.'

'Maybe you should take a little rest.' She was kneeling by his chair, and he opened his eyes to blink at her.

'How can I? The conference—'

'Doesn't start until three,' Dulcie interrupted. 'Nancy is already handling all the phone calls, and I can liaise with the rest of the faculty.' She paused, trying to think of an incentive. 'You'd be doing me a favor,' she said finally. 'I'd get to meet the attendees. And that's just busy work anyway.'

'You could rest up and work on your talk,' Nancy added.

He reached for the cup, but she helped him hold it. To Dulcie, it seemed clear that he was not well. If this was a hangover, it was the worst she'd ever seen.

'Mr Thorpe, can you remember what you drank last night?'

'Dulcie—' Nancy started to object, but Thorpe raised his hand.

'No, no,' he said. 'That's a legitimate question.' The

hand went to his forehead. 'Ever since you suggested that I—well, that perhaps I was given something, I've been trying to recall exactly what...' He stopped, and Dulcie feared that he was going to be sick.

'I did have some of that cider,' he said, finally. Dulcie and Nancy exchanged a look.

'That cider was stronger than it looked,' Dulcie pointed out.

'Yes, but...' Thorpe took the cup from Nancy and tried another sip. 'I don't believe I drank that much of it. In fact, I handed the glass back to her.'

'To her?' Dulcie tried not to put too much emphasis on the pronoun.

Thorpe understood anyway. 'Yes, but you can't think...well, maybe.'

'Who gave you the drink, Mr Thorpe?' Nancy's protective streak added an urgency to her question. 'Who was she?'

'Your friend.' He made a limp gesture toward Dulcie. 'You know...'

'Trista?' Dulcie's voice squeaked. Her classmate liked to party. Dulcie had often had to dispose of excess beverages handed to her by her friend, but not in this way... Not Thorpe. 'She wouldn't have slipped you anything.'

'That was your idea, not mine.' His tone was growing peevish, which meant he was sounding more like himself again. 'I'm only telling you what I remember. But no, there were several of us...'

They waited while he took another sip. Nancy had handed him the mug by now, and sat down on the floor by his side. 'By the way,' he said, resting the mug on his knee, 'was your other friend, Chris, able to find anything?'

'He's still looking,' Dulcie replied, with a rush of gratitude to her boyfriend. 'He didn't yesterday,' she felt compelled to add. 'But he is going back to it today.'

'Good.' Thorpe nodded, his eyes closing again. 'Perhaps I should take a rest. If you think you two can carry on…'

'Of course we can, Mr Thorpe.' Nancy pulled herself up and returned to her desk. 'I'll call a cab now.'

Dulcie waited while she dialed. By then, Thorpe was leaning his head back, and in the morning light his face looked slick and pale.

'Mr Thorpe?' She wondered if he had fallen asleep.

'Yes?' His answer was not much more than a breath.

'If it wasn't Trista, then who brought you the drink last night?' That punch had been strong. Had it been this strong?

'Your friend, didn't I say?' With a struggle, her adviser sat up.

'You said it wasn't Trista.' Dulcie wondered if the hangover—or whatever it was—had affected his memory.

'No, not Trista.' He looked over. Nancy was on the phone. 'Your other friend. The Canadian?'

'Cab will be here in a minute,' Nancy called over. 'Dulcie, why don't you get Mr Thorpe's coat and…'

'Got it.' Dulcie sprang to her feet. She was happy to have an excuse to leave for a moment, to let what she'd just heard sink in. No matter how much she wanted Showalter to be innocent, Dulcie couldn't see Thorpe intentionally slandering her. With everything that happened, it would be an easy step to say she had poisoned Marco Tesla, too, and Dulcie knew that couldn't have happened. But, if not, why would Thorpe have said that?

He had a kitten now—a very special kitten, if what Dulcie suspected was true. In which case...

She raced up the stairs to Thorpe's office, where the orange kitten was curled on the window sill. Somehow, the sight of the little cat reassured her. He looked so relaxed. So normal. Of course, one didn't usually encounter supernatural powers in the form of a sleeping kitten. But Tigger wasn't an ordinary kitten. And so she took her time, taking Thorpe's thick wool coat down from its hook and folding it carefully over her arm, all the while wondering how she could interrogate the little creature about his person.

Finally, she settled on the direct approach, abandoning the coat to lift the sleeping feline from the sill and ask her question as straightforwardly as she could.

'Has Martin Thorpe done something?' she asked, staring into the blue eyes that blinked sleepily up at her. It was a vague question, she knew that, but there had been so much going on, she didn't know what, exactly, to ask. 'Is he lying?'

'*Mrup?*' The little feline mewed up at her, asking, she was sure, for a clarification. 'What about Renée Showalter?' She tried to visualize the red-haired academic. The cat was silent. 'Poison?' Nothing. 'Drugs—something in the drink?'

'*Mrew!*' She looked down. A small paw was reaching up through the top of the carrier. Did the kitten want out, or was he telling her something?

'Tigger, do you have a message for me?'

'Dulcie!' It was Nancy she heard, calling from the first floor. 'The cab is here.'

She put the cat back down, wondering how she could stall for more time. 'I'm coming!' she yelled over her shoulder, before turning back to the little cat. 'Tigger, please. Is there anything I should know about?' There had been so many misadventures over the past twenty-four hours, she didn't know where to start. 'Was Thorpe involved with something else? With Stella Roebuck's computer?' She paused, hesitant even to mention the bigger crisis. 'With Marco Tesla?'

'*Naow!*' It wasn't a howl, but it was a protest. And while it could have been simply the sleepy animal waking—or being startled as Dulcie once again hefted the bulky duffel coat—Dulcie held her breath. '*Anaow!*'

'What, Tigger? Please?' She heard Nancy call her again, an edge of worry creeping into her voice.

'Is Martin Thorpe guilty in some way?' she asked again, trying to leave the question as open-ended as possible. 'Did he do something?'

The kitten only yawned and stretched out one paw, showing the pink pads under the orange fur.

'*Another.*' It wasn't exactly the sound the kitten had made, but Dulcie heard the word as clear as a bell. Another—another suspect? Someone else? Or, no, she'd been asking about Marco, Stella's lover.

'Dulcie?' Nancy was sounding a little frantic, so with a sigh Dulcie headed down the stairs, the little cat now chirping quietly to himself as she descended.

'I was beginning to worry,' said Nancy. With her usual efficiency she took the coat from her and bustled him into it, and sent Dulcie on ahead to the cab.

'Tigger, if you can hear me, please send me a signal,' she whispered to the wind as she opened the taxi door.

'You talking to me, ma'am?' The cabbie craned his neck around.

'No, sorry.' She retreated, in time to let Thorpe slide in.

'Take care of yourself,' Nancy called from the doorway. 'If you don't feel up to making the address...'

'I'll be there,' said Thorpe. The cold air seemed to have revived him already. 'I wouldn't miss this for the world.'

Dulcie was standing there watching the cab drive away when Nancy called to her. 'Dulcie, come in! It's freezing out.'

Slowly, she climbed the steps back into the little house.

'What's wrong, Dulcie?' The secretary seemed finally to have noticed her distracted state. 'Don't tell me you're feeling ill, too?'

'No, I'm fine,' she responded. 'It's just...' She shook her head and sat down in the secretary's chair. Somehow she just couldn't bring herself to tell Nancy Pruitt that according to what she had learned, Martin Thorpe might have been involved with Marco Tesla's death. And, from what her adviser had said, that he might have been poisoned by her mentor, Renée Showalter.

THIRTY-TWO

For better or worse, Nancy hadn't forgotten.

'Oh, Dulcie.' Nancy collapsed in the chair Thorpe had vacated. 'You don't think that someone really poisoned Mr Thorpe, do you?'

'I don't know.' Dulcie pushed back from the secretary's desk and considered rising. There was so much she didn't want to say. There had to be another explanation. 'All I can tell you is that he seemed really loaded. And, well, he is really sick today. Unless…' she paused, her mood suddenly lighter, 'you think it was an act?'

'An act? Please, Dulcie, you have already made that poor man's life miserable.' Nancy didn't need to remind her of how she had suspected Thorpe of foul play before. 'You can't really think he'd feign intoxication, can you?'

'I don't know,' she said again. This time with less conviction. After all, Dulcie couldn't explain, not without telling Nancy what Thorpe had said. But she could see the possibility—it would be a neat way for the acting department head to tarnish the reputation of one of the contenders. It would have been a pretty elaborate ruse, however, since it relied on someone else to suggest the very idea of poisoning. But the alternative—that Showalter had really slipped something into Thorpe's drink—seemed even worse. She'd built so many of her hopes around the visiting scholar, and looped Mina in, too.

Slumped in her chair, Dulcie considered the options.

'I'm trying to think of another explanation, another...'
She'd run out of ideas.

Or had she? A tickle of a memory interrupted her
musing. Tigger, the kitten: had he been trying to tell her
something? Something about 'another'. Chris had said
something similar—something he'd heard in a dream,
or no, from Mr Grey.

'*Another...an author*...' Chris had said he wasn't sure
what Mr Grey had said to him. He wasn't even sure it
had been Mr Grey. Dulcie, however, didn't doubt that
her late, great pet had reached out. Especially since
the kitten's vocalization had been so similar. 'Another.
Okay, then,' she said to herself. 'Another author? Another author of what?'

'Excuse me, dear?' Nancy's voice broke into her reverie. 'Did you say something about another offer?'

'What? I'm sorry.' Dulcie backtracked. 'I'm just
thinking of what I have to do today.' *Another offer?*
Maybe that was it.

But what did it mean?

The possibilities were endless. Maybe Mr Grey—
or Tigger—was trying to reach Mr Thorpe to let him
know that he would have another job offered to him.
Maybe, she thought, the message was for Chris—or
for her. In which case maybe it pertained to the message from Paul Barnes. Today, she decided, she would
have to pin him down, whether or not she could talk to
Renée Showalter first. This had gone on long enough.

Of course, she wasn't the only one looking at her options. Stella Roebuck seemed to have been entertaining
offers, if they could be called that, from different suit-
ors. Which brought her back to Marco Tesla.

Sitting with Nancy now, it seemed far-fetched. At

any rate, she couldn't explain the kitten factor to Nancy Pruitt. 'No,' she said now, answering Nancy's question. 'I can't see Thorpe trying to frame anyone. He's not the type.'

'Besides, Marco Tesla wasn't the top candidate for his job,' said Nancy, to Dulcie's surprise.

'Nancy, you have inside information, don't you?'

The secretary blushed. 'I'm sorry. I guess it's that I've spent so much time around you all, I've caught the political bug. And this job is so important to Mr Thorpe that I can't help listening in occasionally.'

'And?' Dulcie waited with bated breath. As much as she wanted Renée Showalter to be hired, she knew it would break her adviser's heart. Then again, if Paul Barnes got it…

But Nancy was shaking her head. 'No, I really can't,' she said. 'I don't really know anything. I've simply heard some things.'

'Please, Nancy.' Dulcie leaned in. 'You've already told me that Tesla wasn't the top candidate. Can you tell me anything more?'

'Well, I really shouldn't be talking about this.' Nancy suddenly seemed very interested in the papers on her desk.

'Nancy, please.' Dulcie didn't want to annoy her, but still…'This could be important. It could be a motive.'

When Nancy looked up, her eyes were large with sorrow. 'That's what I'm afraid of, Dulcie.'

'Oh no,' Dulcie said. 'I knew it. Thorpe still has the edge!'

'No, that's not it at all.' Nancy cut her off. 'And I really shouldn't be talking about this. I only know about it because Mr Thorpe had me type up some notes from a meeting.'

'A meeting?' Dulcie was beginning to feel like a parrot.

Nancy nodded. 'It's cruel, really. But as the acting director of the department, he sits in on the planning committee meetings. Unless, I gather, they are discussing his candidacy specifically.' The papers on her desk could not be neater, and she sat back down. 'It just isn't fair.'

Dulcie agreed, in principle. Right now, however, she just wanted to hear what Nancy knew. 'Yes?'

'Well, it seems that, on the strength of her presentation, the general feeling was that Stella Roebuck might be chosen for the job. There was so much talk about her groundbreaking research and the new directions of her theories, and all. As if novelty were by itself a good thing.' The way Nancy sniffed a bit at that last pronouncement reminded Dulcie of Thorpe. The sentiment, she was sure, had been adopted from the balding scholar, probably in sympathy. 'If it weren't for this paper, however, I gather that Mr Thorpe would have about even odds—or, at least, the same odds as your friend from Canada, Professor Showalter.'

That was interesting. But Dulcie felt she was missing something. 'So nobody would have had a professional motive to harm Marco Tesla.'

'Exactly,' Nancy jumped in. 'And now, that poor Ms Roebuck. I heard that she's having problems with her paper—and now she's lost her boyfriend? That's just a lot to bear.'

'It is,' Dulcie thought. It was also a damned good way to unsettle the top contender for a job everybody wanted. She didn't know what had happened to Marco

Tesla, but if both Martin Thorpe and Renée Showalter were running a close second to Stella Roebuck, she had to consider that maybe more than one crime had taken place at the conference. And that her preferred candidate, Renée Showalter, had as much motive as anyone else.

Before the silence could grow any more uncomfortable, the phone rang again, and Nancy was back to business, communicating with the surviving presenters. All, Dulcie could hear, were in agreement that the conference should proceed.

'I'm sure Mr Thorpe could say something in the opening address,' Nancy suggested in one of the lulls. 'But after that...'

She'd shrugged. Dulcie wasn't really surprised, although the departmental secretary did seem a little deflated by the participants' unflagging enthusiasm.

'The show must go on, Nancy,' Dulcie had offered. 'It's best for Mr Thorpe, too.'

That had won a grudging nod from the departmental secretary, who had gone back to the phone, making sure that every campus representative knew that the three o'clock address was still on. Dulcie, meanwhile, headed to the Science Center. She didn't know if she'd be able to find out anything else before the conference started. But at the very least, she'd do what she could to make sure nobody else got hurt.

The building was strangely quiet, so much so that at first she wondered if the conference had indeed been canceled after all. It was the construction, she realized after a moment. It had stopped. Although parts of the lobby still seemed to be sheathed in dropcloths, the noise and clatter of the last few days had been at least temporarily curtailed as promised. For that small relief, Dulcie whispered her thanks.

'Dulcie!' She recognized Chris's voice calling to her as she walked into the big lecture hall. She turned to see him climbing down from the sound booth. 'You got my message.'

'No.' Dulcie shook her head as she dug around in her bag for her phone. Sure enough, he had called while she was meeting with Nancy and Thorpe. 'Sorry, I guess I didn't hear. What's up?'

'I may have found something.' Her boyfriend was whispering, but his whisper was as loud as his regular voice. 'On that laptop?' He nodded over toward the front of the auditorium. There, down by the stage, stood Stella Roebuck. All in black, the visiting scholar would have been invisible in the dark if not for her pale, almost luminous face and her hands, which were waving around as she spoke to a young man—a student, Dulcie thought, from his skinny build and too-long hair. Neither of them seemed to have seen her, and Dulcie paused. She ought to check in, she knew. But Chris's news was too tempting. She took her boyfriend's arm and pulled him back toward the auditorium door.

'What did you find?' She leaned in. Chris wouldn't be trying to be quiet if it was something he could share. 'The paper?'

'No.' He shook his head. 'And, to be honest, I'm not sure what it means.'

'Ah, Ms Schwartz? There you are!' Damn, they should have stepped outside. Stella Roebuck had spotted her and was hailing her down toward the stage, that white face looking up expectantly. 'Ms Schwartz, we've been waiting.'

'I'll tell you later.' Chris nodded. 'I'll be in the booth.'

'Coming!' Dulcie descended the ramp. This was what she had signed up for, she reminded herself: to be the contact person for the conference. That meant being at the beck and call of the guests. 'How may I help you?'

Stella Roebuck held up her hand for silence. She wasn't through with her other companion yet. 'And you're telling me that outside media has to go through this university? Through your media office?' She kept questioning the skinny man, who Dulcie now recognized as someone who worked in the dean's office.

'Yes, Ms Roebuck, but—' His Adam's apple bounced as he spoke, and he was going pale beneath his freckles.

'*Professor* Roebuck,' she cut him off, and Dulcie noted the signs of strain that had aged her overnight. 'And so you are responsible for interceding with the press?'

'Well, yes, but—' Another swallow, another bounce.

'Professor Roebuck?' Dulcie knew she was interrupting. It seemed like Freckles could use the help. 'May I be of assistance?'

The hand came up again, and Dulcie wondered if she could go back to Chris. But just as she was about to turn away, the scholar addressed her.

'No, wait,' she said. 'Maybe you can.'

'Excuse me?' Dulcie knew that this woman had been through a trauma, but it still took an effort to be nice. The dean's skinny assistant, she noticed, was slowly backing away.

'I've heard there are people…' She paused, and Dulcie found herself looking up into heavily mascaraed eyes. 'People asking about me.'

Dulcie nodded. Of course there were. 'Because

of the—' She wasn't sure how to phrase it. 'Because of Marco?'

Stella nodded once, quickly. 'The press.'

'Wow.' Dulcie hadn't thought about media. Then she remembered what she'd overheard. 'But it sounds like the university is handling all of that,' she said. 'I'm sure that the dean's office will do its best to shield you from any—'

Stella was shaking her head so rapidly that the peaks of her hair wobbled. 'No, no,' she interrupted Dulcie again. 'It's what they're saying about Marco. It's just not true.'

'What are they saying?' Dulcie felt like everything was going too fast. 'And who?'

'They're saying he was a cheat.' She blinked, and Dulcie could see tears welling up behind the black lashes. 'That *he* stole my paper, that he sabotaged me—for the job. That he did it for this job. And then he…he took his own…' She bit her lip, as if holding back more.

'Who is saying this?' Dulcie repeated. Perhaps she'd been at the university too long, but none of this was making sense. The outside world took notice of deaths—suspicious or otherwise. But it wouldn't care about an academic scandal, would it?

'I've been getting calls.' Stella turned away and blinked again, and Dulcie had to resist the urge to reach out to her. 'But I know who's really behind it.'

Dulcie waited. 'It's Paul,' said Stella, her voice dropping to a husky whisper. 'Paul Barnes. He's jealous, always has been. Ever since I worked for him. And now he's out to ruin Marco's good name.'

'You worked for Professor Barnes?' This was news to Dulcie.

'Researcher, so-called.' She dismissed her history

with a wave of her hand. 'Years ago. It never amounted to anything, of course. But we—'

'Ms—Professor Roebuck?' The assistant was back, a cell phone in a hand that was also spotted with freckles. 'I have the dean on the phone for you.'

Dulcie turned toward him, her mouth open, then back to the visiting scholar. She was nodding, and looking at Dulcie as if she expected a response.

'Um, I didn't know.' It was the best she could come up with. 'Should you take the call?'

Stella took the phone and walked toward the side of the stage, leaving Dulcie to digest what she'd just heard. It didn't change anything; Dulcie knew that. Of course Paul Barnes had had other scholars working with him. Dozens. And those would include other female scholars, of course. If anything, she told herself, it was a good sign. Stella Roebuck was a rising star, and she'd gotten her start with Barnes. That boded well.

Stella's dismissive wave, however—that and her tone of voice. As if Professor Paul Barnes had been the one to owe her. And the implication that the esteemed professor was simply a jealous lover?

No, Stella Roebuck had reason to be distressed. First her paper disappeared, then her boyfriend died. If, on top of that, someone was trying to spoil his good name, then she would be crazy not to be angry. Blaming Paul Barnes, however, was going a bit far.

Unless it wasn't Barnes she was lashing out at. Dulcie stood there, looking at Stella Roebuck's back. Some women, she knew, didn't like working with other women. Maybe Stella Roebuck was one of them. Had Roebuck heard that Barnes had expressed interest in working with Dulcie? Had, perhaps, seen more in Dulcie's work than in Stella's oh-so-hip new paper?

'*Dulcie...*' She heard the voice, but she didn't need to ask what it was about. She knew. Roebuck wasn't jealous of her, not by a long shot. If only Trista were here, she'd be able to get another woman's take on the pixie-like academic. The blonde Trista was, in her own way, just as stylish as the visiting professor. But she'd never looked down on Dulcie. Or Suze: Dulcie's long-time room-mate was as accomplished as any of them; this year, she was clerking for a non-profit law firm that handled some of the highest-profile cases in the country. And she'd never have disparaged her chubbier friend.

'*You have Chris.*' She smiled in the darkness. Yes, she also had Chris; a more true and loving mate she couldn't have asked for. In fact, while Stella was occupied she should check in with him again. Maybe he'd figured out what was going on—then he'd be the hero of the day. She turned, only to see the dean's assistant still standing there, as if mesmerized by Stella Roebuck's back.

'May I help you?' She couldn't just leave him.

'What? Oh, no.' He seemed a bit flummoxed.

'She's quite a handful,' said Dulcie. After all, the freckled man had gotten an earful. 'But, well, she's had a rough time of it.'

He was nodding, so she assumed he agreed—though with which statement she couldn't be sure. 'Are you okay?' He was so thin and so pale, he must be frail.

'Yeah.' He was stunned all right. He turned toward Dulcie, his eyes wide. 'But I think I'm in love.'

Dulcie bit her tongue, hard, to avoid saying something rude, and walked back to the sound booth in search of Chris. Times like this, she almost wished she was back on the commune. Her mother, she knew, would have choice words for those who misappropriated the gifts of the goddess, or something like that.

Then she saw Chris up in the booth and relaxed. So one visiting scholar had been rude to her. That meant nothing. At least she had a live boyfriend. She waved up at his sweet face and waited for him to come down.

And waited. He was talking, she could see now, his face animated and his hands moving as they did when he got excited. And nodding in rapt attention was the media tech, Kelly.

'Yo!' Dulcie had been banging on the booth door for a good ten seconds.

'What?' Chris, looking confused, opened the door for her and stepped back as she clambered in. 'What's wrong?'

'I've been waiting,' Dulcie started in—and caught herself. Here, inside the booth, she could see how dark the auditorium was through the glass. Only the stage was fully visible, illuminated by the safety lights at its sides. 'I'm sorry, Chris. I think the pressure must be getting to me.'

'Working with that one,' Kelly nodded toward the front of the auditorium, even as she rolled a chair toward Dulcie, 'could rub anyone's nerves raw.'

'She's not that bad.' Dulcie sat and looked at where Kelly had gestured, a stab of guilt flooding her with remorse. 'I mean, she has been through a lot.'

'More than you know,' Chris chimed in from near their feet. He was rummaging under the control board now. 'Hang on.'

'So, Kelly.' Something about the limited view sparked a thought in Dulcie's head, and she craned to see as a taller person would. 'You can't really see the auditorium from up here, can you?'

She shook her head. 'It's designed that way. We need light in here to work. If the window were too big, it would shine down on the seats. Besides, we're supposed to be focusing on whatever's up on that stage. Why?'

'I was just wondering.' She looked out at the stage again. The area right before the stage was visible, barely. From what she could see, Stella Roebuck was still on the phone, the skinny assistant still standing by, transfixed. Meanwhile, Chris had surfaced, taking the seat behind theirs. The laptop in his hands reminded her of what she had been half thinking. 'So you couldn't really see who was in the auditorium yesterday, could you?'

'No.' Another shake of her head. 'Not at all. Believe me, Roebuck down there kept asking. But no such luck.'

'Maybe it's just as well,' Chris chimed in. They both turned toward him. 'Dulcie, I heard what she's been saying—that someone has been bad-mouthing that other guy. The one who died?'

Dulcie nodded. 'Yeah, she's really upset about it.'

'I gather.' Chris and Kelly exchanged a glance. Neither seemed as besotted as the assistant. 'But she might be fighting a losing battle.'

'Why?' Dulcie rolled her chair toward him. 'What do you mean?'

'Well, look at this.' He touched the keyboard, and then turned it for Dulcie to see. 'What do you think?'

The page was white, with the rows of symbols and squiggles that Dulcie identified with a corrupted file. 'Is this her paper?' She turned toward her boyfriend.

'What? No, sorry.' He reached over and touched a few keys. The file scrolled down, and Dulcie could see typing. 'This was in her email.'

Dulcie read: '… Not possible…can't go on…' Then more symbols. When she nodded, Chris reached over to make the page scroll down again. 'Ending it,' she read. 'Betrayal.'

'I know she doesn't want to admit it,' Chris said, as she drew back with a gasp. 'It looks like she even tried to erase this. But it's an email from Marco Tesla, and it sure sounds to both of us like it's a suicide note.'

THIRTY-THREE

'HOW COULD SHE?' Dulcie was aghast. 'Doesn't she know that the police think this is a murder?'

'What?' Kelly obviously hadn't heard.

Chris turned to her. 'There's a detective who's sweet on Dulcie.'

'Detective Rogovoy isn't...' She shook her head. 'Never mind. What matters is that Stella Roebuck has tried to destroy evidence.'

'Is it evidence if there was no crime?' Kelly asked. Chris seemed to be considering this, but to Dulcie it was clear as day.

'It's exculpatory.' She'd learned the term from Suze.

'I don't think that means—' Chris shut up when Dulcie swung around to face him.

'Maybe they'll decide it was an accident.' Kelly was playing peacemaker, but Dulcie was shaking her head.

'They're already looking at Renée Showalter,' she said.

'Damn.' Chris slapped his thigh. 'I'm sorry, Dulcie.'

'It's okay,' she responded. 'I doubt they'll—'

'No, I mean, she called.' Chris continued. 'When she couldn't reach you, she tried me.' Seeing her confusion, he explained. 'I guess you weren't answering, so she called the departmental office, and Nancy suggested she try me. I guess it was urgent?'

'Uh oh.' Dulcie dug out her phone. She still hadn't called Lucy back, but her mother could wait. Meanwhile, she had three new messages: the first from Chris, but the other two from a Montreal exchange. 'Excuse me, please.' She turned away from her colleagues and dialed.

'Professor? It's Dulcie.' She bit her lip as she waited for a response. Showalter had said she might have a few minutes to chat today, and Dulcie was afraid she'd missed her chance.

'Oh, hello.' The professor was distracted. Dulcie could hear it in her voice. 'Did you get my message?'

'Just that you'd called.' She looked down at her phone. She probably should have listened to the voice-mail before hitting return. 'I gather you were trying to reach me. I hope I'm not too late and we can still get together. Did you maybe have a chance to look at my paper?'

'Yes, yes, I did.' From the sounds in the background, Dulcie thought the professor was outside. 'It was very impressive, but I did think we ought to talk before you presented it. Some of Ms Love's work on the genealogy of your author seemed especially promising as a new focus of research.'

'I see.' Dulcie stopped herself from saying more. Mina's work had been intended as a minor addition to the paper, a little bonus. Not the focus.

'I'm not saying that the rest of the work doesn't have merit.' Even over the phone, the visiting scholar must have picked up something from Dulcie's reaction. 'Only I've just learned that, well, that there may be some questions about the provenance of some of the research I passed along to you.'

'Questions?' Dulcie barely got the word out. It didn't seem like the professor had heard.

'And so, going forward,' she was saying, 'I think

you may find the genealogy particularly interesting to research. That material is sound as a bell.'

'Okay.' It was all the enthusiasm she could muster, but as soon as the words were out of her mouth, she could have kicked herself. Here was a senior scholar who had gone out of her way to help, even making sure that new documents were made available to Dulcie and Mina. It wasn't her fault if the new material hadn't been properly vetted. That should have been Dulcie's first step. Basic academic discipline, and she'd muffed it.

This was her problem, not Showalter's, and she owed the scholar an explanation, if not an apology. 'I'm sorry,' she said. 'I guess I didn't do my homework. It's just that Thorpe thinks I'm overextended as it is, and he is my thesis adviser.' She paused, wondering how much more she should offer. After all, Showalter was hoping to win Thorpe's job. 'He thinks I should focus on the text,' she said, finally. 'On the accepted text, that is. He's very big on strict textual analysis, with an emphasis on structural procedures.' What she'd said was true, but it felt like she was stabbing her adviser in the back to say it. The word 'traitor' sprang into her mind, or rather...

'That would be a betrayal of your instincts,' Showalter snapped back. That was the word: betrayal. 'Of everything you've been working for.'

'That's what I think, too.' The confirmation was invigorating. They were clearly on the same wavelength. That word, though...'Professor, did you know Marco Tesla?'

Too late, Dulcie remembered Trista's gossip. She hadn't been able to visualize her mentor with the young fop, that didn't mean they hadn't had some kind of relationship—some romantic connection.

'That poor man.' To Dulcie's relief, Showalter didn't

seem unduly upset. 'No, I knew him by reputation, and I had something I wanted to discuss with him. Well, I guess that's not pressing now. You might speak to Stella Roebuck about him, if you're curious. Or Paul.'

'Paul Barnes?'

'Why, yes. They've been talking about a project,' said Showalter. Dulcie could hear what sounded like a bus in the background. Her next words were almost drowned out: '...very confidential.'

'I'm sorry.' Dulcie raised her own voice. 'I'm having trouble hearing you. You said Paul Barnes and Marco Tesla worked together?' She paused, unsure how to phrase her next question. 'I thought maybe there was some conflict between them.' She didn't want to say Stella Roebuck's name.

'You mean about Stella Roebuck?' Showalter didn't seem so easily fazed. 'Yes, there was some history between them.'

So that was what Dulcie had missed. 'She accused Paul Barnes of sabotaging her—of erasing her work.'

'Of *erasing* it?' Dulcie wasn't sure, but she thought she heard Showalter laugh. 'He wouldn't do that. And, well, I know he was in communication with Marco these last few days. I believe he's the reason Tesla came to the conference.'

'Really?' This was news, and she strained to hear more over the traffic.

'I believe it was something to do with his latest paper,' said Showalter. 'I'm not entirely sure. He and I have been discussing another matter.'

This was Dulcie's opening. 'He called me, you know.' She waited a moment. 'I was hoping we could talk.'

'I was, too, Dulcie,' said the professor. 'It's—well, it's complicated. We should speak in person. I'm sorry.'

For a moment, Dulcie thought the professor was apologizing for the noise. She wasn't. 'I'm afraid I'm going to be busy up until the conference starts. That's what my message was about. I thought this morning would be good, but I'm running around.'

'So I hear,' said Dulcie, her hopes sinking. 'Maybe I can meet you?'

'I've got to run out to the airport,' the professor explained. 'Though I should be back by the opening address. Three, isn't it?'

'Yes.' Dulcie was reduced to monosyllables.

'I'll bring your paper along then. At the very least, we can go over my notes.'

'Thanks,' said Dulcie, and let her go.

'What was all that about?' Kelly was the one to ask. Chris only looked at her with sympathy.

'Showalter.' Dulcie shrugged. 'We keep missing.'

'I'm sorry, hon.' Chris reached out to put his hand on her shoulder. 'It seems like everyone is running around like a headless chicken today.'

She nodded. 'Maybe it's just as well that Showalter isn't here this morning. I'm supposed to get Paul Barnes set up and—' She stopped. 'Did you know that Paul Barnes was working with Marco Tesla on a paper?'

Both her colleagues shook their heads.

'Isn't that strange?' Dulcie asked. 'I mean, if they were both in love with Stella Roebuck?'

'Oh?' Kelly looked interested. Chris only smiled.

'Dulcie,' he said. 'I doubt anyone was really in love with that woman. She just likes to think they are. Maybe some of them play along.'

'I don't know, Chris.' Dulcie was already thinking ahead. Neither Kelly nor Chris were privy to the departmental gossip. 'I mean, if she drove Marco Tesla to suicide…'

'You think that was because of her?' He touched the laptop, waking its screen. 'Betrayal. I don't know, Dulcie, that could mean a lot of things.'

'Trust me on this, Chris.' Dulcie looked over at the glowing words. 'In this case, I'm pretty sure it was a betrayal of the heart.'

Kelly, perhaps wisely, stayed out of the discussion. And Chris, ultimately, bowed to Dulcie's superior knowledge of the players. But neither seemed convinced that Stella Roebuck had had any part in her colleague's death.

'Beyond hiding its cause, of course,' Chris had concluded. Once Dulcie had brought Kelly up on the investigation, however, they had both agreed that Rogovoy should be informed. If they were even considering questioning Showalter—or anyone—about a possible homicide, this email was important.

'Do you want me to take it up to him?' Chris had offered. 'I mean, I know you're busy.'

'No.' She shook her head. 'I'll have to explain.' She caught herself. 'I mean, Chris, Rogovoy knows me. He knows that I always get involved.'

'True.' He smiled back at her. 'I just thought, with Ms Stella down there…'

'Good goddess.' Dulcie jumped up. She'd not meant to be away this long. 'I should get back.'

'No rush.' Kelly was looking through the glass, and the other two followed her line of sight. 'I think she's occupied.' Sure enough, Stella Roebuck was deep in conversation with a tall, grey-haired man.

'Who is that?' Chris leaned over Dulcie. 'He's not from the university, is he?'

'No,' said Dulcie softly, and a little sad. 'That's Paul Barnes.'

THIRTY-FOUR

'PROFESSORS.' DULCIE HAD on her best cheery voice. 'May I help you?' This was her opportunity. Her chance to talk to Barnes. Yes, Showalter had suggested that she and Dulcie should confer first, but Dulcie couldn't let a chance like this go by. Besides, it was her responsibility to help the conference attendees.

'There you are.' Stella sounded annoyed.

'I'm sorry.' Dulcie tried to smile. 'I was actually speaking with the computer tech about your laptop.'

'Ah, Ms Schwartz, is it?' Dulcie smiled and nodded. 'Ms Roebuck was telling me about her problems.' Paul Barnes sounded unnaturally formal. That might, Dulcie thought, be why Stella Roebuck turned to stare at him. 'With her paper?' he added.

'Yes.' Dulcie looked from one to the other. Just yesterday, Stella Roebuck had accused Barnes of sabotage. Today it didn't seem like she was going to pursue that charge. 'She told you about it?'

'Yes.' He nodded. 'So regrettable, these computer viruses.'

'Is that what Chris said?' Dulcie kicked herself. She should have asked her boyfriend what he had told the scholar.

'Chris?' Stella's face lit up, the fatigue gone. 'Is that his name?'

'Yes.' Dulcie waited, determined not to be annoyed.

'He's your sweetheart, isn't he?' asked Stella. Dulcie hadn't expected that, and with horror realized she was blushing.

'He's the best in the department,' she responded. 'I mean, he's not a media tech, but when it comes to computer sciences...' Her ears were growing hot.

'Well, I'm afraid he hasn't said much of anything to me.' Stella seemed to have moved on. 'We were simply assuming it was a virus.'

'But yesterday...' She paused. Paul Barnes was standing there, listening.

'Yesterday, I was very upset.' Stella sucked on her wine-dark lips, as if thinking over her next words. 'About work, I mean,' she said. 'Today, well, today everything looks a little different.'

'Of course it does.' Barnes wrapped an arm around her shoulders. 'We're all shaken.'

Dulcie looked from one to the other. She had wanted to ask Barnes about his phone call, to urge him to file his application to work in the Mildon, but her job had to come first. 'So you don't think the—ah—loss of your paper was intentional?' She wasn't going to repeat what Stella had said. It didn't matter; the woman was shaking her head so vigorously her spikes bobbed.

'No,' she was saying. 'I wasn't thinking. I'd been—I was worried about a friend.'

That was Dulcie's cue. 'About Marco Tesla?'

It seemed that Paul Barnes' arm tightened around Stella's shoulders as she nodded, biting her lip. It was a wonder, Dulcie noted, that the woman had any lipstick left on at all.

'Don't you think you should say something then?' Dulcie suggested. 'Just to help everyone understand?'

'Understand what?' Paul Barnes was looking at

Stella Roebuck. 'You said it was nothing. That she couldn't be involved.'

'She?' Dulcie had missed something.

'I'm sure I was just raving.' Stella pulled away and walked toward the stage. 'I've just been out of my mind with grief.' She stopped and turned to Dulcie. 'Marco and I were close, once upon a time.'

Dulcie nodded. 'I heard,' was all she said.

'Yes, but you're not the one who had it out for him, Stella,' Paul Barnes was saying. 'The one who stole his work. That was Renée Showalter, and soon everybody is going to know it.'

THIRTY-FIVE

DULCIE COULDN'T GET out of there fast enough. It was all she could do not to interrupt. The shock must have shown on her face, because Stella had turned toward her in surprise.

'Are you feeling all right?' Dulcie hadn't even realized she'd been wobbling until Stella reached for her. 'Do you need to sit down?'

'No.' Dulcie wasn't sure what she was responding to, but she repeated the word anyway. 'No.'

'Let me get you some water,' said Barnes. 'This has been too much for all of us.'

As he strode quickly out of the auditorium, Dulcie let herself be guided into one of the seats.

'Poor girl,' Stella said, her voice as soft as the hands on Dulcie's shoulders. 'I really do wonder at the university for allowing this conference to go forward.'

'We thought it was for the best.' Dulcie knew her response was weak. 'So many people had come here, and it wouldn't be fair.'

'Huh.' Stella sat down beside her. 'Like any of us can concentrate now.'

'Well, you in particular.' Sitting this close, Dulcie could see the fine lines on the scholar's face, under her eyes and around her mouth. Even her hands looked rough close up, red scratch marks raked in the dry white skin.

'Why me?' Stella must have seen her looking.

She pulled the sleeves of her black jersey down over her hands.

'Well, you and Marco…' Dulcie felt suddenly awkward. Maybe everything she'd heard had been wrong.

But Stella sniffed, audibly, and Dulcie took that as confirmation. 'It was complicated,' she said. 'He was… so supportive.'

It wasn't what Dulcie had expected, but just then Paul Barnes reappeared, pressing a paper cup of water into her hands. 'Drink this,' he said.

She nodded and took a sip.

'I don't know what the dean was thinking.' Barnes was looking at her with concern.

'The dean?' Stella's grief had turned to scorn. 'Blame that Martin Thorpe instead.' Another sniff, though this one sounded like a scoff. 'This is all about his ego.'

Now Roebuck was attacking Thorpe? It was all too much. Dulcie closed her eyes as a wave of dizziness hit her.

'Dulcie?' The voice sounded like it came from miles away. 'Are you all right, Dulcie? What did you give her?'

'Nothing. Water.'

She opened her eyes to see Chris staring down at Paul Barnes. She hadn't realized how tall her boyfriend was, or how fierce, compared to the academic.

'I'm okay.' She didn't want to stand, not yet, but she had work to do. 'I just felt a bit faint.'

'I'm taking you home.' Chris took her hand and almost pulled her out of the seat. 'Come on, Dulcie.'

'No.' She tried to wave him off. 'I've got to help set up.'

'I can take it from here.' Kelly had descended from

the booth. Now she looked at the two academics. 'That all right with you guys?'

They nodded, cowed. But Dulcie had more to say. 'I'll be back before Thorpe's address. And if anyone else comes by...' She stopped herself. Clearly, Professor Showalter was not in high favor around here. Plus, she'd said she'd be at the airport.

Didn't matter. Kelly understood. 'I've got your numbers,' she said. 'Don't worry about it.'

'Come on,' said Chris. 'Put your arm around me.'

Dulcie let herself be led out of the auditorium, but she stopped Chris by the big glass doors. 'Hang on.' She slumped against the wall.

'Should I call an ambulance?' Chris hovered, concerned.

'No.' She shook off his concern. 'It's not that. I'm actually feeling better.' She wiped her brow, as the feeling passed. 'I guess I just needed to get away from those people with all their negativity.'

'Negativity? Is that what you're calling it?' Chris's tone made her look up. 'I don't know what it is, Dulce, but I don't like either of them.'

'What?' Dulcie asked. The nausea was fading, but she knew her thoughts were still fuzzy. They had to be, because she couldn't make sense out of what Chris was saying. 'What are you saying, Chris?'

'Well, that woman, with her carping and bossing you and Kelly around. You'd think she was queen of the prom, instead of just another struggling academic. I mean, we're all in this together, aren't we?'

Before Dulcie could respond, he went on.

'And that Paul guy, Dulcie. I don't trust him.'

'I know you thought he might be a suspect, Chris.'

Her head was swimming. 'But after that note? Don't you think Tesla might have, well, done it himself?'

'I don't know, and frankly I'm not sure if I care.' Chris sounded angry. She craned her neck up to look at him, his face as set as she'd ever seen. 'I think he gave you something, Dulcie. I really do.'

'What do you mean?' Even though her head was clearing, Dulcie was more confused than before.

'I saw him, Dulcie. When he got that drink for you.' She shook her head, confused.

'He didn't go downstairs to the water fountain. He filled it from a bottle. And when he saw me, he tucked it behind a seat. I swear, Dulcie, he looked guilty. I didn't put it together until I saw you start to sway, but I don't trust him. I mean, I know academia is supposed to be cut-throat. But this is ridiculous.'

THIRTY-SIX

DULCIE DIDN'T KNOW what to believe. Over Chris's protests, she had sent him back to work on the computer. What he'd already found had gone a long way toward proving that Marco Tesla might have killed himself. And, really, except for that tragic occurrence, all of the bickering and gossip was probably more or less normal. Academic conferences were always stressful, from everything she had heard. She'd expected a goldfish bowl. What they'd gotten was more like those tiny tanks of Siamese fighting fish. Still, what more harm could they do?

Chris had been trying to answer that, when she silenced him with a kiss. She felt fine, she'd said. And since she'd been sprung for a little bit, she wanted to get some work done. What she hadn't told him was what Professor Showalter had said; she figured that still fell under the rubric of doing her own research. After all, she still had a paper to present in two days.

He hadn't liked it, but he'd finally accepted it, though she was aware of how carefully he had watched her walk out. As soon as she'd turned the corner, she had slowed down, still feeling a bit unsteady. As she headed across the Yard, she tried to sort it out. The dizziness had receded—the frosty air helped—but despite her loud disclaimers, she couldn't entirely discount what Chris had said.

She hugged her coat closer, thinking. None of it made

sense. For starters, she couldn't see Paul Barnes drugging her. Why would he, when he had only the day before called and practically invited her to work with him? It wasn't like she had turned him down. They simply hadn't had a chance to talk. And it wasn't like she was going to speak out against him, for any reason. Granted, she'd rather have seen Renée Showalter get the position, but he didn't necessarily know that.

Or did he? She paused, waiting. But the only voice she heard was calling for a Frisbee. So much for winter. The sun wasn't doing much to warm her, but at least it was out. The day was bright and clear.

But the auditorium hadn't been. No, she shook her head. There was something else going on with her boyfriend. She'd been up in the booth with Kelly and Chris. She'd seen how limited the visibility was.

Chris had had an explanation, of course. He'd gone to check the door, he'd said. The one Kelly said had been forced open. He'd admitted that, almost shyly, when Dulcie had asked how he'd managed to see Barnes with the bottle.

'I was coming back in,' he'd said. 'And he was startled, I know he was.'

She hadn't known what to ask then, or if this had any connection to his strange absence the night before. Now, as she climbed the steps to the library, she wondered what was really going on with Chris. Maybe there really was some strange, fast-moving virus going around.

'Ms Schwartz.' Griddlehaus, at any rate, looked pleased to see her. 'I didn't think you'd be able to get away until next week.'

'Neither did I,' she admitted, as she handed him her bag. 'But I really needed the break,' she said. 'Plus, well, I had a question.'

The bespectacled clerk went through her bag in an almost cursory manner, opening the cabinet to lock it away before turning back to her. 'Shall we?'

She nodded, following him back to the reading area. Before donning the white cloth gloves, however, she reached up as if to take the quiet librarian by the arm.

'Mr Griddlehaus?' She didn't touch him. They didn't have that sort of relationship.

He did pause, however, as if taking in the gravity of the situation. 'What is it, Ms Schwartz?' Behind their thick lenses, his brows creased with concern.

'Probably nothing.' Just being here made her worries seem insubstantial. 'I just, well, things are crazy out there, and someone said something.'

He waited, not speaking, for her to finish.

'Mr Griddlehaus,' she said finally. 'Is there any chance that the latest acquisition—the Philadelphia bequest—could be, well, something other than what we have thought?'

These were the papers Showalter had brought to her attention—the papers that she had also been instrumental in getting donated to the Mildon. These were also the papers—a combination of journal entries, letters, and some fragments of a novel—that she had warned Dulcie about, only a few hours earlier.

'Why? What do you mean?' Griddlehaus looked honestly confused.

'Could they be, well, fake?' Dulcie's voice dropped on the last word, as her mouth went suddenly dry.

'Well.' Griddlehaus pulled out a chair and sat in it, something Dulcie had rarely seen him do. 'We may have a dilemma here. After all, Ms Schwartz, I thought that you were working on their authentication.'

She nodded. That was the crux of the problem. 'I

know, Mr Griddlehaus, I know.' She tried to swallow. 'And I've been so sure, too. But it has been suggested to me that they are not, well, that they are not what they appear.'

The clerk did not respond, and the two sat there in silence for a moment. Finally, he spoke. 'I can check their provenance again,' he said. 'Although, of course, we did confirm the paperwork when they came here, and everything seemed to be in order. Would that help?'

'I guess so.' Dulcie felt like she should be more reassured. 'I mean, I know that their authorship is speculative, and it might always be.'

'Now that's not true.' Griddlehaus seemed to have a little verve back. 'I have a good feeling about those papers, Ms Schwartz. And about your work here.'

'Thanks.' Dulcie tried to take heart. 'It's probably nothing.'

He got up, as if the matter were resolved, and started toward the archives. 'What on earth caused you to question them, Ms Schwartz?' He paused. 'I mean, if Professor Showalter is so confident in them, then what would raise an alarm for you?'

'Professor Showalter?' Of course. The little clerk knew Showalter's name from the provenance.

'Yes, she came by this morning to check them out herself,' said Griddlehaus, his voice carrying as he went through to the archives. 'One of the few who bothered.'

THIRTY-SEVEN

How COULD I have been so deceived? Was the fair face, the voice so gentle-born, that Compelling? Would that I had known what Evil lay behind the gracious form! I would have brought myself, nay, not Here unto this Wasteland, to be Storm-toss'd and all but Broken upon the Rocks, but to another Kinder soul, for Kinder souls must still exist... Yet know you of my sorrow and my Shame, which brought me hence at great Expense and no little Effort, so that I am as Bereft as any Moon-mad sprite, toss'd upon the wilds of Nature, unsure e'en of my night's peace. Uneasy must I rest and wait, guilty only of the Sin of Trust, where such a Gift unwisely bestow'd was...

DULCIE STARED AT that document in front of her, and the document might as well have been staring back. Fifteen minutes had passed, at least, since Griddlehaus had brought the stained and faded letter out to the reading area, ten since Dulcie had placed it carefully on the table in front of her. And although she had carefully followed the usual regimen of handling the delicate and aged paper—gloves barely touching the protective casing—she might as well have taken out the sports section of the daily *Globe*. Or no, she corrected herself as she tried to focus for the umpteenth time. The newspaper would have had some social value. It would have given her something to share with Chris.

'*The Sin of Trust...*' Or maybe it wouldn't have. As much as she wanted to dispel her suspicions, she had to admit her boyfriend had been acting strangely. She was, she knew, reading too much into this letter. The events it chronicled happened more than two hundred years before. What mattered was the text's relevance to her research, not what it might imply about her own life. She needed to forget her own problems, at least for a little while. She needed to focus.

As it was, she was sitting and staring, her brain a jumble of conflicting thoughts. What had actually happened to poor Marco Tesla? Who might have wanted to hurt him, or his erstwhile girlfriend Stella Roebuck? And why would Renée Showalter have lied to her about her whereabouts this morning?

Beneath all of these, Dulcie could sense a little niggling fear—something about Chris and what he'd been doing, or, really, what he might be hiding. But she couldn't deal with that. Not right now, not when he undoubtedly had an explanation. But Showalter—that one hurt. If the academic had simply wanted to check out the papers, couldn't she have asked Dulcie? Dulcie could have done it for her—or at least enjoyed her company. In truth, she had fantasized about bringing her new mentor to her old home. Making the introduction between Griddlehaus and the professor was the kind of connection she dreamed of and now that was not to be. Worse than that was the feeling that the academic had been avoiding her. And maybe, although Dulcie told herself she just might be imagining this, Showalter had something bigger—and more deadly—to hide.

'Ms Schwartz?' She looked up, startled to find Griddlehaus standing over her, worry creasing his face. 'May I ask if there's a problem?'

'No, I'm okay. I'm sorry,' she said. 'I'm just a bit distracted today.'

'The conference, of course.' The little clerk turned away. 'I shouldn't have bothered you.'

'It's nice you asked.' Dulcie was honestly touched. Despite their deepening friendship, she recognized the mousy man's reticence to touch on anything more personal than a preference for a certain kind of gum eraser. 'I appreciate it.'

'Oh. Well.' She had gone too far. He was blushing. But as she turned back to the page before her, determined to get something done before it was time to leave, the shy clerk cleared his throat.

'Mr Griddlehaus,' she spoke as softly as she could, as if he were, in fact, the small rodent he sometimes resembled. 'Is there something you would like to say?'

'Well.' He examined his hands, as if surprised to find them empty, and then blinked up at her. 'I'm not sure how, exactly, to phrase this.'

Dulcie smiled in what she hoped was an encouraging manner. 'Yes?'

'This Professor Showalter.' He was again addressing his hands. 'You would like to work with her, am I correct?'

'You are.' Dulcie found herself taking care with her voice. There was no need to air her latest concerns, not when Griddlehaus was already having trouble speaking.

'So, you must find her honorable.' He stopped.

'Honorable?' She was confused.

'Honorable. An honest academic. An honest *person*.' His eyes, wide behind those glasses, stared at her intently.

'Yes,' she replied. 'Yes, I do.'

'Then perhaps you might answer a question for me.'

He paused and she realized he was waiting for confirmation. She nodded. 'I'm wondering, Ms Schwartz, why a scholar, especially one whom you hold in such high esteem, would have tried to disguise her identity when another scholar came to visit.'

THIRTY-EIGHT

THAT WAS IT. Dulcie gave up. Although she couldn't come up with a credible explanation for the visiting scholar's strange behavior, she did manage to get more details from Griddlehaus before she left.

As she walked back to the Science Center, Dulcie mulled over what he'd said. What the little clerk had told her didn't help make things clear and was, she'd had to agree, strange. In brief, he'd said that Renée Showalter had come in and asked to see the papers that she had been instrumental in obtaining for the Mildon. Griddlehaus, thanks to Dulcie, was very aware of her part in the donation, and he had been quite thrilled to seat her in Dulcie's regular place and to bring out the papers in their protective box for her to peruse.

Dulcie had almost interrupted him, then, to ask what reason she had given for dropping by. But perhaps her own warning to Dulcie was explanation enough. As for what she had said about the airport? Well, Dulcie was willing to forgive that as a well-intentioned deceit. Clearly, Showalter had been worried about the material. Perhaps she wanted to check it out herself, to clear up the mystery. But what had happened next just muddied the waters more.

As Griddlehaus had explained, the visiting professor had gone through one box of papers. 'Rather quickly,' he said later, although his slight sniff of disapproval may have been influenced by what had happened next.

At any rate, he had gone back into the archive, looking both to replace the original box and to retrieve the next in the series, when he had heard a noise.

He looked up to find Showalter behind him. 'Ms Showalter!' he had exclaimed. 'I'm sorry, Ms Schwartz,' he had added, *sotto voce*. 'In my confusion, I forgot that she is of course a full professor at her own institution. At any rate, I was startled to see her there behind me, in what is clearly labeled as an area not open to the public. And then...' He paused and swallowed. Dulcie watched his eyes close and reopen like a frog's. 'And then she shushed me, Ms Schwartz. She *shushed* me! In my own archive!'

'You probably startled her, as well.' It was the best she could come up with.

'Hmph.' He sniffed. 'Perhaps I would have thought so if she hadn't nearly refused to leave. It was only when I'd finally managed to back her into the reading room that I discovered the reason for her trespass.'

Dulcie had waited. Griddlehaus did have a sense of drama.

'Another one of your visiting scholars, a tall gentleman, had been waiting by the entrance. And I had not been there, and so he had walked away.'

That, Dulcie had realized, was the real cause of Griddlehaus's pique. For him, dereliction of duty was unheard of. Indeed, he had been presented with a dilemma. Although he had seen the other guest walking away down the hall, he had been loath to run after him. 'Not once I'd seen what erratic behavior Professor Showalter was capable of.' Although he had called after the departing visitor—'in a reasonable tone, for a library'—he had failed to catch his attention. Instead, he had been forced to see the tall man enter the elevator and take it up, presumably to the ground floor and the library's exit.

'I felt simply horrible, Ms Schwartz,' he concluded. 'And as I was standing there, wondering if perhaps I could send someone after him, she left.' He leaned over, his voice dropping even more. 'I confess, I went over the materials she'd been looking at. But I am happy to inform you that despite her erratic behavior, nothing seemed to be amiss. Only, well, she was clearly hiding. And I'd like to know why, Ms Schwartz. That is, if you can tell me.'

She hadn't been able to, and now she just found herself dreading her return to the Science Center. This conference, she was realizing, was becoming just as terrible as Martin Thorpe had feared.

'Hey, kiddo!' She looked up. Trista was jogging to catch up with her. 'You heading to the snake pit?'

'Why do you call it that?' Dulcie heard the sharpness in her own tone—and saw her friend's reaction. 'Sorry, this whole thing…'

'Tell me about it.' Trista fell into step with her, matching her longer stride to her friend's. 'So you must have heard the scuttlebutt on poor old Tesla, right?'

'I heard something.' Dulcie was wary. 'I don't know if it's true.'

'From the horse's mouth.' Trista raised her right hand, as if taking an oath.

'Really?' Dulcie knew her friend had admired the dead academic—or, to be honest, had found him attractive. She didn't know they had been confidants.

Trista nodded. 'I guess I shouldn't say anything about it. I mean, what's the point now in ruining his reputation?'

'No, you have to.' Dulcie grabbed her friend's hand. 'Don't you see? The police still think it might be murder.'

Trista stopped short. 'Wait? Murder? Dulcie, are you sure?'

The question caught her short. 'I think so,' she said. 'The detective in charge was asking me questions about who Tesla had been with at the party—and who he might have had a beef with.' She paused, trying to remember his exact words. 'He implied that he'd been pushed.'

'Well, yeah.' Trista's calm was not what Dulcie had expected.

'You knew this? But you just said...'

'Pushed emotionally.' Trista emphasized the last word. 'He was near the breaking point. His work had been stolen. He was fighting with his girlfriend. She was going to leave him...'

'Stella?'

Trista nodded. 'Yeah, at least I think she was his girlfriend.' She turned toward Dulcie. 'I'll tell you, Dulcie. Some of these senior fellows? They're worse than freshmen at a mixer. I mean, what is up with that professor of yours?'

Dulcie opened her mouth to defend Showalter. But all she could think of was what Griddlehaus had told her. Renée Showalter had hidden from Paul Barnes, the man she was supposedly involved with. The man who had all but accused her of stealing Marco Tesla's work. 'I don't know, Tris,' she said instead. It was the best she could do.

THIRTY-NINE

BY THE TIME they got back to the Science Center, the world—or at least their particular segment of it—had convened. Dulcie could see Raleigh and Lloyd, and figured that the rest of her department was lost in the milling crowd. Between her colleagues and the visiting scholars, and a bunch of undergrads who looked like they had shown up hoping for free food, the lobby was thronged with more people than Dulcie had expected. And if this had the welcome consequence of warming the space, it also raised the volume to way above study levels.

'Well, this is cool.' Trista yelled above the noise. 'You think you'll get a crowd like this for your talk?'

'I wish,' Dulcie replied, swallowing hard. She didn't really, and the thought of speaking before a crowd this large was more than a little intimidating.

Trista must have picked up on some of that, because she draped her arm around her friend's shoulders. 'You'll do great. You'll see,' she said, her voice barely audible in Dulcie's ear. 'Once you get into your paper, the audience won't matter. And it'll be fantastic preparation for when you have to defend your thesis.'

'Great.' Dulcie knew she was speaking too softly to be heard. The fact that she was facing the floor didn't help either. She knew Trista meant well, but the pairing of this crowd and her eventual defense did nothing to make either less frightening.

'Oh, come on, Dulce.' Trista might not have heard her response, but she had certainly intuited it. 'It won't be that bad.'

Before she could think of a response, Dulcie heard her name being called and turned to see, deep in the crowd, an arm waving.

'Yo!' For a moment, the crowd parted, and she could see Mina, on the far side of what did indeed look like a caterer's folding table.

'Wait there!' Dulcie called back, before the undergrad was swallowed up by the crowd. She liked to think that people would make way for Mina if they saw her cane, but it would be easier for her to make her way through the mob, especially if that mob was intent on little cubes of pimento cheese. 'It's Mina,' she yelled up at Trista. 'She and I need to talk.'

'Go.' Trista waved her off. 'Just watch out for the cheese ball. I swear they recycle it from party to party.'

With those words of wisdom, Dulcie began to make her way through the crowd.

'Hey.' It hadn't been far, but she felt slightly breathless by the time she got to Mina.

'This is crazy.' Mina was looking around, wide-eyed. 'Are all the conferences like this?'

'I think they're all pretty crazy, but this is the first one I've been to,' Dulcie admitted. 'We haven't hosted the ELLA since I've been here, and I've never had a paper to present before. Which reminds me,' she leaned in to make sure Mina could hear her as she lowered her voice, 'I haven't been able to talk to Professor Showalter yet. In fact, I'm a little worried—'

'There she is!' Mina probably hadn't heard her, Dulcie decided. As it was, the undergrad was waving frantically again. Looking up, Dulcie could see the tall redhead near the edge of the crowd. 'I'm sorry, Dulcie. What were you saying?'

'Never mind.' Dulcie looked over at Showalter. The visiting scholar had seen them and was making her way through the crowd. If Dulcie had hoped to grab a private moment with Showalter before the conference opener, she'd have to act fast. 'Let's try to grab her.'

Despite her cane, Mina proved adroit at working through the crowd, and Dulcie ended up following her as they made their way out to where the professor waited.

'Professor!' Mina yelled up at her. 'I wanted to thank you for all your help.'

'It's nothing.' The red-haired academic smiled at her. Dulcie found herself hanging back. There was so much she wanted to ask about, and so little privacy in which to do it.

'We didn't get to meet,' she said now, as much to Mina as to Showalter, before checking her watch. 'And I'm supposed to be helping Thorpe get ready. But I've got maybe fifteen minutes. Do you think we can talk?'

'Of course.' Showalter, the tallest of the three, looked around. 'I don't think they're letting people into the auditorium yet, but the corner over there looks relatively quiet.'

They used up at least two of her free minutes getting through the outer edges of the crowd. The free cheese was proving to be a stronger than usual draw. But finally the three found themselves over by the auditorium's back doors. Closed, they made a little alcove, where Dulcie could actually hear herself think.

'Professor Showalter,' she began. 'I was just over at the Mildon...'

'Oh, I don't want to be rude,' Mina interrupted.

'But since our time is limited, could we talk about the paper?'

'Why, yes.' With a glance at Dulcie, Showalter turned toward Mina. 'I was beginning to tell Dulcie earlier that I was wondering about using the genealogical material.'

Mina's face fell, and Dulcie's heart went out to her. 'Of course,' Mina said, her enthusiasm a little forced. 'Dulcie's paper should focus on the literary interpretation of the newly discovered work. As an undergrad, it was an honor for me to even be involved—'

'No, it's not that,' the professor interrupted. 'Your work is solid. Quite good, in fact.'

Mina only looked more confused, and Dulcie broke in. 'The professor told me this morning that she had doubts about the other material,' she explained as quickly as she could. 'There may be some problems with the papers from the Philadelphia bequest. In fact,' she paused, wondering if Showalter would step in, 'I believe she was checking them out today. Perhaps to see if they could be verified?'

The professor didn't say anything for a moment, but from the way she looked at Dulcie, Dulcie knew she'd hit home. 'Yes, yes, they looked good,' she said finally.

Mina looked from one to the other. Dulcie ignored her. 'Professor, can you tell me why you—' She didn't want to say 'lied'. 'Why you said you couldn't meet me this morning?'

'Dulcie,' Mina broke in. 'You heard her. She was verifying our material for us.'

Dulcie shook her head, but kept her eyes on the professor. 'I could have met you at the Mildon,' she said.

'I needed to see for myself,' Showalter began, and then stopped. Putting her hand up to her face, she took a deep breath. 'It's the oddest thing. I thought maybe it was a dream. I—I don't know why I wanted to check that material. Only that I had a strong sense that something was wrong with it.'

Had it been anyone else, Dulcie thought, she would not have believed it. But dreams had a way of being true, in her experience. And if she and the professor were as strongly connected as she suspected, it was just possible that dreams were more than night-time fancies for her as well. Still, she needed to know more.

'A dream?'

Showalter only shook her head again. 'I'm sorry, I can't remember. It may have been because of the party. I'd been talking with Marco…'

'Marco Tesla?' Mina chimed in, and Dulcie wanted to shush her. Of course, Mina hadn't heard the gossip about Showalter and the younger academic.

'Yes.' Showalter's brow furrowed as she concentrated. 'It was so strange, because we hadn't expected to run into each other. Not here.'

Dulcie nodded and leaned over to Mina. 'He was a late addition to the schedule, you know. I don't think Nancy even had a title for his talk.'

Showalter had heard her. 'No, she did. Even though his paper had been stolen, he was working on re-creating it from his notes. He'd given her a title. He seemed to think it was quite important, though he may just have been a bit tipsy.'

'You were drinking with him?' Mina latched on to that. 'Did he seem, you know, drunk?'

Showalter shook her head. 'No. Angry, maybe. But not drunk.'

Dulcie froze. 'Did he say who—'

'Dulcie.' At the sound of her name, she spun around.

Chris was there, his hair mussed up as if he'd been running. 'I'm so glad I found you.'

'That you did.' The attention was flattering, the timing inopportune.

'Can we talk?' He had his hand on her arm, as if to draw her away. ''Cause I may have—'

'Chris, this is Renée Showalter. Professor Renée Showalter.' Surely he couldn't have forgotten about the woman she hoped would become her mentor? 'You know Mina.'

'Hi, Mina.' He bobbed his head. 'Professor. But Dulcie—'

She closed her eyes, just briefly. 'Chris, I'm in the middle of a—'

'*Be wary, little one.*' The voice shocked her into opening her eyes—and stopped her complaint. '*Pay attention!*'

'Chris, Professor Showalter was just about to tell us about Marco's last—'

'Marco?' She spun around. Stella Roebuck was blinking at her with a look that threatened tears. 'Are you talking about Marco?'

'We were merely reminiscing.' Professor Showalter must have noticed the watery eyes, too. 'How are you doing, dear?'

'I still can't believe it.'

Chris pulled on her sleeve. 'Dulcie.'

'Chris, I was on the verge of hearing something,' she whispered. 'Mr Grey wants me to be alert.'

'We were colleagues as well as lovers.' Stella was blinking furiously now, but still one fat tear rolled down her cheek. 'There, I've said it.'

'Marco won't be forgotten,' Showalter began. 'What we know of his work will help us understand—'

Stella cut her off. 'That's so kind of you. Especially because of where you are, and what you study. Marco and I—Marco was forward-looking. Always breaking the boundaries.'

'Oh, brother.' Dulcie couldn't help it. This deconstructivist drivel couldn't be what Mr Grey wanted her to hear, could it?

'Dulcie!' Luckily, only Mina seemed to have heard her.

'Dulcie?' Chris's voice had taken on a whining tone. 'Please, this is important.'

'I was just telling these students here about him.' Showalter had upped her volume. 'About my last conversation with him.'

'Dulcie.' Chris again. Dulcie shook him off.

'Dulcie!' This time it was Mina, her voice taking on a note of urgency that was near panic. 'Look at the time!'

'What?' She turned. Somewhere back behind the scaffolding was a big clock. Unless it had been taken down. 'Chris, do you have the time?'

'I gather you don't, Ms Schwartz.' A new voice broke into the mix from behind Dulcie. She saw the faces look up, and she turned.

'Mr Thorpe.' She choked out his name. *Pay attention*, indeed. 'I'm sorry. Do you need me?'

In response, he pointed. She followed the line of his hand where, yes, the big clock could be seen, high above the draped ladders. Three fifteen. She turned and looked around. The lobby was nearly empty. The caterer's table, where the cheese platters had been, held only crumpled napkins and what appeared to be a discarded hat.

'I'm so sorry, Mr Thorpe.' She shook off Chris's grasp. He had to understand. 'Shall we go in?'

He nodded and turned, and Dulcie scurried after him. This was supposed to be Thorpe's big moment and not only had she forgotten it, she had forgotten it because she'd been in conversation with his rival. He deserved better.

'This day can't get any worse,' she heard him say.

'HOW ARE YOU FEELING?' Less than five minutes later, she was clipping the small microphone to his jacket collar. Although they hadn't had time to do a proper soundcheck, Kelly had handed her the mini-mic with a reassuring nod. 'Any better?'

'I'm fine, thank you.' His words boomed out, and she rushed to adjust the controls. 'Or I would be,' he went on in a stage whisper. They both paused. No, his words were not amplified. 'If I had had proper time to prepare, that is.'

'I'm so, so sorry.' She patted down his jacket and did a quick inventory. His talk was on the podium. She could see it from here, under the directional lamp, which was already turned on. There was a hand-held microphone somewhere—Dulcie would have to find it—but odds were, there would be no questions from the audience. A keynote speech didn't usually draw that kind of response and, frankly, Dulcie didn't think impromptu interaction was Thorpe's strong point anyway. Nix the hand-held, she made a mental note. What else?

'Mr Thorpe, there is a box of tissues in the podium, if you need them.' She worked to keep her voice calm. Yes, they were late. And, yes, her adviser was already panicking, the last-minute nature of their preparation adding to his already considerable stage fright. Underneath his wool jacket, he was sweating, Dulcie could tell. She considered grabbing another box of Kleenex for him to wipe his face and, after a moment's hesitation, decided against it. Better not to make him even more aware of his pre-presentation jitters. 'Do you need anything else?' It was a more open offer. One that she hoped sounded friendly and helpful.

'Some water would be nice.' He licked his lips. 'There was supposed to be a bottle.'

'Of course.' Dulcie looked over. She could see the paper, pages bright under the light, where she'd placed them only moments before. She could even see the box of tissues. And beyond, she could make out the waiting crowd. Nothing in the university started exactly on time, but it was close to three thirty now, and she could tell they were getting impatient. 'Right on it.'

She darted out, the stage lights in her eyes, and ducked down to peer inside the podium. Empty. What did she expect? She was supposed to take care of the day's preparations. She would have to figure something out, and fast.

'Hold on, Mr Thorpe.' She walked quickly past him, back into the depths of the auditorium. Surely there was a water cooler somewhere—no, of course not. The plumbing work was behind schedule. The closest working water fountain was down in the basement. 'Hello?' Weren't there supposed to be staff here? Someone to help out.

'Ms Schwartz.' Thorpe's stage whisper caught up to her. 'I don't think we should dally much longer.'

'Dulcie.' Renée Showalter appeared out of the shadows. 'Is everything okay? People have started asking.'

'Oh, thank the goddess.' Dulcie could have hugged the older woman. 'Yes, I just should have been back here…' No, this was not the time to explain. 'Did you see a bottle of water somewhere? Maybe a case of them?'

'Why, yes.' Showalter looked around her. 'I just did.'

Dulcie could have swooned with relief. Instead, she waited as the visiting professor ducked behind a curtain and emerged, holding an opened plastic bottle.

'Is this yours?'

'It'll do.' Dulcie grabbed it and stopped. The bottle wasn't sealed. Someone, Kelly maybe, must have seen it and thought it was unclaimed. There was a virus going around.

'Ms Schwartz?' Thorpe's voice was ratcheting up in pitch, and Dulcie made a decision.

'Here you go, Mr Thorpe.' She twisted the top off and handed it to him. He took a deep drink and handed it back. Well, the damage was done. She didn't say she'd opened a new bottle. Odds were, it would be fine. 'Do you want me to put this out there for you?'

'No, no.' He waved her off. 'I'll just spill it.' He fished a handkerchief out of his pocket and mopped his brow. Between the water and the wipe, he looked better or, at least, ready to go.

'Break a leg, Mr Thorpe.' She squeezed his hand and watched, holding her breath, as he took the stage.

'Good evening,' he said, to a buzz of feedback. 'Or rather, good afternoon.' The crowd laughed, and Dulcie smiled. Good. Let him make a joke about the delayed start. It would warm up the crowd.

'We are all gathered here today…' He paused. This time, the joke fell flat. Kelly had corrected the sound, and now there was silence. 'I mean, thank you all for coming. Today's lecture is on…' He looked down at his pages.

'Come on, Thorpe. Play it straight.' Dulcie spoke under her breath. Uneasy public speakers like Thorpe shouldn't try to improvise.

'I'm sorry.' The handkerchief came out again, in reaction to the beads of sweat that could clearly be seen on his brow. 'I seem to have gotten my notes out of order.'

It was not an auspicious beginning, and it was Dulcie's fault. She had checked that his talk was there, but not its order. Though she seemed to recall seeing, in fourteen-point type, a more conventional opening.

'Good afternoon,' Thorpe began again. 'And welcome to ELLA.' Yes, that was it. Straightforward and direct. As long as Thorpe continued to read from his pages, he should be all right. Dulcie began to relax.

'Over the following three days, we will hear…' A pause, and Dulcie felt her shoulders tense up. 'We will be hearing presentations by some of the most distinguished scholars in their fields.'

He was launched. She turned to go. And that's when she heard it—the collective gasp of several hundred startled scholars. And the thud, as Martin Thorpe hit the ground.

FORTY

He wasn't out long. By the time Dulcie got to him—and that was fast—he was already blinking awake. By the time she was joined, in rapid succession, by Professor Showalter, Paul Barnes, and a hefty young man who explained he'd had CPR training, Thorpe was talking. Protesting, in fact, quite loudly.

'Please, I'm fine.' Still lying on the ground, he raised his hands to push his well wishers away. 'Just a moment of weakness. It's nothing.'

'It's not nothing, Mr Thorpe.' Dulcie's dissent was echoed by Nancy and Showalter. The young CPR champ was too busy trying to listen to Thorpe's chest.

'It is. Get off!' That last bit was directed to the would-be EMT, but the gesture—which looked a bit like he was doing the breast stroke—served to move them all back.

'Please, Mr Thorpe.' Dulcie made a last attempt. 'We only want to help you.'

'You can help by helping me up.' Thorpe reached for her hand. At the front of the stage, Paul Barnes was addressing the audience.

'Everything is under control,' he was saying. 'Please remain calm.'

'Man, he's good.' Kelly had reached her by then. 'I couldn't have gotten through the crowd if he hadn't calmed them down.'

'Great,' Thorpe muttered, his face knotted. Dulcie

didn't know if that was because of the effort of sitting up or the praise for Barnes.

'Are you sure you should be getting up, sir?' The student had a point. Dulcie looked from him back to Thorpe, and saw how ashen his face had grown.

'He's right, Mr Thorpe.' Even his grip on her arm had grown slack.

'Emergency, coming through.' She looked up. Two real EMTs had shown up, the first one carrying what looked like a tool box. 'What's the problem here?'

'There is no problem.' Thorpe's temper was lively, at least. 'I have a talk to give.'

'I think you'll find that the auditorium has been cleared, sir.' The second EMT, a woman, had begun wrapping a blood pressure band around Thorpe's arm. She nodded to her partner and he disappeared, returning a moment later with a portable wheelchair. Dulcie stepped back to let him through.

'Can you sit up, sir?' He seemed to be lifting Thorpe bodily into the chair.

'Oopsy daisy,' said the other. 'Here we go!'

Dulcie didn't hear what Thorpe responded. All she knew was that the conference had started off with a colossal disaster, and it very well might be her fault. That open bottle—who knew what was in it, what she had given him to drink.

'Dulcie, what happened?' She turned. Chris was behind her.

'Thorpe fainted.' She could barely get the words out. 'Chris, I think maybe I did it. I mean, I wanted to get him something to drink, and I...'

'Dulcie.' He wasn't buying it. 'Please don't beat yourself up.' He held her shoulders and looked down into her face. 'He's been sick, right? He's probably got that stomach flu that's going around, and the way he worries...' He smiled encouragingly, and she found herself smiling back. 'If it weren't for you, he'd have collapsed long ago.'

'Thanks, sweetie.' She leaned into him and realized just how tired she was. To her surprise, however, he didn't relax. Didn't hold his arms around her like he usually did, and so she looked up. 'Chris, what is it?'

'I didn't get to tell you.' He lowered his voice. 'I don't even know what it means. But Dulcie, I've been looking at that laptop, and it's the strangest thing.'

'You found the paper?' She didn't dare hope. Maybe the conference could be salvaged.

But he was shaking his head. 'Nope, it's weirder,' he said. 'It wasn't a virus. I'm pretty sure of that. And whoever did it must have had the laptop for some time.'

She didn't even know how to ask and simply waited.

'That woman—Professor Roebuck—was right. Someone went into her system and carefully erased her work. Destroyed all traces of it, as a matter of fact. But whoever did it took a lot of time and care, and really did it properly.'

'Great.' This might be a breakthrough to Chris, but to Dulcie it was just more bad news. She heard his soft protest as she broke away, and turned to explain. 'I'm sorry, Chris. This is all getting worse and worse. Can you—is there any way you can find out more?'

He nodded. 'I'm running a program now. I should be able to find out when it was done, and that will help us figure out who did it.'

'Thanks.' Dulcie noted his use of the word 'us'. 'I love you.'

'I love you, too, sweetie.' He reached for her again,

but this time only to deliver a peck to her forehead. 'I should run myself. And you?'

'I better get to the health services.' She looked around. The EMTs had vanished. 'Poor Thorpe.'

'He's lucky to have you,' said Chris. 'I'll call whenever I find out anything. Or call me.'

Somewhat heartened, Dulcie walked into the wings. Nancy was there, with Showalter and Barnes, and gestured for her to come over.

'Dulcie, are you going over to see about Mr Thorpe?' Worry made her look ten years older.

'Do you want to join me?' She'd shrugged on her coat and saw that Nancy was reaching for hers.

'If I may.' She turned back to the other academics. 'I appreciate your help with this. The dean will make his decision soon, I'm sure.'

'What was that about?' Dulcie asked as they left the auditorium. The winter dusk was already deepening, and she shivered in the cold.

'The entire conference…' Nancy shook her head, pulling her own coat closer. 'Professor Roebuck didn't even stay for the talk. She's very upset with us, with the university.'

'But that's not fair,' Dulcie protested. 'Thorpe pulled in every resource to help her. It's her own fault for not backing up and for…for making enemies.' She didn't want to gossip, but really, the way Roebuck mixed and matched lovers was asking for trouble. 'We're not responsible for Tesla—for that poor man's death.'

'The heart has its reasons of which reason knows nothing,' said Nancy. 'Love is a funny thing, Dulcie.'

Dulcie stopped and stared. Somehow, she had never imagined the plump departmental secretary speaking out in defense of passion. Was it possible? 'Nancy, are you and Mr Thorpe...?' She could not even finish her question.

'I respect him deeply,' the older woman said. 'And, frankly, with all the pressure that's been on him, I'm not surprised that he collapsed.'

Slightly stunned, Dulcie followed in silence as Nancy led the way across the Yard to the health services.

'Martin Thorpe?' Nancy asked at the front desk. Dulcie, meanwhile, tried to process. Nancy and Mr Thorpe...well, why not? The man had a heart, after all. She knew that because of the way he had taken to Tigger. Maybe Tigger was only the first of many changes. Maybe, she paused to consider, Thorpe might even open up in other ways. Could he really be the kind of adviser she had hoped for? The kind of chairman the department needed?

It was too much to consider. Besides, first she had to deal with this crisis. Chris was right, she knew, that she shouldn't blame herself. Thorpe had been ill earlier. After all, that was why she and Nancy had sent him home. However, Thorpe had asked her to be his right-hand person, and therefore she had to see what she could do to salvage the conference.

'What did they say?' As soon as Nancy had turned away from the desk, Dulcie approached. If Thorpe would be released soon, it would make her job a lot easier. If not, she would have to make plans.

'They're keeping him here for observation.' Plans, then. She looked up and saw how stricken Nancy looked.

'Is it bad?' Dehydration, stress, the stomach flu. Dulcie went over the possibilities.

'There you are!' She turned in time to see Paul

Barnes barging through the door, Renée Showalter behind him. 'How is he?'

'We came as soon as we'd spoken to the dean,' Showalter said, addressing Dulcie. 'He's decided to suspend tonight's events, but said he'd wait until we heard about Mr Thorpe's condition before going beyond that.'

'And Professor Roebuck?' If the third star of the conference could be talked into participating, the conference could still be saved. Besides, Dulcie had news—or reason to hope, anyway. With Chris on the case, Stella Roebuck's work would be found.

Showalter and Barnes looked at each other. It was Barnes who answered. 'I don't know.' He made a little cough, as if he were clearing his throat. 'She was very upset.'

'But I may have news for her.' She looked up at Nancy. The secretary had turned away and seemed to be having an earnest discussion with a woman in a white coat. 'Do either of you have her contact information?'

Showalter looked at Barnes. He coughed again and pulled out his cell phone to show her the number. 'You can try her.' He sounded doubtful.

'If I were back in the office, I'd have her number anyway,' Dulcie said. This entire conference was only supporting her belief that romance was best outside one's own discipline.

'You have news?' Showalter asked.

'Sort of.' Proud of Chris, Dulcie explained. But instead of the relief she expected, she saw concern—or was it confusion?—on the academics' faces.

'I'll see what the latest is before I call her,' Dulcie decided, and punched in Chris's number. The call went directly to voicemail. He was probably leaving her a message.

'*There's more at play than meets the eye.*' The voice sounded so real she started to turn. '*Pay attention, Dulcie.*'

She shook her head. What wasn't she listening to? She looked at the phone in her hand. 'Excuse me,' she said, turning away, and hit voicemail.

'Dulcie, about that shape shifter...' The old message from Lucy. Dulcie skipped ahead.

'Hey, Dulce. Chris here. I may have found something.' Bother: she'd heard this one. She clicked to the next. 'Dulcie, Professor Showalter here.' Was this another old message? She was about to erase that one, too, when the next words stopped her. 'We need to talk. I'm sorry, but this isn't what it seems.'

'What isn't?' she asked the phone, but the message had ended. 'Professor Showalter?' She looked up, but the professor was staring at her, shaking her head ever so slightly. 'What did you mean?'

'Dulcie...' The professor took a step toward her, her arm outstretched as if to take Dulcie's arm. 'I can explain.'

She never got the chance. Just then, a cry went up and they both turned.

'Oh no!' It was Nancy; her hands were covering her mouth. Her eyes had filled with tears.

'Nancy!' Pulling away from Showalter, Dulcie ran over to the secretary. 'What is it? What happened?'

'It's Mr Thorpe,' she said, her voice breaking.

'He's not—' Dulcie couldn't even say it. 'He's...'

'He's been *poisoned*,' said Nancy, her usually calm voice rising to a shriek.

'Come, here.' Showalter was there, her arm around the other woman. 'Let's sit down, shall we?'

Dulcie stood there, frozen, until a beeping sound

woke her. Chris's voicemail, once again. She hung up
and tried again. 'Chris, where are you?' Another try.
'Chris, call me, please. As soon as you get this.'

Showalter had Nancy over in the waiting area now.
Her arm was around the other woman, who was bent
forward, her body racked with sobs.

'Oh, Nancy.' Dulcie put her phone away. What wasn't
what it seemed? Had she been wrong about Showalter all along? Her questions would have to wait. She
started toward the chairs, unsure about Renée Showalter's intentions—and determined to extricate Nancy
from her grasp.

She didn't have to. The plump secretary must have
had the same response because, as Dulcie approached,
Nancy pulled herself from the professor's embrace and
stood up.

'Nancy?' Dulcie had never seen her so distraught.
Nor, the thought struck her, so strangely determined.

'Dulcie, I'm...' Nancy wiped her face with one sleeve
of her cardigan as she blinked back the new tears that
threatened. Then she turned to look at Showalter and
the various medical personnel who had gathered. 'I'll
be back,' was all she said, and with a determined stride
made for the door.

Dulcie started after her. The secretary was in no
shape to be alone, at night, in the city.

It was the thud that stopped her. The thud and the
way the receptionist vaulted over his desk to run past
her. Showalter and even Nancy looked up, and Dulcie
turned.

Paul Barnes had crumpled to the floor.

FORTY-ONE

DULCIE COULDN'T HELP IT. She turned to Professor Showalter, her voice rising in panic. 'What was in that bottle,
professor? What did you give them?'

'Them?' One of the aides who had rushed over
looked up. Dulcie ignored him.

So did Showalter. 'What did I? Wait, Dulcie, you
can't think…'

'I don't know what to think.' Dulcie's head was reel-
ing. 'You said that you'd explain—but you haven't.'

'Haven't what?' The gruff voice caused them both
to turn. Detective Rogovoy, his craggy face looking as
rough as he sounded, was standing there. His eyes, although small, focused in, first on the visiting professor and then on Dulcie. 'Someone better tell me what
is going on.'

'Detective Rogovoy.' Dulcie struggled to regain her
composure. 'What are you doing here?'

One eyebrow went up. It wasn't an attractive look. 'I
get a call about a possible poisoning, you think I don't
look into it?' He looked from one woman to the other
again. 'Especially when it turns out that our jumper
from the other night might have had some help?'

'Marco?' Showalter's surprise sounded genuine to
Dulcie, who remained silent. In fact, she turned toward
Dulcie now. 'And you think that I had something to do
with this?'

'I—' Dulcie didn't know how to respond. It was

Rogovoy who had first suggested that Showalter might have been involved in Tesla's death. Now, considering that Stella Roebuck had been effectively taken out of the running and both Thorpe and Barnes were laid low, it only seemed natural to look to the red-haired professor.

'Wait here,' said Rogovoy. It was a command. Not that Dulcie could have moved. She felt rooted to the spot as the detective lumbered over to speak to one of the white coats who had taken Paul Barnes away.

Renée Showalter, at least, seemed to have use of her wits.

'Dulcie,' she said, 'I meant what I said—I can explain. *Now*, I can—I needed to confirm something. But there's something else going on here. I didn't have anything to do with—with any of this.' She was speaking softly but quickly. 'All I know is that something is very, very wrong.'

'You weren't at the airport.' It was weak, but it was all Dulcie could think of.

Showalter nodded. 'I know. I lied, and I'm sorry. But it has just been so odd.' She glanced over at the desk, where several other medical types were talking with the detective. 'I've told you the truth about the documents, though. Someone—something—put the idea in my head that they weren't to be trusted. Weren't "true", in a way. And since I'd given them to you—to you and Mina—I felt like I had to check them out. But I couldn't tell you why I had those suspicions. Not then...' Her voice trailed off.

Something about her story, however, had alerted Dulcie. 'You heard a warning?' She bit her lip. 'Have you ever heard anything like this before?'

'I'm not sure,' she said, slowly. 'Why, Dulcie? What do you know?'

'Professor Showalter?' Rogovoy was walking toward them, his face grim. 'I'm going to have to ask you to answer a few questions.'

'Dulcie?' The professor pleaded. 'Please?'

'I can't explain right now.' Dulcie was thinking fast. 'But I do know where to start.' She looked over at Rogovoy, but the detective was clearly focused on the professor as he made his way toward them.

Dulcie took a deep breath, weighing everything she could. Something, the professor had said, was not what it seemed. Well, it seemed like she was guilty. And what had Mr Grey said?

We are not what we seem. She made a snap decision.

'I'm going to get to the bottom of this, Professor Showalter,' she whispered to the professor. Looking up at Rogovoy, she pasted on a smile. 'I'm just going to use the facilities.'

There was something sharp in his gaze that made her hesitate. But he muttered, 'Don't be long.'

Ducking out of the health services, Dulcie reached for her phone. 'Please pick up.' No use; she'd gotten Chris's voicemail again. 'Chris, please, call me back.' She'd passed the shelter of the building by then, and the wind made her cringe. Turning back, into the light, she checked: no messages, no texts. She fired off one of her own: 'Help pl? Lk 4 bttl bkstage Aud A left.' She paused, then added, 'DONT DRINK!' That should do it. But to make sure, she hit dial one more time. 'Chris, if you get this, I need you to look for a water bottle. It was on a chair stage left of Auditorium A.'

Nothing for it. While she'd hoped her boyfriend would be on hand to help, she was certainly capable of returning to the Science Center—and finding that bottle. Not that she knew what it would prove. But somehow she couldn't believe that Renée Showalter had consciously poisoned Thorpe—or Paul Barnes.

In fact, it had been Paul who had given her a drink, before she'd gotten ill. At least according to Chris. Where was her boyfriend anyway? Dulcie put her collar up against the cold. Could Chris have fallen ill, too? Maybe he was alone, in the lab. Or worse, out here in the dark. Not even six and it might as well be midnight.

She called again. 'Chris, I'm getting worried.' She remembered how dizzy she had felt. How nauseous. 'Please call me, okay?'

Pausing under one of the Yard's tall lights, she tapped out a text, her fingers cold and awkward in their gloves. When another attempt to call led to an announcement that her boyfriend's voicemail was full, she began to panic.

'Mr Grey, are you out there?' Stepping through the arch on to the open plaza, she looked up at the sky. 'You wouldn't let anything happen to Chris, would you?' The clouds racing above her parted, showing the bright face of the moon. 'Mr Grey?' No other answer came, however, and so she hurried on to the light and warmth that human works promised.

'Kelly!' She should have gone straight to the stage area of the auditorium, she knew that. Every minute meant more chance that someone would have found that bottle, could have thrown it away. For all she knew, it had been tossed hours ago, as the custodial staff came in to clean up after the aborted opening address.

Still, she couldn't help it. As soon as she'd entered the brightly lit building, she headed straight for the sound booth. As dark as it was outside, it wasn't that late.

With the rest of the conference still on hold, someone had to be working.

'Kelly?' The door wasn't locked, but the booth inside was empty. No Kelly, and more important, no Chris.

Had they both become ill? Dulcie forced herself to stay calm as she left the vacant booth and stepped back into the lit lobby. A young woman in a custodial uniform was still mopping.

'Hello? Excuse me.' Dulcie ran up to her, and she turned, tucking a long blond plait behind her ear. 'Can you tell me, did you see a tall guy, dark hair?' She held her hand up above her head, palm flat. Chris was over six feet, taller than either of them. But the woman just shook her head.

'I'm sorry.' She smiled apologetically. 'There are just so many people.'

Of course. Dulcie licked her lips and thought. 'You didn't see anyone taken away by emergency personnel, did you?' She held her breath.

The other woman lit up, her dark eyes opening wide. 'Yes. Is that what you were asking about?'

Dulcie nodded, unable to speak.

'It was about an hour ago? No, more like two hours.' The blonde held out the mop and started waving it like a pompom. 'Over there, in the big auditorium.' Not waving, she was pointing with it. 'I think it was someone from the conference?'

Thorpe. Dulcie exhaled, the tension flowing out of her. 'Oh, yeah, thanks. Nobody else?'

'No.' The dark eyes looked confused. 'Isn't one emergency enough?'

'More than enough.' Dulcie managed a smile. 'I'm sorry, I just thought, well...' The blonde had gone back to her cleaning, her hair once again hiding her face. 'Thanks, anyway,' Dulcie said backing away, embarrassed.

The basement was no better. The computer lab was bustling with students. Final projects didn't understand holidays or weekends, but Dulcie saw no familiar faces. Even the grad student on call—the job Chris had held regularly for the last two years—was someone new.

'Chris Sorenson?' He blinked up at her with the wide, watery eyes she had come to recognize as the sign of the sleep-deprived programmer. 'I don't think he works here any more. Girlfriend, you know.'

'Yeah,' she said, turning away. 'I know.'

She checked her phone as she made her way upstairs. Still no new calls or texts. Then it hit her: of course! If Chris had gotten her messages, he wouldn't have paused to reply. He'd have gone looking for the bottle. Racing up the last few steps, she sprinted back to the auditorium. Pulling the door open, she took a moment, waiting for her eyes to adjust.

'Chris?' she called down to the stage. 'Chris, it's me, Dulcie. Are you there?'

She saw a movement. The faint emergency lights behind the auditorium didn't do much to illuminate the seating area, but up front, she could make out shadows—a figure. Someone was on the stage, and she began to run. 'Chris! I've been so worried!'

'Where is he?' Stepping into the faint blue glow was Stella Roebuck, center stage, a look of utter panic on her face. 'I can't find him either!'

'You can't?' Dulcie didn't want to believe it. Climbing up to the stage, she passed the visiting scholar to look through the stage's left wing. Nothing. No Chris, even though the lighting was more effective here. But

stage directions could be confusing, she reminded herself, and raced to the other side. Nothing there either,
except that empty blue glow, even though she was careful to check the corners, where someone, say taken by a
bad cramp, might have curled up in pain. 'He's not here.'

'That's what I've been saying,' Stella was right behind her. 'And there's nobody in the booth either. Not
even that girl, what's her name?'

'Kelly.' Dulcie recited it by rote. She looked around.
In the blue light, the other woman looked ghoulish. This
wasn't making sense. Where was Chris?

'Yeah, well, she's not here either.' Stella started poking around the tiny backstage area, her slim body casting long shadows. 'It's a liability issue. I mean, this is
just too much.'

'What are you talking about?' Dulcie watched her
as she poked behind a curtain and ducked down to look
beneath that chair. 'Are you looking for the bottle, too?'

'What?' Stella stood up, her face blue-white. 'No.
What bottle?'

Dulcie just shook her head. It was gone. Chris was
gone. She didn't know what to do next. 'And you haven't
seen Kelly?'

'No, and I'm wondering if they're in cahoots.' Stella
crossed her arms and stared at Dulcie like she was waiting for something.

'I don't understand.' Dulcie stared back.

'Look, I know he's your boyfriend. That's one of the
reasons I trusted him.' Stella shifted her weight, ap-
praising Dulcie. 'That's why I don't know if I should
say anything.'

'Please,' Dulcie said. 'If you know where he is.'

'I know what he's been doing,' said the other woman.
'And I bet he's off with that Kelly woman. I'm sorry.'

This was because Dulcie's mouth had fallen open. 'I mean, who else but a computer person would have known how to plant fake evidence on my laptop? I told him—told them—that I wanted it back, immediately, and he said he'd go get it. And now they've taken off, and they've taken my laptop with them.'

FORTY-TWO

IT WASN'T POSSIBLE. There had to be another explanation. But faced with an enraged Stella Roebuck, Dulcie couldn't quite explain what that other explanation was.

'No,' was all she said. 'No way. Kelly, maybe, but...' No, Dulcie didn't know the media tech well, but she'd liked her. 'There must have been a problem. Maybe one of them got sick. Or both of them.'

'Of course you'd think that.' Stella was nearly spitting. 'You still think you can trust a man.'

'But...' Dulcie stopped herself. What she'd been going to say wouldn't have helped. She had been about to point out that as far as she could see, the men in Stella's life had been trustworthy. She'd been the one to trade partners like a square dancer. 'I can't imagine that Chris would take your laptop,' Dulcie finally managed to say. 'Why would he?'

Stella shrugged. 'Maybe he was working with Paul.'

Dulcie's confusion must have shown on her face.

'Paul Barnes.' Stella had grabbed her bag and was scanning the rows of seats before them. 'That sleazebag is capable of anything.'

'You don't know then,' Dulcie said, realization growing. Stella turned toward her and shook her head. 'Paul's at the health services. He—he's been poisoned, too.'

'Poison?' Stella's eyes went wide.

Dulcie nodded. 'That's what they're saying, and the

police are looking into it. So it couldn't have been Paul Barnes who took your laptop. Are you sure it's missing?'

'I think so.' The self-assured academic suddenly didn't sound that certain, and Dulcie saw her peek inside her bag.

'If your laptop is actually in there…' Dulcie began. The other woman looked up.

'No, I don't have it.' She threw her head back, making her pointy 'do' bounce. 'Believe me, I'd know if I had my own laptop.'

'Then there's another reason for it to go missing.' Dulcie checked her phone again. Nothing. Both Chris and the water bottle were missing. 'You haven't seen a water bottle around here, have you?'

Another shake of the head. 'What are you talking about?'

'It's complicated,' Dulcie said, as she gave the backstage area another once over. 'But I'd left a message for Chris…' She paused, as another possibility hit her. Maybe he had gotten her messages. Maybe he'd found it. If he were on his way to the health services, he might not have bothered to call her back. He might be talking to Rogovoy now.

'What did you say?' Stella's voice carried from the other side of the stage.

'Hang on,' Dulcie yelled back. 'I'm calling this cop I know.'

'What?' Stella's voice rose in panic. 'Dulcie! Come quick. Help!'

And the room went black.

FORTY-THREE

'STELLA, WHERE ARE YOU?' If the lighting had been dim before, now it was impenetrable. 'What happened?'

'Dulcie!' Stella's panic was audible, but without the blue lights Dulcie had to move slowly, feeling the floor before her with her feet as she made her way across the stage. 'There's…there's someone here.'

'Where?' She reached out and felt something cool and smooth. It jerked away and Dulcie realized she'd grabbed the other woman's bag. Stella had jumped. 'It's okay, Professor Roebuck,' said Dulcie. She felt Stella's hand reaching for hers. 'It's just me.'

'Oh, thank God.' Stella sounded breathless. 'What happened?'

'I don't know.' Dulcie looked around, blinking, but the blackness was absolute. 'You didn't see anything, did you? I mean, before…'

'I thought I heard something,' the other woman said, a little breathless. Could Stella Roebuck be afraid of the dark? 'I'm not sure.'

'Well, let's get out of here.' Dulcie took a firmer hold on the other woman's hand. 'I've been in here enough. I ought to—oh!' Dulcie stumbled as her foot hit something heavy and soft. Only Stella's grip kept her from falling, and she pulled herself upright. 'Hang on.' Dulcie had to pull her hand out of Stella's, the other woman was holding on so tight. 'Let me move this.'

Kneeling, she reached down, feeling for the bag or

the box or whatever it was that had tripped her. She felt cloth—a bag, then—and then warm skin. 'It's a body!' she yelped in surprise.

'Let's get out of here!' Stella was picking up on her nerves. But with the initial shock out of the way, Dulcie's more analytical mind kicked in.

'No, wait.' More cautiously, she felt along the lump in front of her. It was warm, therefore… Yes! *It's alive!* She stopped herself; even Mary Shelley hadn't descended to such a hackneyed phrase. Besides, the mass before her had just moved and, yes, groaned.

'Stella,' Dulcie called. 'Help me. It's hurt.'

'I don't know.' Dulcie could feel Stella moving away. She didn't care; this was no time to be afraid.

Instead, Dulcie focused on the person before her, who had started to stir in earnest. 'Can you sit up? Wait, maybe you shouldn't.'

'No, I'm—I'm okay.' It was Kelly. 'Dulcie, is that you?'

'Uh huh.' Dulcie helped the tech sit up. 'What happened? Did you trip on a cord?'

Maybe it was her eyes, growing accustomed to the dark. Dulcie could make out that the other girl was shaking her head.

'Oh, wow.' Kelly gasped in pain. 'Sorry. I don't think so. My head…'

Dulcie could just make out Kelly's outline and watched as she felt the back of her head.

'Something must have fallen,' she said. 'Why is it so dark?'

'Power must have gone out,' Dulcie said, as she squinted around. Was it her imagination, or was the darkness lessening? 'We were trying to get out of here when I stumbled over you.' Kelly's hand went to her back, where Dulcie's foot must have made contact. 'Sorry.'

'It's okay,' she said, sounding more like herself. 'We?'

'Stella Roebuck is here too.' Dulcie paused, listening to the darkness. The little light that entered showed her Kelly's profile, alert beside her, but didn't penetrate much beyond. 'Ms Roebuck?'

'I'm here.' The voice came from a little ways off, at least as far as Dulcie could tell. Between the backstage curtains and the dark, she no longer had a clear sense of distance. 'I think I may have found something.'

'Hang on.' Dulcie didn't want to risk any more injuries and stood, helping Kelly to her feet. 'Keep talking,' she said. 'We'll follow your voice.'

'I'm here,' Stella responded. 'There's a curtain and then, well, I don't know what it is. Can you come to me?'

'I think so.' Leading Kelly, Dulcie edged toward Stella's voice. 'Keep talking.'

'I'm here, Dulcie.' Stella's voice had gotten softer and the light fainter. 'But I'm—I don't know…'

'Stella?' Dulcie stopped, afraid to miss something in the dark. There was no reply. 'Ms Roebuck? Are you there?'

Nothing.

'Wait, there.' Kelly, at her side, was whispering.

'What?' Dulcie turned toward her.

'I don't know.' Dulcie could feel Kelly looking around, straining her eyes to see. 'I thought I heard something—something soft. A little thud.'

'A little…?' Dulcie stopped herself. A little thud.

It had to be a coincidence. Kelly must have meant a footfall, or a door somewhere out in the lobby closing. For a moment, however, she thought of the sound a cat makes when it jumps on to a soft blanket. The sound Mr Grey would make when he joined her in bed. 'Mr Grey?' She barely breathed the words, and then held her breath, waiting.

'Ms Roebuck?' Kelly called out beside her, not much louder. 'Professor?'

The two girls had clasped their hands together, and Dulcie could hear Kelly breathing. Of one mind, they stepped forward once, twice. Then—

'Ow.' Kelly cut off her exclamation.

'What?' Dulcie turned toward her, then dropped toward the floor. Running her hand over the dusty surface, she half expected to feel warm flesh. 'Is it Stella?'

'No, it's…' Kelly paused. 'I don't know.'

Dulcie's hands touched something rough and low, and she heard Kelly kneeling beside her, running her hands over the coarse and gritty surface.

'A cinder block?' Kelly asked. 'But why here?'

'Do you keep them here for some reason?'

'Well, yeah.' Kelly stayed on the floor, as if feeling for something. 'They're useful as weights, but they're usually stacked in the back, along the wall.'

'Maybe Stella tripped over this.' Dulcie reached past the rough concrete. 'Maybe she knocked herself out.'

'Knocked herself out?' Kelly sounded skeptical.

Even though she couldn't see her, Dulcie turned to the woman at her side. 'What do you mean?'

'Dulcie, I don't think I tripped,' Kelly explained. 'I don't know what's going on, but it's the back of my head that's sore. I think somebody walloped me.'

'Oh great.' Dulcie strained to make out something, *anything* in the dark.

'I mean, I sort of didn't know what was happening for a few moments there,' Kelly continued. 'Then, when I heard you and Stella, I figured whoever it was was long gone. But maybe…'

'Shush.' Dulcie knew Kelly couldn't see her. Still she instinctively waved her down. 'Is anyone out there?'

Nothing.

'Stella?'

Silence.

'Maybe she's gone.' Kelly pulled herself to her feet. From the sound of her breathing, it took effort. 'At any rate, Dulcie, I'm ready to blow this popsicle stand.'

'Wait, we can't just leave her.' Dulcie made herself breathe. 'If someone knocked you out, and then jumped Stella Roebuck.'

'They want something, Dulcie.' Kelly was thinking along the same lines. 'There must be something here.'

'Or in her laptop.' When Kelly didn't respond, Dulcie explained. 'Stella said her laptop was missing. She blamed Chris, but he wouldn't take it.'

'So someone did,' Kelly said slowly. 'You know, I wasn't sure I believed her. But this…'

Dulcie nodded, then realized that the other woman couldn't see her. 'Yeah, something was on it.' Chris's message. 'And Chris knew, too.'

Her mouth went dry. If Chris had discovered what was on the laptop, he was in danger, too. 'We've got to find her, Kelly,' she said. 'And we've got to get out of here.'

'We can't find anything in this dark.' Dulcie could sense the other woman putting her hands out, feeling the space in front of her. 'And I don't think we're going to find Stella Roebuck unless you trip over her like you did me.'

'Sorry,' Dulcie muttered.

'Don't be.' The other woman had taken a step or two away, and Dulcie followed. 'But I think we have to get out of here and turn the lights back on or get a flashlight or whatever. Unless we can see, we can't help anybody.'

'But if she's hurt…' Dulcie didn't like the idea of leaving anyone, not even Stella Roebuck.

'I was knocked out, that was it,' Kelly was saying. 'So either she's out cold, too…or they took her.'

Dulcie didn't want to add the third possibility. That Stella Roebuck was in mortal danger—that the stylish academic had been the intended victim of the party defenestration. But why? Surely nobody would kill Stella Roebuck for whatever was on her laptop? Surely nobody *could* kill someone without a sound. Could they?

She asked a different question. 'Can you find your way out?'

A little laugh. 'I should. I know this place like the back of my hand. Just…' She took a step forward. 'Just step carefully.'

Holding hands, the pair stepped around the cinder block and into the dark. 'The door's here someplace,' said Kelly, letting go of Dulcie's hand. 'See if you can find it.'

Dulcie reached in front of her, moving forward as she did so until she felt something solid. The wall. 'Which way?' she asked.

'Let's see.' Kelly was quiet for a moment. 'That block threw me off. Let's go to the left. Toward you,' she said.

Shuffling, the pair worked their way along the wall until, wonder of wonders, Dulcie felt the raised surface of the door frame. 'Got it!' Stepping to the side, she felt the push bar and leaned on it. The bar moved. The door didn't. 'Kelly, help me,' she called. 'It must be stuck.'

'Great.' The other girl joined her and together they pushed. The door creaked and moved, letting in a splinter of light. But no more. 'What the—?'

'What?' Dulcie had a sinking feeling that she knew what the other would say.

'It's not supposed to be locked.' Kelly was rattling the door, making the sliver of light appear and disappear as she did so. 'It's a fire safety issue. All these doors should push open.'

'It's not just stuck?' Dulcie asked hopefully.

'No.' Up against the illuminated sliver, Kelly dropped to her knees. 'Hello!' she called through the crack. 'I think someone put something up against the door. Maybe drywall? Hello!'

'Kelly.' That slight opening had made Dulcie notice something, something she would rather not have. 'Do you smell something?'

'Don't ask,' the other girl said, her face pressed against the crack. 'This place is filthy.'

'No, I don't mean that.' The construction, Dulcie remembered. The scaffolding. The power tools. 'Kelly?' she asked, her voice growing tight. 'When they were painting, would they have disabled the smoke alarms?'

She didn't need much light to see the shock of horror on the tech's face.

FORTY-FOUR

'THEY COULDN'T HAVE,' said Kelly. Dulcie just shook her head. By now, her eyes were itching and she could smell the strangely bitter scent.

'Hello!' Kelly put her mouth to the door's slight opening and yelled. 'Hello! Is anyone there?'

Dulcie turned away. Even with the faint light, the interior of the auditorium looked darker than it had before, and she screwed her eyes shut for a moment, hoping to reaccustom them to the dark. Shadows danced before her—images on her lids, perhaps, or phantoms drawn from the increasingly acrid air. Ignoring them, she tried to picture the stage. Where were the stairs down to the seating area? Where—she sniffed the air—was the fire? It was a long walk to the back of the auditorium, and already her eyes had started to water. There had to be another, quicker way out.

'Kelly?' She reached behind her for the other girl's shoulder. 'Is there another exit back here?'

'What? Yeah.' She could feel the tech stand. 'Follow me.'

With a sigh of relief, Dulcie let the other girl lead her back across the stage. 'Watch it,' Kelly warned. 'I don't know who—' Too late, she fell, her hand pulled from Dulcie's.

'Kelly!' Dulcie dropped to her knees. 'Are you all right?'

'Yeah, I think so.' The tech pulled herself up and took Dulcie's hand again. 'It should be—'

She stopped so quickly, Dulcie bumped into her. 'What is it?' Dulcie's voice had again dropped to a whisper. But before Kelly could answer, she knew. The smell was stronger here—foul and bitter, like plastic burning.

'I don't think we should go that way,' Kelly said. 'Let's try for the back of the auditorium.'

'Good idea,' Dulcie said with more enthusiasm than she felt. But as they turned, they heard it: a crackling and a pop. The air grew thicker, and in the dark, Dulcie could see bright sparks. Grey smoke rose around them. Grey wisps curled and fell.

'*Dulcie!*' She stopped, listening. The smoke coiled away to the right, beckoning. '*Dulcie, this way!*'

'Kelly!' She grabbed the tech's hand. 'Follow me.'

'No!' The tech pulled back. 'The back of the auditorium. It's safer!'

'*Dulcie!*' The smell, the chemical burn, had turned the sparks green. The smoke curled to the right. '*This way!*'

'There's fresh air this way,' Dulcie yelled. 'Look at the smoke. Look at it!'

Kelly paused, a dead weight as Dulcie pulled. Then, as suddenly, she turned. 'You're right. The fire—it's down by the main doors.'

Holding Dulcie's hand, she forged ahead. Dulcie pushed aside a curtain, and Kelly kicked a chair—that same folding chair—and then they saw a thin strip of light. Together, they threw themselves at it, and it gave way, opening on to the cold and moonlit night.

FORTY-FIVE

'STELLA!' AS SOON AS she'd gotten her breath, Dulcie turned back toward the building. 'We've got to get Stella out!'

'Not us,' said Kelly. 'Them.' As she spoke, Dulcie heard the sirens and they ran around to the front of the building in time to see the fire truck pull up.

'Over here!' Dulcie hailed a large man in full gear.

'Are you the person who called this in?' He was bigger than Rogovoy.

'What? No,' she said. 'But we just got out and Stella—Stella Roebuck—is still in there.'

'In where?' He motioned for a colleague to join him.

'I can show you.'

A large hand landed on her shoulder. 'No, you can't. Tell us, and we'll take a look.'

'In the main auditorium—number one,' she said. 'Has the fire spread?'

'Why?' The face looking down at her scowled. 'Are you a student here?'

'Well, yes, I am.' Dulcie was getting impatient. That smoke—that thick, dark smoke. 'But—'

'And your name is?' He leaned a little closer.

'Dulcie, Dulcinea Schwartz. I'm a grad student here.' She paused. 'Well, not *here*, here. I'm in English and American Literatures, but one of our visiting scholars—'

'There you are.' The gruff voice behind her was familiar, and she turned. 'She's okay,' said Rogovoy.

'Well, I am, but Stella Roebuck—' A big hand cut her off.

'She's fine, too.' The big detective looked down at her and then back at his colleague. 'This one's with me.'

'Are you sure?' Dulcie looked up at the big detective. 'We lost her in the back of the lecture hall.'

'I'm sure,' he said. 'She came out before you did, and she's been taken to the health services. Where you, I believe, were supposed to be.'

'I'm sorry, detective.' She had to make him understand. 'Only, when Paul Barnes collapsed, I realized that I'd left crucial evidence behind.'

He paused only to fix her with a skeptical eye. 'Really.' It didn't sound like a question.

'And besides, if it hadn't been for me going back, you might not have known about the fire.' She looked up at him. 'The whole place might have burned down.'

'Or the fire might have never been set.' Rogovoy's voice was low, almost a grumble, but Dulcie started.

'Set?' She turned to the big man. 'You mean, arson?'

'Look, Ms Schwartz, just do me a favor, okay?' His voice sounded tired. 'When I ask you to stay someplace, please just stay there. For your own safety.'

'Okay,' she replied, somewhat abashed. The big man must be exhausted. 'It was just, I was looking for Chris.'

'I thought you were looking for your other friend?'

'Well, yes.' Dulcie looked up at him. 'To get her out.'

He stopped and turned toward her. 'What do you think happened, Ms Schwartz?'

'There was a fire and the alarm had been disabled.' She knew she was getting it all out of order. 'Someone knocked Kelly out, and then Stella disappeared.'

'Disappeared, huh?' With one hand on her back, he ushered her over to a squad car.

'We were locked in.' Dulcie needed to make him understand as she took a seat. 'And Chris is missing, too.'

'Uh huh.' He leaned over the open door. 'Let's start with this fire.' He drummed on the car roof, and Dulcie winced. 'First of all, what were you two doing in a locked auditorium?'

'I was looking for the bottle,' Dulcie began. 'You said that Mr Thorpe had been poisoned, and, well, I'd given him a drink from a water bottle I found backstage.'

Rogovoy's eyebrows went up at that. 'Just some random bottle?'

'Yes,' Dulcie lied. 'You said they'd been poisoned?'

'No, *you've* been saying they were poisoned,' the detective said. 'All I'm willing to say is that certain substances were found in their system. Could have been intentional. Could have been an accident.'

'But… Marco Tesla and then Thorpe, and now Paul Barnes?' Dulcie was confused.

'Dulcie,' the detective's voice had gotten softer. 'Don't you have enough to deal with right now? I mean, isn't your department running a conference?'

FORTY-SIX

ROGOVOY HAD A POINT. Without the bottle—or Chris—
Dulcie really should get back to work. Or, at least, figure out what was going on. The detective agreed to let
her go, after giving her a stern warning. After all, as
Dulcie pointed out, it wasn't as if he wouldn't know
where to find her.

'May I offer you a ride home?' Rogovoy asked in a
rather pointed fashion.

'No, thanks.' She looked over to where Kelly was
talking to one of Rogovoy's men. 'I'll walk. I'll walk
with Kelly. We'll be okay.'

Rogovoy raised his eyebrows, but she refused to add
more.

Dulcie hung back until the detective had left. By
that time Kelly was no longer being questioned, and
she had come over.

'Well, that was weird.' The tech kept her voice low.

'Tell me about it.' Dulcie looked around. 'They seem
to think we set the fire.'

Kelly only shook her head. 'Maybe we overreacted.'

Dulcie thought of the smoke—and of Mr Grey leading her out. 'I don't think so. Do you?'

'It's been a really long day.' Kelly sounded exhausted. 'You want to get out of here?'

'I was hoping to catch up to Chris.' With everything
going on she hadn't had a chance to check her messages,
and she reached into her bag for her phone. Two mes-

sages. Her heart raced. Neither from Chris. 'He still hasn't called me. Kelly, do you know what's going on?'

'Hey, don't look at me,' the tech said. 'He's a nice guy and all but he's not my type.'

'No, I didn't mean—' It had been a long day. 'Let's get out of here.'

They walked out the door and, although Dulcie had half expected some fireman or cop to stop them, found the plaza deserted.

'Wow, it's cold.' Kelly wrapped her arms around herself. 'Hey, look at the moon. It looks like a street light.'

A glance up showed Dulcie what she meant. Oversized and bright, it cast everything around them into sharp relief. 'It makes me think of home,' she said, a little wistful.

Kelly looked at her. 'You're not from the city, are you?'

Dulcie shook her head. Just then, they heard it—a mournful cry. 'Neither are they.'

'Is that a dog?' Kelly looked around. 'Who would leave a dog out in this weather?'

'I don't know.' It was too hard to explain. 'But we should get moving.'

Because Kelly lived down by the river, they agreed to walk back across the Yard together at least as far as the health services. From there, Kelly could catch a shuttle and Dulcie could figure out what to do. At the very least, she wanted to check in on Thorpe—and also Paul Barnes. If both of them were still incapacitated, it would have grave implications for the conference. Nancy might have returned, too, and it would be useful for them to confer.

At least, that's what Dulcie told herself as they hurried across the Yard. In reality, she knew, she was hoping to find Chris there. The lack of a return call was worrying, but he would undoubtedly have a reason for that. Out here in the dark, with those howls echoing around her, an explanation after the fact was the least of her concern.

'Kelly, you know when you said something had gotten in?' Dulcie scurried to catch up. Deep in thought, she had let the other woman get ahead. 'Something had scratched the door?'

'Or someone.' Kelly's teeth were starting to chatter.

'Do you think…' Dulcie didn't even know how to phrase it. 'Do you think… Chris?'

'Oh, don't be silly.' Kelly put her head down and forged ahead. 'That woman has made you all jealous.'

'No, it's not that,' Dulcie said to the other woman's back, as she hurried to catch up. But she couldn't explain exactly what she meant.

'Hey, look.' Kelly stopped suddenly and turned to face her. 'Do you mind if I just take off?' Her hands still clasped around her body, Kelly nodded off to the right. 'The shuttle takes forever this time of night, and this way I can duck down Oxford and save a few blocks. And you're almost at the health services anyway.'

'Yeah, that's fine,' Dulcie said. 'It's as light as day with that moon and all.' It was true about the moon. What was also true was that it was cold and the Yard was deserted with all the undergrads gone, but she needed a little time alone with her thoughts. Still, as she watched the other woman walk quickly off into the night she had a moment of misgiving. Something about that light wasn't natural.

Since she still had her phone out, she hit Chris's number. The mailbox she had selected, she heard once more, was now full. She hung up just as a gust of wind hit her, and she bent into it. No wonder Kelly had wanted to take the shorter way home.

'Chris, where RU?' She couldn't walk quite as fast while she texted, not while cradling the phone like this. Still, it seemed like a good thing to do. 'Heading 2 HS.' She hit send as the wind buffeted her again, howling between the buildings.

'Where are you, Chris?' She spoke out loud. There was no way her voice would be heard above this wind, and there was no one around to hear her anyway.

Or was there? 'Mr Grey?' On a whim, she turned around and got a mouthful of grit. 'Are you there? I know you saved me. Saved us,' she said, her hair whipping across her face. Maybe the fire hadn't been dangerous. Rogovoy hadn't said, and the fire chief had looked more annoyed than anything. But she knew what she had experienced—and how she had felt. Mr Grey had saved both her and Kelly. Maybe he had saved Stella Roebuck, too.

'Mr Grey?' The wind had died down, and with it an eerie quiet had fallen. She started walking again, aware of the crunch of frozen dirt beneath her feet. Somewhere, blocks away probably, a siren went off. A car—a taxi, she'd bet—honked in an angry blast. She started walking again. Of course Mr Grey wouldn't come to her here. She didn't need him. She wasn't in danger. Besides, he had been a house cat, after all.

The wind again. It pushed her forward this time and sent her staggering toward the gate. A low light suspended from the arch made the short brick passageway look cozy, almost like shelter, and she made for it gratefully. Just a moment out of this wind would be welcome. Then she'd pass out of the Yard and cross the street; in just a few minutes, she'd be in the plaza. There was a café just beyond the health services building. Maybe she should stop off there first. Get something to eat. It would be warm there.

But if she expected the gust to pass, she was mistaken. After the briefest respite it picked up again, pelting her with grit and the last of the leaves, plucked from the low-lying holly that bordered University Hall. She bent down, hurrying for the archway. For shelter. It pursued, pushing her like a giant hand at her back. And then she heard it: the howl.

FORTY-SEVEN

DULCIE FROZE, THE cold forgotten. Her heartbeat loud in her ears, she made herself breathe, and then she looked around. The archway, the nearest shelter, was only a few hundred feet away. A minute's walk. Less. She started toward it, moving quickly. But it was dark, the moon covered by a passing cloud, and the frozen ground crumbled beneath her, throwing her off balance. She stumbled and caught herself. And then, as she righted herself and began walking again, the cloud passed, racing across the sky, and out of the corner of her eye she saw…what? Maybe nothing. A patch of dark on dark, moving quickly as the cloud crossed the sky. A shadow, undoubtedly, cast by the once again bright moon, stretching out from the buildings to her left. Stretching and changing shape as the wind cleared the remnants from the sky, it was nothing—a shade—only ever so slightly darker than the frosted sod that lined the path.

Nerves, Dulcie told herself. Nerves and suggestion, and the memory of a scary tale echoing in her mind. It was a shadow, cast by the racing wisps of cloud. Nothing more. Only this shadow seemed to be moving toward her. Coming to cut her off.

Out of the shadows it ran. Too big for a dog, it moved low to the ground, loping and stretching as if cast by the moonlight. And as it grew closer, Dulcie saw, it was too solid to be a shadow. And not grey at all. Rather, rust-colored—bloody almost. The moon shone down, glinting off a cold eye. And Dulcie ran.

The race was impossible. The *thing* had too much of a head start, but still she ran, pounding against the cold path as if it could propel her high above the dangerous ground. Somehow she passed it, running hard. Through the archway and across the sidewalk. She didn't pause to look as she leaped into Mass Ave and sped up more as the health services came into view. Arms outstretched, she pushed through the door, only to crash into an older woman and send them both tumbling to the floor.

'Doctor! Are you hurt?' A slim orderly came running as she clambered to her feet. But he wasn't talking to Dulcie, and instead helped the other woman to her feet. 'Here, let me help you.'

'You.' He looked over his shoulder at Dulcie. 'You stay there.'

'What happened?' Another orderly, barely her height, had come running. He grabbed her arm. 'Why did you attack Doctor Xi?'

'I didn't.' Dulcie leaned on him, panting. 'I fell. I—it was chasing me.' She started to turn, to pull away. To make sure it had not followed.

'Wait a minute, miss.' The orderly was stronger than he looked.

'No, please.' She managed to turn. There was nothing behind her. Nothing outside the door. 'I'm fine,' she said finally. 'Really.'

'Dulcie!' She turned to see Chris running toward her. 'Are you okay?'

'Chris!' Pulling away from the orderly, she threw herself into her boyfriend's arms. She could feel his heart racing as he held her close. 'Where have you been?'

'Here.' He pulled back to look at her. His cheeks

were flushed, his hair more disheveled than usual. 'I was talking with Stella Roebuck.' He turned, but the modish academic was not visible among those who now crowded around. 'What happened, Dulcie? What's going on?'

'I—' She stopped. Her boyfriend would understand. The bystanders gathered round them, however, wouldn't. 'You've been here?'

He nodded. 'I got your message, and I was afraid I'd missed you.'

'You just got here?' Somehow, she couldn't make the words come out. He nodded. 'Chris, are you...' She didn't know how to ask. Not here, with all these strangers present.

'What?' He was definitely breathing heavily as he pushed his hair off his face. 'You look upset.'

'Chris, are you... You're not...' She dropped her voice to a whisper. 'You're not a wolf, are you?'

'Come with me, miss.' Someone grabbed her arms from behind. 'Let's have a seat, why don't we?'

'Let go of me.' She pulled, but the hands were strong. Behind Chris, she saw the orderly nodding.

'Really, she's fine.' Chris looked up. 'Please.'

'She was hysterical,' said the orderly. Still, the arms released her, and she turned to see a uniformed policeman behind her.

'I was *upset*,' Dulcie clarified, rubbing her forearms in what she hoped was a dramatic gesture. 'It has been a trying day, and I was out and it was dark, and...' She paused. How to explain it all? She looked around. 'Stella?' She spied the academic heading toward the door and waved. 'Professor Roebuck, you're okay!'

'No thanks to you.' Her voice was terse. 'Now, if you don't mind...'

'No, wait.' Dulcie spluttered. 'Stella, we lost you.'

'Yeah, I know.' Sarcasm dripped from her words. 'Thanks so much.'

'We looked for you.' Dulcie found herself on the defensive. 'Honest.' Something was out of whack. 'Wait, how long have you been here?'

'I really don't know.' She raised one pale hand to her forehead. 'I'm exhausted.'

'Miss, please.' The orderly was reaching for Dulcie again.

'No, I'm curious.' Dulcie pulled away, her eyes on Roebuck. 'What happened?'

'Dulcie, please, come with me.' Chris was by her side. He took her hand, but his next words were to the cop. 'She's had a really stressful couple of days, officer. I'll take her home as soon as I get my things.'

'Wait a minute, Chris.' Dulcie kept her eyes on Roebuck. 'Did you know she accused you of stealing her computer?'

'What?' Chris shook his head.

'Oh, please.' Stella turned once again toward the door.

'No, wait,' Dulcie called, but Chris held her.

'Dulcie, don't do this—'

'Do what?' They all turned to see Nancy Pruitt coming through the door with what seemed to be a large box by her side. Despite the knitted throw that covered it, Dulcie recognized it as Tigger's carrying case. 'I'm sorry, what have I missed?'

'Nancy!' Dulcie couldn't explain the wave of relief that washed over her. The sight of the motherly secretary—and the implication of the kitten—just seemed to make everything better. 'Thank the goddess, it's you! It's been terrible.'

'It isn't—Mr Thorpe...' The color drained from Nancy's cheeks. She dropped the box with a thud and sank to the floor.

The orderly ran toward her, pushing Stella Roebuck out of the way.

'Nancy!' Dulcie followed, but the orderly waved her back.

'Let's just give her some air,' he said. 'Shall we?'

Chris drew Dulcie aside. 'What's going on with Thorpe?'

'Thorpe and Paul Barnes—they both drank something. Rogovoy said they may have been dosed with something.' Chris shook his head in disbelief. 'You don't know, Chris. You weren't here.'

Another orderly had arrived by this time, rushing a wheelchair over to Nancy, who still sat slumped by the door.

'I was trying to help you, Dulcie.' His whisper had an edge to it. 'And help Thorpe. And I found something.'

'So you said, before you disappeared.'

He sighed and pushed his bangs back once again. 'Dulcie, I was working.' Nancy seemed to be arguing with the wheelchair orderly. She was sitting up and had taken the kitten's carrier into her lap.

Dulcie wanted to go to her. At the very least, she wanted to ask about Tigger—surely Nancy had brought him for a reason. Her boyfriend, however, was waiting.

'Okay, I know how you get,' she said. 'But Chris, I've been trying to reach you for hours. You said you'd found something...'

'I said I *thought* I did.' He seemed to think this made a big difference. 'And I had to go check it out. I've been in the computer lab all day.'

'Wait, you were in the Science Center?' He nodded. 'But what about the fire?'

'The fire?' It took a moment before anything registered, and Dulcie glanced back toward the door. The second orderly had begun folding the wheelchair. 'Oh, the false alarm. We heard that and ignored it. It happens so often.'

'It wasn't…never mind.' She shook her head. Nancy was being helped to her feet, still clutching the plastic carrier. 'I looked for you.'

'I was in the clean room,' he explained. 'I wanted to get at that laptop's hard drive and, well, it probably wasn't necessary, but I figured there'd be hell to pay if I messed anything up. So I went into lockdown—vacuums on, air filters, you name it.'

It made sense. So much so that Dulcie wondered at not having thought of it. Except for a few nagging doubts.

'So don't you want to hear what I found out?' He looked so happy, though. Much more puppy than wolf.

'Sure.' She shelved her fears. There'd be time enough later for them to talk.

What he said didn't make sense at first, although it did serve to distract her from what seemed to be a growing argument about the kitten. Nancy should have known no pets would be allowed in the health services.

'Dulcie, are you listening?' She made herself turn away. Chris was explaining, for the umpteenth time, how hard it was ever really to erase any file from a computer. Between the caches and the memory, he'd explained to her before, there was almost always a ghost of a file somewhere on a machine. That was why she'd been surprised when he hadn't been able to find Stella Roebuck's file originally.

'But she told me she hadn't backed anything up.' Dulcie looked up. Nancy seemed to have won at least one victory: the second orderly was pushing the unwanted wheelchair away.

'No.' Chris was smiling now. 'What you told me was that she no longer trusted those systems. Not that she *never* had.'

Dulcie shook her head. Anglo-Saxon had been easier. 'There's a difference?'

A triumphant nod. 'That was what I was hoping, and sure enough, there is. You know what an ISP is, right?' He seemed to want confirmation, so Dulcie nodded. He didn't look convinced. 'Think of it this way, Dulce. Everything leaves a trail of some kind. Like... computer footprints.'

She nodded again. 'You don't have to talk down to me, Chris.'

He opened his mouth and shut it. She leaned forward and kissed him. 'That was a joke.'

He seemed doubtful, but continued anyway. 'So, I was betting that she had sent her file someplace. I mean, it sounded like she had, and maybe, I was thinking, even if it wasn't on her computer, it would still exist on someone else's. Or on the server.' He must have noticed the blank look on her face. 'You remember what I told you about how, when you send a file, the server basically makes a copy, right?'

Another nod. 'Kind of.'

'Bingo.' He was beaming. So much so that Dulcie felt a bit like a heel for her next question. Before she asked, she looked around. The staff and Nancy seemed to have reached a truce: the first orderly was escorting Nancy over to the chairs, while the second fetched a paper cup of water. Tigger, his case still covered by the throw, remained by the door. Stella had retreated during all the fuss and now hung back behind the seating area. Dulcie and Chris might as well have been at home alone.

'Chris? So...what does that mean?' Her head down, Stella walked by them, past the chairs.

'I found it.' Chris interrupted her next words, raising his hand. 'No, no. I'm exaggerating. But I know where there probably is a copy. I just have to track down a computer belonging to an Associate Professor MT at Cal.'

'Marco?' Dulcie wheeled around. Stella Roebuck was almost at the door. 'Stop her!'

'Dulcie?' Chris reached for her arm again.

'Miss, please!' The orderly with Nancy just looked annoyed.

But it was the box by the door that stopped them all. Somehow, in the commotion, the knitted throw had fallen off, revealing the plastic cat carrier and the tufts of orange fur poking through. Even from the chairs, they could all see the box shaking, its inhabitant rocking it back and forth. And from inside, the most ferocious growl.

Even Stella stepped back.

'Stop that woman.' Dulcie stood, pulling free of Chris. 'She's guilty. Don't let her leave! The kitten proves it.'

FORTY-EIGHT

WHAT HAPPENED NEXT was like a scene from a nightmare. One in which the ones you trust turn on you. Nancy had, of course, jumped up. But racing past Dulcie she had thrown herself on her knees by the kitten's carrier. Within moments she had the tiny orange fellow in her arms. No longer growling, no longer agitated, the kitten seemed as meek as milk, cuddling in the secretary's lap.

'Mew,' he said, his blue eyes focused on Dulcie's.

'Tigger, Nancy.' She looked from the little creature to the woman cradling him. 'Nancy, you know…' The orderlies were approaching, with a slow and steady caution. 'Tell them why you brought the kitten here.'

'For Mr Thorpe, of course.' Nancy held the little tiger closer. 'I thought it would be a comfort for him.'

'Dulcie, please,' Chris, meanwhile, was pleading with her. 'Not here.'

'Chris, you of all people…' She stopped. Looking around, she saw that he was right. Whatever she suspected—whatever she *knew*—about Tigger, this wasn't the place.

'ISP tracking—that's brilliant!' Stella, at least, had not fled. In fact, as Nancy had been lifting Tigger from his case, she was stepping forward, a strange smile on her face. A smile she directed toward Chris. 'It sounds like maybe you're my hero.'

Dulcie opened her mouth to object. Only a few hours before, Stella had been accusing him of sabotage and theft. She had been, Dulcie was quite sure, about to flee. But when she turned to Chris, she saw her boyfriend flush and stammer under the full force of the academic's gaze.

'It was nothing really.' He turned toward her as she took the chair to his right. 'I'm only sorry I didn't think of it earlier.'

'Wait a minute.' Dulcie was willing to admit she'd rushed to judgment, but still she knew something was wrong. Tigger's display had confirmed it. 'Stella, what is going on? If—if...' She wasn't sure even how to phrase what she suspected, and so she backtracked to what Chris had explained moments before. 'Tell us, why did Marco Tesla have a copy of your paper?' Something wasn't kosher.

'Because I sent it to him.' She said it as if it were the most natural thing in the world. 'An early draft. We were in the same field, you know, and I valued his feedback. That's what couples do, you know.' She turned to face Chris, a conspiratorial smile on her face. 'When they can understand each other's work, that is.'

'But, but...' Something was wrong. Very wrong, and for starters Dulcie didn't like the way Stella Roebuck was leaning over toward Chris. 'I thought you two were rivals.'

'We were, after a fashion. As well as lovers.' She smiled and shrugged. 'I wouldn't expect you to understand.'

'I understand well enough how you operate.' She stood, to find Chris standing also. 'Chris, don't...' That would be too much. If he took this interloper's side against her. If he...

'Look!' He was pointing over to the entrance. At the huge, hairy beast that had appeared at the door.

FORTY-NINE

FOR A MOMENT, the kitten—the computer—all were forgotten, as the creature pushed open the door with its shaggy head and padded into the lobby. Big, too big for a wolf, even, it stepped slowly into the light, eyes glowing bright against the dark red fur. For a moment it paused, jaw opened slightly, as it took in the room. Those fangs, each the size of Dulcie's hand, disappeared only briefly as a huge red tongue lapped over the black muzzle. Then it came forward again, unafraid of the humans before it. And with each step it seemed to shrink, its hairy bulk diminishing as it approached.

'Come here, girl.' Chris got down on his knee and held his hand out, palm up, toward the intruder.

'What are you doing?' Dulcie couldn't help it. Maybe her imagination had gotten the better of her. Maybe this—this *thing*—had never been as large as her fears had made it. Still, the dog—if dog it was—had to be the same animal that had chased her through the Yard. And it was large, bigger than any dog Dulcie had ever seen, and its coat was such an odd rust red. 'You,' she yelled over to the guard. 'Do something.'

'I'm not animal control.' The orderly must have thought she was talking to him. 'Besides, I think it's just tired.'

'Tired?' Dulcie turned to see the dog staring at her with large, yellow eyes. No longer glowing, they did indeed look tired. But as she watched, its great jaw opened once more. Teeth, curved and sharp if not quite so huge, and then a long, red tongue.

The dog—for now it was clear that the beast was a dog, simply a large dog, and not that large now that she had had a good look at it—was panting.

'Not tired,' Chris was saying. 'It's thirsty. *She's* thirsty. Come here, girl.'

'No wonder she's thirsty,' Dulcie said, half to herself. She'd been pretty winded by that run, too. But Chris wasn't listening. Instead, he was reaching into his bag. Pulling out a bottle of water, he poured some into his cupped hand. The dog, for surely it was a dog, took one step closer and stopped.

'Come on,' said Chris, his voice soft and kind. 'It's okay, girl.'

The dog looked up at Dulcie, as if seeking her approval. Dulcie found herself smiling at the animal, as if it could read a human face. Everyone else, even the kitten, she realized, had gone silent.

'She's afraid,' said Chris. 'Can everyone step back?'

Dulcie hesitated. 'What if it has rabies?' She looked at the gathered medical professionals and then at Chris. 'What if it bites you?'

'She won't.' Chris held his hand out further, but the movement seemed to spook the animal. It turned, as if to run, then paused. Still panting, it looked up at Dulcie and then again at Chris.

'Hang on.' Chris grabbed the bottle again. Cradling it against his body, he leaned forward while clasping his hands. Water sloshed out, spilling on to the floor, but also filling the larger cup made by his hands. Once the bottle had emptied he let it fall, and as it rolled away he once more extended his hands.

'It's okay.' The big dog eyed the impromptu basin.

'Here, look.' Eyes on the dog, Chris brought his hands back in. He bent his face over his hands and paused. Dulcie looked at the dog, but the dog—instead of looking at Chris—only looked up at her. As if, she suddenly felt, it was waiting for something.

'Come on.' Chris extended his tongue and bent his head over his hands. 'Like this.'

'No!' Dulcie couldn't have said what made her yell, but she did. 'No, Chris!' She ran toward her boyfriend and pushed him, so that he fell on his side. Water splattered all over the floor. He stared up at her, confused, as once again the orderly moved in.

'That's enough, miss.'

'No, wait.' Chris righted himself. 'The dog!'

She turned. They all did. A feral animal wasn't to be ignored, especially one that size. Dulcie felt a moment of fear. If she had startled the animal…if she had scared it and it attacked…

But despite her own racing heart, the dog seemed unaffected by her outburst—or by the loss of its drink. If anything, the big beast seemed to be waiting. For a moment they all stayed silent as those huge yellow eyes took them in, moving from one to another as if to take their measure. They lingered longest on Dulcie and then, she was sure, it nodded. Then it turned silently on those big paws and made for the doors again.

'Stop it!' someone—one of the orderlies?—yelled. But nobody moved, and the big animal pushed against the glass door and slipped out, into the night.

FIFTY

'DULCIE, WHAT WAS that about?' Chris was standing as she turned back to face him. His jeans were splattered with water and he looked concerned. 'I thought you liked animals.'

'It was the water, Chris.' She didn't know how to explain. 'That bottle. Where did you get it?'

'You asked me to bring it.' He reached for the empty, which had rolled over by the wall. 'I got your voicemail when I came out of the clean room and found it. I thought you wanted it.'

'It's poisoned.' Dulcie thought back. 'Didn't you see my text?'

'No, sorry.' He looked down at the bottle in his hand, then back up at her. 'Poison?'

'You're the one.' Stella stepped forward. 'You poisoned Marco, and then…then, you tried to implicate me.'

'Wait, what?' Chris looked from one woman to the other, clearly confused. 'What are you talking about?'

'How dare you!' Stella's voice went shrill, and she turned to the guard. 'Arrest him. He's been involved with this since the beginning. He has the bottle. He has my computer, too. Somewhere.'

'I told you. It's in the clean room,' Chris was saying as the orderly came toward him with a menacing look. 'Oh, come on.'

'Wait, everybody.' Dulcie stepped forward. 'Someone, call Detective Rogovoy. He knows all the details.'

The orderly had Chris's arm by now and stepped behind him, the more easily to get him into a full restraining hold. The guard, meanwhile, seemed unwilling to take matters into his own hands.

'Please,' Dulcie entreated. 'Call him. Or I will.' She took a step toward her own bag and saw everyone flinch. 'I just want to get my phone,' she explained.

Slowly, so as not to startle anyone, she reached into her bag and extracted her phone. All eyes were on her as she dialed.

'Detective?'

Voicemail.

For a moment, she thought she could fake it. She thought she could leave a message and make it sound like she was holding a conversation. But one look at Stella, and she realized she wasn't a good enough liar.

'Okay, then.' The orderly had Chris from behind and the guard was approaching. 'No, wait.' Dulcie stepped between them. 'It's her you want to arrest.' She pointed at Stella. 'Not Chris.'

'You can't take his word over mine.' From the tone of Stella's voice, such a choice would be unthinkable.

Only it wasn't. 'Yes, I can,' said Dulcie. Time was slowing down. 'And I do. You keep saying Paul Barnes is a cad, that he's so jealous he would sabotage you. And I believed you, even though he's been nothing but a gentleman to me. In fact, when I felt ill he went to get me a drink of water. Only the water fountains aren't working on the first floor of the Science Center, so when he wanted to get me a drink of water he took the bottle out of your bag. Didn't he?'

'You're crazy,' Stella said, her voice so calm that

it seemed only reasonable to believe her. She looked around. 'Isn't this a hospital? Isn't there someone who can take care of this poor girl?'

The orderly looked from Stella to the doctor, waiting for a cue. The doctor opened her mouth and then closed it. Stella stepped into the gap.

'What are you waiting for?' she snapped. 'The poor girl has clearly lost it.'

That was it. The dropped word—and Dulcie suddenly realized what she should have noticed all along. 'Lost it?' she asked Stella. '*Lost* it?' Dulcie wasn't much for drama, but she envisioned scorn dripping from her words like so much ice water. When she realized that her attempt at sarcasm was only drawing concerned looks from the assembled medical staff, she switched gears.

'You're the one who was saying you "lost it",' she said. 'Meaning your famous paper, of course. Only you didn't, did you?'

She'd gone too far. The doctor nodded at the orderly and he took a step toward her.

'No, that's not what I meant.' Dulcie took a step back. Right into the considerable bulk of Detective Rogovoy.

'I was on my way back here anyway.' The large man put both hands on her shoulders to steady her. At least that's what Dulcie hoped was his intent. She didn't dare pull away—not yet. Not until she'd explained herself. Instead she looked up at him. To her great relief he smiled. 'Go on,' he said. 'I'm enjoying this.'

Swallowing hard, she turned. It helped that those big hands were on her shoulders as she turned to face her adversary.

'You say I lost it. Well, maybe I have,' she said. 'But you didn't. Not in that way. That paper you've had Chris looking for? The one you claimed Paul Barnes stole. Or, I don't know... Professor Showalter? They didn't. They couldn't, because you never lost it.'

She paused for breath. Chris was looking at her. Everyone was, but he had an expression of confusion on his face. 'I love you,' she mouthed, as she silently willed him to wait. To believe in her. Then she continued, speaking once again to Stella Roebuck.

'You never lost your great presentation, because you never had one. Not one of your own. Marco Tesla, your lover, was a late invite. I don't know what you were thinking—that he wouldn't know and that he wouldn't find out. But you stole his work. And when he showed up, you realized you couldn't present "your" work, because it was really his. You erased it. You hang out with so-called gearheads, so you know how. But to muddy the waters, you blamed Professor Showalter and Professor Barnes. You blamed anyone—even Chris. But somehow Marco found out about it. And you...' She paused. The water bottle.

'Detective Rogovoy?' She looked back at him. He nodded. 'Can you test that water bottle for drugs?'

'The lab can,' he said.

'That's not my bottle.' The petite academic was sounding panicked. 'You can't prove it is.'

'No, but I can prove that work on your computer came from Marco Tesla's.' Chris stepped forward. 'And I'd swear in court that the paper was intentionally deleted by someone who had at least an hour to do so.' He shrugged as he looked at Dulcie. 'That's not much, but it does mean someone didn't sneak in while Kelly was doing her soundcheck. And that means that Dulcie is right: Stella Roebuck deleted her own paper.'

FIFTY-ONE

IT WAS ALMOST ENOUGH: Chris's testimony, along with the ill-will generated by Stella Roebuck's high-handed manner. Nobody wanted to come to her aid. Even Nancy's eyes sank to the little cat in her arms as Stella looked around the room for support.

'You're crazy. All of you.' Dulcie had to give it to her: Stella Roebuck could act. 'You really think I'm some kind of criminal mastermind?'

'I think you're better with computers than you let on,' said Dulcie. 'And that you'd let Chris be blamed for what you did.'

'You have a theory. That's all.' Stella was calming down. 'That's nothing. One girl's theory.'

'That's not all.' They all turned. Nancy was still looking at the floor, but it was her voice they had heard.

'Nancy?' Dulcie was thinking of Tigger, thinking of the kitten's reaction when Stella had tried to leave. Tigger had known something. His outburst had to have meant…something. Out loud, however, she voiced the question on all their minds. 'Would you tell us?'

'The titles.' Nancy seemed to choke on the word, then repeated it a little louder. 'For the papers. It was my responsibility to gather the titles of all the papers that were being presented. For the conference program, you know.'

She stroked the small cat, then continued. 'I had forgotten about it—about them—until just a little while ago.' She glanced up at Rogovoy. 'We've been keeping Mr Thorpe's kitten at the departmental offices, and I went back after he became ill to retrieve the little fellow. I have a spare key to his office in my desk; when I went to retrieve it, I saw the list again.'

'But I thought they were incomplete?' Dulcie didn't understand. 'You told us they could still be changed.'

Nancy was nodding now. 'Yes, that's true. But I had working titles and rough ideas. Nothing published yet, but you know how Mr Thorpe is.' She paused. 'We like to be prepared.'

'I'm sorry, Miss—' Rogovoy broke in, his voice gruff. 'Miss Pruitt? How does this pertain to the matter at hand?'

'When Marco Tesla called, saying he was interested in attending, I asked him for a title. He explained that he was trying to re-create a work that he had lost, that had been erased from *his* computer systems, but that he believed he'd have ready by Saturday. He was calling it 'The Look of Love: Deconstructing the Appearance of Affection in Late Twentieth Century Gender-Specific Romance'.

'But I thought that—' Dulcie stopped and turned. She and Nancy were both staring at Stella Roebuck, who had gone even paler.

'I can explain.' Her voice was a hoarse whisper.

'Dulcie?' Chris turned to her.

'That's why she erased it, Chris,' Dulcie said. Beside her, Nancy nodded. 'She stole Marco Tesla's work and was going to present it as her own. Only when he showed up here, she had to get rid of it. That's why she panicked when you were close to tracing it. Why she knocked Kelly out and tried to make it look like you two stole her laptop. She needed to ditch it—'

'Okay, I've heard enough.' Rogovoy was clearly losing patience. 'You're going to have to come with me, miss—Professor.'

'It wasn't like that,' Stella yelled, pulling away. 'Marco and I were lovers. Collaborators. We shared everything.'

'Is that why you drugged him?' Nancy had taken on an unaccustomed vehemence. 'Mr Tesla, and Mr Barnes and Mr Thorpe too?'

'What? No.' She was shaking her head. 'It was Barnes who turned Marco against me. Barnes who was with Marco before I got there. Ask him.'

'I'm sure we will, Ms Roebuck.' Rogovoy nodded to a woman in uniform and she came forward to take Roebuck's arm. 'If he ever wakes up.'

FIFTY-TWO

'NANCY, YOU SHOULD go home.' The waiting room had cleared out by then, leaving only Dulcie and Chris to sit with the secretary. 'You need some rest.'

'I need to be here.' She blinked and sat up straighter. She had retrieved Tigger's box by then and placed the sleeping kitten back in it. The orderly had given up. 'For when Mr Thorpe wakes up.'

Dulcie sighed and exchanged a look with Chris. There wasn't really a case to argue here. She'd have done the same.

'Why don't I get us something to eat, then.' Chris looked from one woman to another. 'It might be a long night.'

'Thanks, Chris.' She reached out to take his hand as he stood. 'And thanks again for finding that bottle.' Rogovoy's people had taken it, as well as Chris's statement. He'd been warned about staying in touch, but nobody seemed seriously concerned that he had done anything other than retrieve it.

'Glad I could find it,' he said, zipping up his coat. 'But, you know, it's funny. I still don't know why she did it.'

'What do you mean?' Dulcie kept her voice low. Nancy had nodded out again, her chin on her chest, and Dulcie didn't want to wake her.

'She'd pretty much destroyed the evidence. I mean,

she didn't know I'd be able to find it. Why drug Thorpe—
or Barnes?'

Dulcie shook her head. 'I don't know. Maybe Barnes
was on to her? Maybe he was going to give her away?
Maybe he'd said something to Thorpe?'

'It's like she just wanted to ruin the conference. But
she had so much riding on it.' He pulled his knit cap
over his ears. 'Pizza okay?'

'Pizza would be great, Chris. Thank you.'

It was nice to have someone looking out for you,
Dulcie thought, and with a stab of guilt thought of her
mother. Lucy did her best, and she did it alone. Well,
Dulcie corrected herself, with only the help of her sister 'crones' at the commune. And Dulcie couldn't even
be bothered to call her back.

Pulling the phone from her bag, Dulcie made a silent
promise. Yes, her mother was nutty. But Lucy loved her.
From now on, Dulcie would make more of an effort to
keep in touch. For starters, she could at least listen to
her messages.

'Dulcie, about that shape shifter,' the message began.
As Dulcie suspected, her mother had picked up their
last conversation right from when they'd gotten disconnected. Now, she tried to remember what her mother
had been saying: something about the kitten and about
'shape shifters' not all being bad?

'They can seem threatening, but that may be part of
the protective aura. The wolf in the dog, so to speak.'
Lucy was rambling. 'I see one close to you. Close to
your mission, Dulcie. I see it—her—clearly. That kitten is orange, right? Kind of reddish?' Dulcie shook her
head. Her mother meant well, but there was no logic
in her view of the world. 'That may be key. And there
may be others.'

Tomorrow, she'd deal. It had been an exhausting day. The gentle purr emanating from Tigger's carrier was soft and rhythmic, and Dulcie found herself beginning to doze. She'd only closed her eyes for a moment, she was sure, when she opened them to see Professor Showalter in front of her.

'There you are.' Professor Showalter's auburn bun looked a little messier than usual. They'd all been having quite a day. 'I came back here as soon as I heard. That nice detective wanted me to go back to the hotel, but I can't believe…' She scanned the room.

Dulcie nodded in silent agreement. 'It's been crazy,' she said finally. Then, taking in her mentor's late arrival, she asked, 'If you don't mind me asking, what were you doing—yesterday and this morning in the Mildon?'

'I had to verify the Philadelphia letters.' Showalter actually blushed. 'I felt responsible, you see, since I'd passed them on to you.'

'The Philadelphia letters.' It felt like a million years ago that Dulcie had worried about them. She certainly didn't want her mentor to feel bad about them. 'I never did know why you doubted them.'

Showalter shook her head, her brow furrowed. 'I should know better,' she said with a new determination. 'It was something Paul had said, something about how he'd looked at that research and dismissed it, out of hand. Plus, I got that strange, well…that strange feeling that something was wrong. I thought that was about the papers, at first. It seemed the most likely option. But once I heard that Barnes had asked you to collaborate, I realized there was another possibility.'

'He wants to get his hands on those papers, doesn't he?' The realization hit Dulcie with a dull thud. 'It's the papers he wants access to, not me. He didn't know that he could apply for access, that he could have gone to the Mildon himself and done his own analysis.'

'Not exactly.' Showalter's voice was gentle.

For a moment, Dulcie felt hope spark again. 'You mean, he never applied because he *did* want to work with me?'

'He should have.' Showalter was shaking her head. 'It would have been more seemly. But no, it wasn't because he wanted to work *with* you that he didn't apply. He wanted you to do the work.'

Dulcie's heart sank as Showalter continued.

'There was no way for you to know, Dulcie, but I'm afraid that's his modus operandi. Get a brilliant grad student and then claim credit for her work. That's why I wanted to speak with you about his so-called offer. Why I've been trying to talk him into coming clean. Why do you think there's such bad blood between him and Stella Roebuck?'

'She was his grad student? But that must have been years ago.'

Showalter nodded. 'Some people say she was the real author—uncredited, of course—of *So Many Cities, So Many Hills*.'

That took a moment to sink in. 'If that's the case, then why did she switch? I mean, nothing could be more different from eighteenth century prose...' As she was forming the words, the answer came to her. 'Marco Tesla? She met Marco and adopted his style—and his area of expertise. And then she stole his work?'

'It's how she was taught.' Showalter's voice was gentle. 'They were lovers, so perhaps she felt entitled.'

'But Tesla knew. He knew she was the one.' Dulcie didn't understand. 'I think Paul Barnes must have told him.'

Showalter looked at her, about to interrupt, but Dulcie kept talking.

'You missed it,' Dulcie said. 'Chris found proof—well, as good as we're going to get—that Stella had erased her own paper. She had to. Marco was here, and he would have exposed her.' The reality hit her. 'Unless she killed him.'

'Marco wouldn't have exposed her.' Showalter was shaking her head. 'He knew about Stella because I told him. I'd figured out what happened, from her history. From what I've seen Paul do. But Marco only wanted to talk to her. That's why he came here. He wanted her to step down, of course. He'd emailed her. I know he felt betrayed. But he loved her, in his way, and he was hoping for a private opportunity to confront her. I still think it must have been some kind of horrible accident.'

'Maybe he was drunk. Those drinks were strong. Thorpe—' She stopped. Thorpe had been made a fool of. With Stella discredited and Thorpe humiliated, Tesla was the obvious front runner. Unless...

'Oh, dear Bast,' said Dulcie, not noticing the gentle smile her invocation provoked. 'Paul Barnes was in Cambridge early. He must have been hoping to get Stella alone. He knew what she was capable of, and he was trying to blackmail her. Then he drugged Martin Thorpe and set you up for it. Thorpe said you handed him the glass, but Barnes was at the party with you, wasn't he? He drugged me, because I was becoming too nosy. And then he dosed himself, just when the police started asking questions.

'He must have drugged Marco Tesla, too. I don't

know if he meant to make a fool out of him, or what. But if Tesla already knew about Stella and they fought…'

'What?' Nancy had woken up and was staring at her. 'Dulcie, what are you saying?'

Dulcie looked up at Showalter, the horror of it all hitting her. 'Chris saw it.' It was all becoming clear. 'He saw Paul Barnes with the bottle. I just assumed—but it was Barnes all along. He was trying to frame you for Marco's death, wasn't he? That would have made him the best remaining candidate, even if he hadn't published in years. If it hadn't been for that dog…'

Dulcie turned toward her mentor, about to explain, when it hit her. Lucy's message. Shape shifters. Her mentor's flushed confusion when questioned. Could it be…?

Renée Showalter was looking at the floor, blushing slightly, as she tucked one loose red strand behind her ear, and Dulcie just closed her mouth, happy to let one mystery remain unsolved.

FIFTY-THREE

Through no Malice of Man could Nature be delayed. No ill-will nor seeming Fairness would suffice. The pale Dawn reached above the stony Peak, sifting through the barren branches of the Forest, seeping through the mists. Despite her utmost fears, into her Chamber stark and chill, its Light began its lowly work, fixing first upon her own hands and then beyond upon her work. She knew it then for what it was, saw with unclouded Eyes that which had seemed so fair. And if the Terrors of the Night were then dismissed, so too her greatest Hopes. The journey would continue, upon hard Stones and far by Water. So, too, would this undying Hope illuminate her years, a comfort in the coldest days, bringing warmth to a world cold and Grey. Even on the coldest days, the Journey would continue.

DESPITE THE PIZZA, Dulcie slept soundly. Even her dreams, as vivid as always, took a hopeful turn, and she woke in the morning more refreshed than she would have expected.

'Chris.' She nudged her boyfriend and, in the process, dislodged Esmé, who had commandeered the pillow beside him.

'Mruf.' The muffled reply soon gave way to a gentle snore, and so Dulcie slid out of bed. Esmé landed with a thud beside her and together they made their way to the kitchen. Without another word, Dulcie opened a can for the cat and was rewarded by the soft press of fur against her bare shins.

'You're welcome, Esmé,' she said, and proceeded to set up the coffee. 'I do appreciate loyalty, you know. I was simply worried.' She paused. 'Not without reason.'

The cat, digging into the moist food, didn't look up.

'You could have helped me out more, Esmé. I mean, "Not Chris"?' Dulcie looked down at the young cat. 'Was that the best you could do?'

'*I know what I know.*' The voice was faint compared to the sound of lapping. '*You don't...*'

'I don't what?' Those scratches on Chris's hands. They could have been the kitten's doing. A virus. 'Esmé?'

With an almost imperceptible shrug, Esmé stopped eating and began to wash. And Dulcie, now that it was daylight, decided to let her wilder suppositions go.

'I wasn't that taken by Paul Barnes.' The cat ignored her. 'It was just...' Dulcie paused. What had come over her? Was it simply that a big name, one that she knew from his book, had taken an interest in her? Or was it the famed conference madness getting a hold on her, after all? Nobody else had taken him seriously as either a scholar or a candidate for the job. Not while there were any other candidates standing. And this morning, she knew, he'd have slept off the drug's effects and wakened to find himself facing criminal charges. A last desperate act by a man at his wits' ends.

'At least he won't take advantage of any other graduate students,' she said to the preoccupied cat.

'He? You mean "she", don't you?' Chris shambled into the kitchen, still half asleep and looking particularly shaggy. 'I mean, it was that Roebuck person who had me running in circles. Well, her and Thorpe.'

'It was the conference, Chris.' She poured the coffee. 'Too much pressure on everyone. It's enough to make anyone crazy. Not that that excuses what she did.'

He accepted a mug and sat, nodding, one hand rubbing a slightly heavier than usual beard. 'Maybe so. But what's going to happen to the conference?'

Dulcie shook her head. By the time Rogovoy had heard the story last night, Martin Thorpe was resting comfortably. The resident on overnight hadn't wanted anyone to visit, but Nancy had found a way to sneak in—with Tigger—and had emerged blushing to report he'd be back at work in the morning. Renée Showalter had retired, finally, to the conference hotel. But without Paul Barnes, Marco Tesla, and Stella Roebuck, the schedule would be sadly attenuated.

'Kelly will be grateful,' Chris noted. 'At least the scheduling problems will be gone.'

Dulcie drank some of her coffee. It was too hot still, and it burned. But that was better than asking how close Chris had gotten to the slender tech. He hadn't questioned her enthusiasm about the silver-haired academic.

'I just wish I knew…' She left it open. There was, after all, so much that could happen. That might still come to be.

Just then, Esmé jumped up and ran from the room. 'Esmé?' Chris asked, just as a phone rang in the living room.

'I'll get it.' Chris went to retrieve it, leaving Dulcie to her coffee. Another reason, she realized, why living with him was good.

A moment later he was back, a wide grin brightening his stubbly face. 'Here,' was all he said.

'Ms Schwartz?' It was Martin Thorpe, sounding healthier and more confident than she could remember. 'I'd like to discuss some changes with you.'

Inwardly, Dulcie groaned. If he was going to have her run errands again today, after all this…

'The conference will, of course, need to be somewhat curtailed,' her adviser was saying. 'But I've already spoken with the dean, and I believe we've come up with a workable plan.'

Dulcie reached for a pen and paper, as he explained about the rescheduled keynote address and how now all the papers would be presented in Lecture Hall B.

'It seems there was a mishap in the other auditorium yesterday,' he was saying. 'Something with cleaning solution and a stray spark, so this is really better all the way around. Besides, this will concentrate the audience; make sure every presentation is heard. But, Ms Schwartz?'

'Yes?' Dulcie could hear the wince in her own voice.

'I am wondering if you would consider moving up your presentation. We need someone to fill in before Professor Showalter's talk and she suggested you.' He cleared his throat. 'Would you—do you think you'd be up to addressing the main hall? Professor Showalter and I could both take some time today to help you prepare.'

'I would love to, Mr Thorpe,' said Dulcie. She looked up and met Chris's grin with a big smile of her own. 'I can be down there in a half hour.'

'And I'll meet you in an hour,' said Thorpe. In the background, a small sound—perhaps a giggle, perhaps a mew. But all Dulcie could hear was the warm whirring of a purr that rose up to meet her, like warmth. Like love.

'*Even on the coldest days*,' the purr seemed to say. '*The journey will continue.*'

* * * * *

REQUEST YOUR FREE BOOKS!
2 FREE NOVELS PLUS 2 FREE GIFTS!

H HARLEQUIN®

INTRIGUE

BREATHTAKING ROMANTIC SUSPENSE

HII5

REQUEST YOUR
FREE BOOKS!

2 FREE NOVELS
FROM THE SUSPENSE COLLECTION
PLUS 2 FREE GIFTS!

YES! Please send me 2 FREE novels from the Suspense Collection and my 2 FREE gifts (gifts are worth about $10). After receiving them, if I don't wish to receive any more books, I can return the shipping statement marked "cancel." If I don't cancel, I will receive 4 brand-new novels every month and be billed just $6.49 per book in the U.S. or $6.99 per book in Canada. That's a savings of at least 19% off the cover price. It's quite a bargain! Shipping and handling is just 50¢ per book in the U.S. and 75¢ per book in Canada.* I understand that accepting the 2 free books and gifts places me under no obligation to buy anything. I can always return a shipment and cancel at any time. Even if I never buy another book, the two free books and gifts are mine to keep forever.

191/391 MDN GH4Z

Name	(PLEASE PRINT)	
Address		Apt. #
City	State/Prov.	Zip/Postal Code
Signature (if under 18, a parent or guardian must sign)		

Mail to the **Reader Service:**

IN U.S.A.: P.O. Box 1867, Buffalo, NY 14240-1867
IN CANADA: P.O. Box 609, Fort Erie, Ontario L2A 5X3

**Want to try two free books from another line?
Call 1-800-873-8635 or visit www.ReaderService.com.**

* Terms and prices subject to change without notice. Prices do not include applicable taxes. Sales tax applicable in N.Y. Canadian residents will be charged applicable taxes. Offer not valid in Quebec. This offer is limited to one order per household. Not valid for current subscribers to the Suspense Collection or the Romance/Suspense Collection. All orders subject to credit approval. Credit or debit balances in a customer's account(s) may be offset by any other outstanding balance owed by or to the customer. Please allow 4 to 6 weeks for delivery. Offer available while quantities last.

Your Privacy—The Reader Service is committed to protecting your privacy. Our Privacy Policy is available online at www.ReaderService.com or upon request from the Reader Service.

We make a portion of our mailing list available to reputable third parties that offer products we believe may interest you. If you prefer that we not exchange your name with third parties, or if you wish to clarify or modify your communication preferences, please visit us at www.ReaderService.com/consumerschoice or write to us at Reader Service Preference Service, P.O. Box 9062, Buffalo, NY 14240-9062. Include your complete name and address.

REQUEST YOUR FREE BOOKS!
2 FREE NOVELS PLUS 2 FREE GIFTS!

ROMANTIC suspense

Sparked by danger, fueled by passion